SOLVING DROOD

A novel by

Mark Wheats

This novel is a work of fiction. Any references to historical events, real people, or real places are used fictitiously. Other names, characters, places, and events are derived from the author's imagination, so any resemblance to actual events, places or persons, living or dead, is entirely coincidental.

Cover design by Nusrat Abbas Awan

First paperback edition December 2022

ISBN 979-8-9871233-1-7

Published by Mark Wietrzychowski

For my two greatest gifts, Stephanie and Becky

Contents

Prologue

On June 9th, 1870, one of the world's greatest literary figures, Charles Dickens, died at his Gad's Hill estate in England.

They say he was halfway through penning his 15th and final novel, *The Mystery of Edwin Drood,* when he met his untimely fate.

They say that the second half of the story was left unfinished and that Dickens took the secret ending to the grave with him.

So, they say.

Solving Drood

Chapter 1

Class

Friday, March 24, 2000

"Settle down, students," exclaimed the professor's Oxford English accent, "it's not spring break *yet*—so settle down!" His eyes glared small and hard, like two black pebbles implanted into a lipless face. "There's no need for you to be in such high spirits." He began passing out test results. "Especially *you*, Mr. Murray." He handed a handsome student a paper branded with a big red **F**.

"Damn," said the boy, slumping into his desk and covering his face with the paper.

"I wonder if some of you ever bother reading the book," said the professor. "Afterall, this is a course in literature, so it would be wise to surmise that reading is involved. One cannot live on notes alone." The professor glanced at a frumpy-dressed girl with thick glasses seated directly behind the boy. "Especially if you are not the one who is taking the notes."

The girl sat frozen.

"Congratulations, Miss Pipple," he said, placing a paper on her desk. "A perfect score. It is too bad that while you so desperately try to help your comedic protégé by lending him your notes, you also hurt him by performing so well. I say this because I have decided to elicit the standard curve on all papers."

Brian Murray slumped further into his desk (and his face further into his paper).

"This is college, not middle school." As the professor spoke, Brian pushed himself up from his desk, gathering his books. "And before any of you have the audacity to interrupt my class and flee to the registrar's office for a drop-add slip, may I inform you that the deadline for dropping this course has expired four-and-twenty hours ago. So, whether you like it or not, we are stuck with each other."

By slow degrees, Brian returned his books and himself to his desk, where he resumed his slumping.

"I know how all of you are looking forward to spring break, so I have a little, shall we say, *going away present* for all of you. Just to keep those feeble minds of yours churning while you fill them with alcohol, cannabis, and other hedonistic extra-curricular activities, I have decided to allow you to work on your term papers over the holiday. They will be due back on *my* desk the precise day that all of you are due back at *your* desks."

The entire class moaned.

"Suffice it to say, if any of you happen to have the misfortune of suddenly becoming ill upon your arrival, keep in mind that for every day your paper is late, your scores will be lowered by one full letter grade."

The class moaned louder.

"But don't worry," he said, casting his black pebbles in the direction of the boy, "for some of you, I doubt that your grades can get any lower."

"What an ass," Brian whispered.

"Pardon me, Mr. Murray? Did you say something? If so, please be so kind as to enlighten the rest of us."

"What a class," he returned.

"Let us not forget, Mr. Murray, 'tis *you* who signed up for English Literature Four O' One, not *I*. And please allow me to remind you that this is a four-credit course. Hence, if I were you, I'd open my notebook and listen quite attentively."

Brian unhappily complied, as did the girl in the frumpy dress, who, along with her notebook, produced a small tape recorder that she set atop her desk.

"Now, Mr. Murray...since you seem to be in such a loquacious mood today, perhaps you can tell the class who *Edwin Drood* is."

"Who?"

"*Drood*, Mr. Murray, *Edwin Drood*."

"Isn't he a wrestler?"

The students roared with laughter.

"Fortunately not, Mr. Murray. Try again."

"Is it a whiskey, like Jack Daniels?"

The students roared louder.

When the professor stopped shaking his head, he turned his eyes on the girl seated behind him. "Miss Pipple, since you are so well rehearsed at helping your friend with his studies, why don't you offer him a clue as to the identity of this mystery person."

She leaned in, whispering in the boy's ear. "He's a fictional character."

Brian repeated it aloud, quite humorously, to the delight of the class. "He's a fictional character."

"A *Dickens* character," she whispered again, leaning closer.

"A Dickens character," he repeated.

As the girl leaned closer and closer toward Brian, there was a dreamy nature in the way her eyes examined the back of his head, where his hair met his neckline, suggesting that her answers were well worth her proximity. "In a book entitled *The Mystery of Edwin Drood*," she whispered.

"In a book titled The Mystery of Edwin Drood," he repeated.

"That will be quite enough," the professor exclaimed over the students' laughter. "Pray tell me, Miss Pipple… have you read the book?"

The girl, her eyes still dreamily bent on the back of Brian's head, whispered her answer to the boy.

"Miss Pipple? I am addressing *you*."

"Oh—um, sorry professor," she said, snapping out of her haze. "What was the question?"

"The book, Miss Pipple. Have you read it?"

"Yes, professor…why, yes—yes I have."

"And pray tell the class, Miss Pipple: what happens at the end of the story?"

"The ending? Why, I'm sure I don't know, Professor Mudgrove."

"I thought you read the story, Miss Pipple?"

"I did, professor, but I only read half of it."

This contradiction of speech had the students roaring again.

A most serious expression betook the professor's face. "Class, you laugh at Miss Pipple, but you should very well be laughing at yourselves, your own incognizance, your own ineptitude. I say this because she is correct."

The students looked at each other in befuddlement.

"Please tell the class, Miss Pipple, *why* you were unable to finish the novel."

The girl nervously adjusted her glasses before timidly responding. "It's actually the only book of his that I've never finished." Her spectacles panned the roomful of students. "You see, Charles Dickens never wrote the ending of The Mystery of Edwin Drood," she explained, "because he died of a massive stroke halfway through completing it. Unfortunately, he took the secret ending of the story to the grave with him."

"That is the bad news," the professor stated. "Now for the good news." His stony face smiled a lipless grin. "Over spring break all of *you* are going to have the pleasure of writing the ending of his novel in no less than five-and-twenty typewritten pages."

A groan befell the room that sounded like the class was suffering from salmonella poisoning.

The professor began handing out guidelines for the assignment. "You may purchase the first half of the novel at the campus bookstore."

"Do we get half-off?" quipped Brian.

"I trust you will read the book this time, Mr. Murray, because I can assure you, there isn't a videotape to be found."

After class, Brian waited for all his classmates to disappointingly file out of the room before approaching the professor.

"Professor Mudgrove," he said, staring straight into his pebbles, "I'd appreciate it if you didn't announce my test results in class."

"Why the University of Maryland allowed you admittance to begin with, Mr. Murray, is beyond my comprehension."

"And I'd appreciate it if you stuck to the syllabus. It doesn't say here anywhere," he paused, searching through his notebook and retrieving a crinkled piece of paper, "that we're supposed to write the ending of any novels."

"As usual, Mr. Murray, your ignorance precedes your actions. If you will only take the time to examine the syllabus in its entirety, you will notice that the asterisk next to the word *term paper* matches the asterisk at the bottom of the page, which clearly states *term paper guidelines and due dates to be announced in class*."

"You never said we'd have to write a twenty-five-page paper during spring break."

"You never asked, Mr. Murray."

"Ya know somethin', Professor Mudgrove, I've been wantin' to tell you this since the first day of class…"

"Pray tell, Mr. Murray…pray tell."

"You're absolutely the biggest—"

Before he had a chance to discharge his insult, the classroom door squeaked open, revealing the frumpy bespectacled girl awkwardly hunched in the ingress with an armful of books.

"Yes, Miss Pipple?" said the professor.

Sorry to interrupt, but…" she shyly pointed over at the tape recorder still sitting on her desk.

"Go ahead, Miss Pipple, but let's hurry along. Mr. Murray was just about to convey something of grave importance."

She walked to her desk, clumsily dropping her books in the process.

Brian went over to assist her, and when he reached down to help gather some of the books, she shoved a note into the palm of his hand, whispering "Don't worry." She secured her belongings then tromped back out, sealing the door behind her.

"A fine specimen that Miss Pipple," said the professor. "So intelligent, yet she cannot see past those Coke bottle glasses on her nose that you are only using her for her mind."

Brian opened his mouth as if to refute this claim…but could say nothing.

"See, Mr. Murray, your ignorance precedes your actions once again." The professor snapped his briefcase shut. "I understand that you need at least a cee-minus on this paper, not only to pass this class, but to remain a student here at the university." He went for his hat. "Now, I believe that there was something you wanted to tell me. Something of grave importance that you have been wanting to tell me since the first day of class."

Brian wanted so badly to discharge his insult, but he could only think about what the girl had said, and what she could have possibly written on that note he was palming.

"Wise choice, Mr. Murray, because I would have most certainly taken it up with the Office of the Dean. Now, I suggest that you get to the Maryland Book Exchange before you are unable to come up with the first half of your assignment, as well as the last."

Brian headed for the door.

"Oh, I almost forgot, Mr. Murray...*have a nice spring break.*"

Chapter 2

The Meet

'*eet me in Hornbake Library.*' That's all the note said, plain and simple. *'Meet me in Hornbake Library.'*

Somehow the boy thought a girl of her type would have written something a bit more informative, a bit more intellectual, a bit more...*literary*. Certainly, she would have written the specifics on precisely *where* to meet in a building of that size—but there it was, inscribed on a plain piece of notebook paper: *'Meet me in Hornbake Library.'*

If the girl, whose face and dress seemed as plain and simple as her words and paper, had chosen anywhere else to meet—the student union, her dorm room, any pub within a ten-mile radius of the college—the boy would have undoubtedly shred the note and ingested its remains! However, since the girl wanted to meet in a place where few people he associates with ever frequent, he found it a safe haven to be seen together.

It was an unusually cold March day, with remnants of a late snow that was swept to the sides of walkways before freezing to ice. Brian shrugged his hands into his black leather jacket, which was no match for the blustery winds that pierced his bones, forcing him to jog up the steps of the library and not stop until he was a good distance into the building.

In searching for the girl, his watery eyes came across the faces of students who stared as if he were in the wrong building.

"Can I help you?" asked an elderly librarian.

"Yeah, I'm looking for a brown-haired girl, about *this* tall," he said, extending his hand, "with sort of a pale face and big round glasses."

"Sorry," replied the librarian, "if she's not on microfiche, I can't help you."

After combing the first level of the building, he took the escalator to the next, being sure to examine the faces of those traveling in the opposite direction. As he searched each floor, the boy's good looks stole some female eyes away from their pages.

"Yo Bry!" called a voice from afar.

Behind these words approached a short, redheaded boy with freckles that invaded every part of his body. There were freckles on his nose, ears, hands, neck, and even his lips.

"Oh shit," Brian whispered.

"Funny seein' you here," said the freckled boy. "I thought you'd be out celebratin' before the big road trip this Sunday."

"You might say I hit a major speedbump—Professor Mudgrove."

"Yeah, I heard…glad I dropped *that* class. Don't tell me you're gonna miss the spring break festivities."

"Pass or fail, I'm there."

"You can ride with us if ya want. We rented an old yellow school bus for the trip; you can't miss it. We got a kegger, and I've got this bud from Jamaica. I swear— one hit—that's all it takes! We'll be baked before we hit the Florida sun!"

"Listen Pat," he said, trying to get away, "I don't wanna cut ya short, but I'm supposed to be meetin' somebody here."

"Let me guess," he replied, his freckles following. "Carolyn Saltus, right Bry?"

"Not exactly."

"Debbie Manette?"

"Nope," he said, hastening his pace in an attempt to rid him.

"Bry! Don't tell me you landed Jennifer Cole?"

Brian walked faster.

"Man! You've got to be the luckiest person this side of the Mason Dick Line! What I wouldn't do to get into Jennifer Cole's—"

"Hello," said a sheepish voice.

Brian stopped, along with his freckled friend (who bumped into the back of him).

Between two bookshelves stood the frumpy bespec- tacled girl. "Go on," said her soft voice to the redheaded boy, "please, finish your statement."

The boy's freckles grew redder.

"You were just saying," repeated the girl, "what you wouldn't do to get into Jennifer Cole's…?"

The flush that came over him filled the spaces between his freckles, turning his face as red as his hair.

"Her *what*?" she asked.

"Better go, Bry," he said. "See ya Sunday." He shot toward the escalator in a red blur.

"My goodness," she remarked. "I seem to have embarrassed your friend."

"You did me a favor. I was tryin' to get rid of him anyway."

"Why?" she inquired, nudging her glasses up the bridge of her nose and moving her pale face closer. "Is there something embarrassing you, as well?"

He ignored the question, changing the subject. "I'm sorry, but I can't remember your name—I mean—I know your last name because Professor Mudgrove always calls you Miss Pipple."

"Ellen," she said, "my name's Ellen." She extended her hand.

"Thanks for bailin' me out back there in class, Ellen. If it wasn't for you, I'd be sittin' in the Dean's office right now. By the way, my name's—"

"Brian," she interrupted. "Yes, I know. Funny, isn't it? How the unpopular always seem to know the popular?"

"Well, it's just that you sit right behind me in class. There's only a certain number of times a person can turn around without gettin' a stiff neck."

"So *that's* why the girls are always rubbing your shoulders at the student union."

"What's this about anyway? What did you mean by that note?"

"I was referring to the assignment," Ellen replied. "Consider yourself lucky, because I'm going to help you with your paper."

"For real?"

"If there's one thing I never joke about, it's literature."

Brian took her hand again, vigorously shaking it. "Ellen Pipple, you're a life saver! And I don't care if my neck's stiff for the rest of the semester, I'm gonna turn around in class every chance I get—I'll even rent a swivel chair if I have to!"

"Now," she said, laughing, "let's not get *too* carried away."

"How can I ever repay you, Ellen?"

"Well," she returned, "for starters you can stop shaking my hand."

"Sorry," said Brian, letting go.

"And secondly, you can meet me back here tomorrow evening at six. Don't forget to get a copy of the book."

"Meet you back here? In *this* spot?"

"Yes. See?" she said, pointing at the bookshelf. "It's the Dickens section." Her finger slowly ran across the various leatherbound titles of the author's works. "They have every one of his novels here. The finished ones, I mean."

"It's the unfinished one I'm worried about," he said.

"But at least we only have to read half of it. *A half a book is better than one,*" he quipped.

"But you're missing the whole point, Brian," she said, her hand now resting on the leathery spines of the books. "Dickens was the best—the all-time greatest! Not reading him would be like…like…"

"Like renting a bus for spring break and not taking it?"

"I don't think you understand."

"Oh, I understand, alright," he replied, zipping up his leather jacket. "You've got your interests, and I've got mine." He started for the escalator.

"But—"

"I'll see ya tomorrow," he called, turning his neck then his entire body around, stumbling onto the escalator backwards. "Six-sharp!"

She shook her head and laughed as she watched him descend among a group of students who were getting onto the escalator, her hand still resting on the leathery books of the Dickens section (as if she knew each one of them by feel).

Chapter 3

Misunderstandings

The winds at six o'clock on that next eve were gusting so ferociously, they could be heard all the way into the Dickens section of Hornbake Library.

The leathery covers of the books did little to conceal the howling gales, as did the leather jacket of the boy who was arriving from the escalator like a block of ice off a conveyor belt.

"C-c-c-o-o-l-l-d-d," he stuttered.

Ellen rushed to his aid with her downy coat, covering him and rubbing his back. "Poor boy," she teased. "Come, warm yourself up a bit." She guided him over to a tiny table hidden between the bookcases. Ellen had the table arranged beautifully. A checkered tablecloth held a small vase with droopy flowers that looked down upon an assorted box of donuts, two steaming cups of coffee capping each end.

"Ahhh," he sighed in relief, receiving his coffee like the Tin Man receiving his oil. "My entire f-f-face is fr-fr-frozen."

"There, there," she mused, giving him a few moments to thaw out.

"Th-th-this place is a long way from my d-d-dorm."

"You need a jacket tailored for warmth rather than image."

A gust of wind howled through the building, sending a shiver through him. "A-a-a-am I on time?"

"I can set my watch to you," she replied, "because you're always twenty minutes late."

"S-s-sorry."

"Well, we'd better not waste any time. Let's start with Dickens's earlier works first," she said, opening her notebook. "From the Pickwick Papers through A Christmas Carol."

"Wh-wh-what?"

"I thought it best to start from the beginning, so you can get a chronological view on all of his writings."

Brian's chiseled looks shattered through his frozen face. "Wait a minute," he said, "I thought I was just comin' by to drop off the story." He drew an old, tattered book from the breast of his jacket and tossed it onto the tablecloth. (The binding of the curious book deserved much credit for keeping the aged pages together.)

Ellen appeared shocked. "Surely you didn't think that I was going to write your paper for you?"

Brian's face melted onto the table. "I did," he said.

"Copying notes is one thing; whispering answers in class is another. But writing your term paper, why... that's plagiarism—academic dishonesty—fraud!"

"I don't feel very well," he said, face down in the

tablecloth (the checkered pattern making him feel worse).

"I specifically told you that I would help you, Brian. I thought we would meet here nightly and work on our papers over the break. You know…*together*."

"Ohhhhh," he moaned, "I think we've got some sorta misunderstandin'."

"Indeed."

"My ticket to spring break leaves at nine tomorrow morning," he said, lifting his head. "There's supposed to be a keg, and someone's bringin' weed from Jamaica."

"But if you stay, you can be assured of getting a good grade, and fill your head with substances far better and much more potent…good literature."

"Ohhhhh," he groaned, "You're startin' to sound like Mudgrove."

"There will be another spring break next year, I can promise you that. But I can't promise that you'll still be in college."

"Now you're startin' to sound like my—wait…what do you mean by that?"

"I work part-time in the Registrar's Office, and… well…I sort of looked you up in student files. I know about you being placed on academic probation. In fact, you're going to have to appear before the Academic Probationary Committee."

"Ohhhhh," he groaned louder. "That's why I need to go. It's the whole point of spring break. You're supposed to leave your mind at school, and your worries along with it. You know, party 'til ya drop."

"Drop right out of college, you mean."

"If you think I'm actually gonna choose to freeze here in Maryland when I could be baking on a beach in Florida—you're the one who needs more schoolin'."

"Suit yourself," she replied.

"Don't worry about me. I'll find some way to pull through," he said, zipping up his jacket. "When I'm standin' in front of that Probationary Committee, there'll be tears in my eyes when I tell them how it would break my sweet dear ol' mother's heart if I was expelled. I'll give the greatest sob story since Oliver Twist. I don't need nothin' from nobody!" He started away, then suddenly stopped and returned, snatching his cup of coffee from the tablecloth.

"Nothing?" said Ellen.

He was about to put the coffee back, but a howling wind reminded him it would be good company, as would a donut that he helped himself to as well. Brian stomped back toward the escalator (without looking back at her).

"Wait," she exclaimed, "you forgot your…" her voice softened, "book," she said, slowly picking it up and gently running her hand over the old leather binding. The spine of the book oddly contained three tarnished snaps. As Ellen cracked open the archaic-looking cover, her eyes grew wider and wider in disbelief. The winds were picking up again, howling louder and louder with each page her tender finger turned.

"I can't believe it," she said to herself, "*Chapman and Hall.*"

It was upon these words, "Chapman and Hall" that *Hard Times, Little Dorrit*, and *A Tale of Two Cities* fell from the bookcase behind her, startling Ellen right out of her chair!

"Who's there?" she said, scared, talking to the giant wall of Dickens' works behind her. "I say who's there?"

By slow degrees, she picked up the fallen books, hugging them against her breast for security as she stepped around to the other side of the bookcase.

All that remained was the distinct odor of a frowsty smelling cologne she had no doubt encountered before. Her thoughts quickly conjured up the redheaded boy's face, the one with the freckles, but she soon dismissed the entire incident on account of the winds, which seemed to be eerily howling her name.

Chapter 4

Decisions

It was a most incredible sight on this rawest of mornings! The temperature outside the fleet of busses was barely twenty degrees; yet inside, the heaters were cranked full blast where students were partying in bathing suits and bikinis. Amid the luxurious litter of mammoth Greyhound busses, there rested an old yellow school bus that appeared like the runt of the litter. The aisles within the Yellow Runt had different activities to choose from. In one aisle, students were batting a volleyball back and forth over a net. In others, drinking games were underway. There was even a Frisbee traveling back and forth, from the north section of the bus to the south (as if foreshadowing their Floridian journey to come), with beach balls being punched in between. The most amazing thing about it all was that the students were playing these games one-handedly—for all of them were clutching a Solo cup of beer with their other.

Brian Murray was the only one not wearing a bathing suit. Arriving twenty minutes late, he was seated in the rear, in t-shirt and jeans, keeping close proximity to a metal keg buried in ice.

"Hi Brian," greeted a shapely blonde-haired girl who seemed to be popping out of the seams of her bikini.

"This is the address of the motel I'm staying at—so don't lose it." She gave him a folded-up cocktail napkin. "Can you do me?" she said, handing him a tube of suntan lotion.

The bodacious blonde situated herself on his lap while Brian squeezed the coconut scented lotion onto her shoulders, rubbing it in with both hands and kissing her neck.

"Brian," she giggled, "that tickles!"

"How about this," he said, applying the lotion somewhere to the lower part of her bikini, causing her to momentarily leap from his lap.

"You're the worst, Brian!" she giggled louder.

"We'll see about that in your motel room," he replied, dipping her into the next seat with a French kiss.

The redheaded boy with freckles caught the Frisbee then pointed at the two. "Whoa!" he said to some fellow students, "Bry landed Jennifer Cole!"

As Brian was kissing her, he heard a faint tapping noise. However, he was so involved with the beautiful girl that he dismissed it. The tapping became louder and more frequent, turning into a rapping sound, but the boy was so full of pleasure that he didn't care what it was or who was precipitating it.

"What's that sound?" asked the bikini-clad girl.

"My heart," he answered, still kissing.

"It can't be," she said, her lips disengaging. "You don't have one."

"Go away," Brian said at the sound, kissing the girl more passionately, "nobody's home."

The rapping turned into banging, so Brian opened one of his eyes, peeping out.

It was Ellen Pipple, standing in the cold on the outside of the bus, her big round glasses spying in. She was banging on the window with one hand while displaying his book with the other.

The blonde opened her eyes and glanced in the direction Brian was peeking. "Who's *that?*" she asked, sitting up and adjusting her bikini top.

"That? Oh…that's nobody," he returned.

Ellen shoved the book against the window, excitingly pointing at it and mouthing something.

"She seems to want you."

"*Me?* I don't know what she could possibly want from *me,*" he said, nonchalantly waving her off with the back of his hand.

"She looks like a bug," insulted the blonde.

Brian finally understood what her frozen breaths were mouthing…she was saying, "Your *book*—your *book!*"

"Ohhh…I know what it is," he explained. "I lent her a book for class and she's returning it."

"*You,*" she said with surprise, "lending someone a book?" Her eyes softened as she hugged his face into her bikini top. "Men who read turn me on."

"Really? I lend books to people all the time—after I read 'em, I mean."

A tapping noise came from the window again.

"I'll be back before you can bleed us another beer," said Brian, handing her the hose of the keg and zipping up his leather.

When the door of the bus opened, students booed Brian for letting cold air into their exclusive beach party.

The boy's lips let go foggy breaths as he exited the bus and jogged over to Ellen who was elatedly smiling. The diesel fumes outside harshly contrasted with the tropical scents inside, forcing him to cough cloudy breaths.

"Thanks Helen," he said, reaching for the book.

"Ellen. My name's Ellen," she returned, holding the book out of his reach.

"Alright then, thanks Ellen," he said, trying to grab hold of it.

"Do you even have a clue of what you've got here?" She juggled the book from one hand to the other, keeping it away from him.

"Do you have a clue of what I've got in *there?*" he answered, pointing to the window of the bus. The girl in the bikini was displaying two Solo cups of beer like a St. Pauli Girl model.

"This is an original!" said Ellen, drawing his eyes back to the book while keeping it away from him. "It's a one of a kind!"

"So is *that!*" he replied, pointing to the girl again, who was now jiggling her bikini top in the window.

The bus door opened, and the driver was accompanied by boos as he leaned out and shouted, "All aboard!"

"I don't have time for this," said Brian, poking Ellen's ribs through her downy coat and snatching the book out of her hands.

The litter of Greyhounds began revving their engines, along with the Yellow Runt—the fumes causing Brian to cough again as he started back for the door.

"You don't understand!" she called.

Without turning around, he lifted his hand, acknowledging his departure.

"It's published by Chapman and Hall!" she shouted.

Brian continued his way down the length of the bus, the back of his hand still raised.

"There's a letter inside!"

His hand turned into a fist, knocking on the door of the bus.

"I think he wrote the second half of the story!"

The door opened with a wheezing hiss.

"Dickens, I mean!"

Brian climbed aboard the Yellow Runt's mouth, the door about to close.

Ellen thought for a moment, then in one last effort to stop him, she shouted, "It could make you rich!"

No sooner did the Yellow Runt's mouth shut than it sprang back open. "Say that again?" he said, leaning out.

The students grew angry, shouting "Close the door!" while hurling empty Solo cups and balls at him.

"It could make you rich," she excitedly repeated. "Finding the second half of The Mystery of Edwin Drood would be like finding a lost Rembrandt painting, or a lost DaVinci—even greater!"

Brian escaped the Runt's mouth, slowly approaching her. "Is this some kind of a joke?"

"No," she returned, the bus fumes making her feel dizzy. "Is this some kind of a dream?"

He glanced at the window where the girl in the bikini was waving him back with the beers. "I wonder."

Ellen held out her hands, and Brian marveled at the book before relinquishing it back to her.

"See," she said, opening the cover. "Chapman and Hall. They're the original publishers. This alone is worth thousands."

One of the windows of the bus opened, and the freckled boy poked his head out. "Yo Bry," he called. "Aren't cha comin'?"

Brian couldn't believe what Ellen was saying. "How can it make me rich?"

"Dickens placed a letter inside, but somehow it never reached its recipient." She revealed a cleverly hidden pocket in the cover. "It was addressed to his mistress. After doing some research, I discovered he wrote the letter while on his last reading tour in the U.S."

"Yo Bry," he called again. "Jennifer's gettin' mad."

Ellen's eyes seemed to get as wide as her glasses. "I don't think Dickens took the surprise ending to the grave with him. I think he wrote it, then hid it!"

"Yo Bry, you're gonna blow off Jennifer for *her?*"

The litter of Greyhound buses started dashing away.

"If this is a trick to keep me from going," warned Brian, "so help me, I'll—"

"I wouldn't do that! If I'm wrong, I'll fly you to Florida—first class—I promise!"

The Yellow Runt slowly began rolling away, as if trying to keep up with the rest of the pack. "Wait here," he said, running after the school bus. He exchanged words with the redheaded boy, who covertly handed him something through the window. Brian then shouted to the blonde in the bikini. "Jennifer, I'll meet ya there!" When the students discovered where the cold air was coming from, they stoned the freckled boy with cups and shoes and frisbees and balls, until he sealed the window.

"You better be right," said Brian with frozen breaths, watching the fleet of beachgoers pull away like a mirage in wintertime. "God help you…you better be right."

All that remained for him in the empty parking lot were diesel fumes, the freezing cold, and Ellen Pipple.

Chapter 5

Unfinished Business

The table that Ellen set up in Hornbake Library seemed untouched since the previous night, as if the librarians themselves dashed off in a hurry for spring break. With the exception of the missing coffee and donuts, everything appeared as Ellen had left it; even the faint odor of that frowsty smelling cologne still seemed to linger.

"Here it is," she said, producing a computer printout listing the chronology of Charles Dickens's works, laying it on the checkered tablecloth. "Now, as you can see, Dickens was a prolific writer. He averaged about one novel every year or two."

Brian pulled his chair closer to the table, decreasing their distance.

"But notice the timeframe between his last completed novel, Our Mutual Friend, and the start of Drood."

"Five years," Brian returned.

"That's right. From eighteen-sixty-five to eighteen-seventy there's nothing but reading tours."

"Some in the U.S.," Brian added, looking over the printout.

"That's where your book comes in," said Ellen, carefully opening it. "By the way, how did you come across this?"

"To tell ya the truth, I wanted to save as much beer money as possible for the trip. So instead of goin' to the book exchange, I hit up that flea market off Route One."

Ellen laughed. "Your frugality may have led to one of the greatest discoveries of the twenty-first century."

From between the pages of the timeworn book, Ellen removed an old letter addressed to a *'Nelly'* by a *'Mr. Tringham.'*

Brian scanned it. "How do you know this was written by Dickens? This is someone else's signature."

"Mr. Tringham was the pseudonym Dickens went by whenever he corresponded with his mistress, Ellen Ternan, who he affectionately called Nelly," she answered. "And look at the paper," she gestured, "Dickens wrote his text on blue stationery just like this, the same size too—seven and a quarter by nine."

Brian's eyes traced the letter. "I still don't understand why you think he finished the novel."

"Simple. Read this paragraph," she said, poking her finger at the letter.

Brian read aloud: *"In regard to the Sapsea prose I mentioned to you, my Dear Nelly, I am arranging it with the purpose of giving the illusion that my demise occurred precisely on that last word, which, as you can see, is the most telltale clue. This last word is the keynote. For within it lies the clue. Not only must those who attempt to solve this mystery be extraordinarily detective-minded, but they must be astute and devout readers of my writings and travels as well."'* Brian looked up at her, and for the first time he noticed her eyes through the thick, bug-eyed glasses. They were a soft shade of brown, with naturally long lashes. For a moment, he stared into them, perhaps admiring them (perhaps beginning to admire the person behind them).

"What's the Sapsea prose?" he asked, continuing to explore her face.

Ellen thumbed through a library book, her pretty eyes widening with excitement when she found the page. "It's what's commonly referred to as the Sapsea Fragment. Here…read these last few paragraphs."

Brian read to himself: *'Come, Poker,' said I, 'let me hear more about you. Tell me. Where are you going to, Poker, and where do you come from?'*

'Ah Mr. Sapsea!' exclaimed the young man. 'Disguise from you is impossible. You know already that I come from somewhere, and am going somewhere else. If I was to deny it, what would it avail me?'

'Then don't deny it,' was my remark.

'Or,' pursued Poker, in a kind of despondent rapture, 'or if I was to deny that I came to this town to see and hear you, Sir, what would it avail me? Or if I was to deny

"It ends with *deny*," said Brian, "is that the keynote?"

"Most certainly. And when he writes, *'You know already that I come from somewhere, and am going somewhere else,'* I think he's referring to his eventual departure from this earth. Dickens wanted this clue to be found posthumously. And when he writes, *'...if I was to deny that I came to this town to see and hear you, Sir, what would it avail me?'* I think he's referring to his last reading tour in America. That's how this book got here."

"I still don't get it."

"Avail means benefit, to profit. And if someone were to go to the town he lectured, it would profit them by—"

"Finding the second half of the novel," Brian finished.

"Precisely. You see, The Mystery of Edwin Drood is really just a metaphor for the mystery of the novel's ending...literally *and* figuratively. The disappearance of Edwin Drood in the story refers to the disappearance of the story itself." She dreamily stared at the letter. "Dickens spun the ultimate yarn. He wove fiction into reality. Everything's connected. Not a cobblestone left unturned." She drew a long breath and sighed, whispering, "What a genius."

If one wanted to argue that it is possible for a person to become jealous of another who is a hundred and thirty years old, this would certainly be proof of the case. For, it appeared the boy suddenly found himself rivaling for the attention of Ellen's pretty eyes; rivaling with, of all things, a dead man! It seemed that each time Brian attempted to garner her gaze, he would find himself talking to the back of *her* head, which she kept buried in the free-flowing words of Charles Dickens.

"Genius? Well, after all, he *did* have five years to plan it," Brian demurred.

Ellen, too busy concentrating, ignored him. "But he lectured in so many different cities," she said. "What is it about the word *'deny'* that's so important? It doesn't spell anything when you mix it up—'neyd', 'yend', 'nedy', I just don't get it."

"You know somethin,' Ellen," he said, still staring admiringly at the back of her head, "I think it's really cool how we met and everything. I'm startin' to wonder if—"

"Please!" she said, her eyes immersed in the pages. "Not now. I think I'm onto something." She slowly raised her head back, closing her lovely lashes to better think.

And, for the first time, Brian noticed the soft pink lips that she was whispering to herself with. He moved in a bit closer, noticing for the first time the strawberry fragrance of her nut-brown hair, and the incorrupt nature of her face—a face that he had never before seen such virtue, and honesty, and intelligence. It seemed as if it would have taken a hundred girls in bikinis to equal one ounce of beauty that Ellen Pipple was exuding at that moment. He moved closer and closer as she continued to whisper to herself, still with her eyes closed, and he was about to place his lips on hers, perhaps to stop them from moving, perhaps so she'd know he was still there, when suddenly her hair fell back and her eyes popped wide open.

"I've got it!" she said (not noticing his proximity nor realizing his intentions). "Deny means *New York!* It refers to New York!" She wrote the word down on a piece of notebook paper. "Look! Break it up—DENY— DE-NY! DE means OF in many countries and NY is the abbreviation for New York! I don't know why I didn't think of it before! It makes perfect sense!"

"It does?" said Brian, falling back into his chair.

"Dickens's last lecture was held in New York. At Steinway Hall."

"I bet that's where he stashed the ending," said Brian.

She started rummaging through her knapsack. "Where's my tape recorder, I must get this down." She took to dumping the contents of her sack onto the tablecloth. "Oh no!"

"What's wrong?"

"My tape recorder—it's not here!"

"Just put it down on paper," he suggested.

"You don't understand! Almost everything I've told you so far is on that tape—that's how I take notes—it's gone!"

"Okay…try tracing back in time. Where were you when you last had it?"

"Where was I?" she thought, "I was…I was…I was right here! I stayed here late last night after I discovered your book was authentic, and I dictated notes into it."

"That solves it," he said. "You must've left it here. Let's check the lost and found."

They inquired about the device at the information desk, where a bird-faced librarian with steel gray hair searched through a cardboard box filled with hats, scarves, gloves, keys, but no tape recorder.

"Sorry," said the lady, "if it has batteries, it usually doesn't stick around long."

"But this was just last night," Ellen pleaded. "Surely you must have another box?"

"The only other box we have is a suggestion box," returned the librarian.

"Come on, let's go," said Brian. "Somebody probably swiped it."

The two headed for the door, Ellen gazing down despondently.

"Don't worry, Ellen, when we find the second half of that book, I'll buy ya a new one—a better one."

"It's not the tape recorder I'm worried about. It's the information."

"Are you kiddin'? Most people wouldn't even know who Edwin Drood is, let alone what you were talkin' about. Even if they did, they wouldn't believe it."

"Maybe you're right," she said. "To understand those notes, they'd have to be as devout and astute as we are, like Dickens said."

"And as crazy."

They looked at each other and laughed.

"Where to now?" asked Brian.

"Looks like your spring break has a latitudinal change in direction," she replied. "Next stop, The Big Apple!"

Upon these words, the ornithic face of the steel gray-haired librarian gave them a squint, as if she intended to file their remarks in the card catalog.

Chapter 6

The Trip

T he two classmates in quest now found themselves within the pick of the litter when it came to busses, as if the Yellow Runt were decommissioned for a brand-new Greyhound intent on traveling northbound. The comfortable coach they were situated in was making good time, steadily scampering up the New Jersey Turnpike. It was quite different from the bus the students occupied earlier that day. The young people in bathing suits and bikinis seemed to be replaced by old people in leisure suits and house gowns. In lieu of beach balls and frisbees flying about, there were crossword puzzles and word finds being worked on. Where multicolored Solo cups of beer were once in hand, there were plain bottles of water and cans of Ensure being consumed. Even the coconut-scented suntan lotion seemed to be replaced by a medicinal wintergreen odor that stung the air.

Brian hopelessly stared out of the window at the passing landscape, which seemed like a videotape that kept rewinding the same highway scenery and playing it back again.

"I've never seen exits so far apart in my life," he said.

"Don't worry," said Ellen, "we'll be there before you know it."

"Now I can see why people are always makin' fun of New Jersey."

"Wait a second," she warned, "I'm from New Jersey."

"Are you serious?"

"I am. And it's a beautiful state, not that you can see it from the turnpike."

"Oh yeah? Then why are people always bustin' on it?"

"The ones who love New Jersey are usually the ones who make fun of it the most. It's called having a good sense of humility. Something *you* obviously know nothing about."

"I have a good sense of humility," Brian defended.

"I know. It's written all over your leather jacket and t-shirt."

"Hey, what are you tryin' to say...I can't take a joke?"

"No. I'm saying that you don't have a good sense of humility."

An old man slogged by, blowing his nose into a white handkerchief.

"See him," she said, leaning in. "Now *that* man has a good sense of humility."

"And what makes you say that?"

The old man blew his nose again, sounding it like a trumpet before opening the bathroom door at the rear of the bus.

"He walked right by us and blew his nose," she said, "that's why."

"So?"

"Well, for one thing, he doesn't mind letting people know he's on his way to the bathroom. And for another, he's perfectly comfortable discharging his nose in front of the entire bus. He could've waited until he was in the bathroom."

"I think you're confusin' good humility with bad manners," said Brian.

"On the contrary. He was gentleman enough to distance himself from his wife before doing it."

He laughed. "I guess if he comes back fartin' you'll say he's musical too."

Ellen gave him an angry look. "Please, don't say that."

"What? Fart?"

"I don't like it."

"You mean to tell me that Ellen Pipple, straight 'A' student and literary connoisseur, never farted?" He doubled over in his seat in hysterics.

"I said I don't like that talk," she angrily retorted.

"I hate to break the wind to ya," he roared, attempting to straighten his torso, "but even your favorite author, Charles Dickens, ripped one every now and then." The laughter overwhelmed him, and his face was once again in his lap.

Ellen ignored his hilarity, soberly staring straight ahead.

A few moments passed before Brian composed himself, but when he heard the toilet flush and watched the old man slog by again, it started him back up. He looked at Ellen—her face still angrily staring ahead.

"And ya say *I* have a bad sense of humility," he roared.

Ellen removed a magazine from her knapsack and started reading.

"I'm sorry," he said, his laughter subsiding. "I won't say *fart* anymore, I promise."

She kept her eyes on the magazine.

"It's just that I never met anyone who took such offense to the word. You should hear some of the sorority girls back at school. They're worse than a group of drunken—"

"I'm not one of your sorority girls back at school," she interrupted, her eyes still buried in the magazine.

"I know you're not," he said, examining her face. "One thing for sure, don't ever play beer pong with 'em. They'll drink anyone under the table."

"I wouldn't know," she said, still reading, "I've never been to any of their parties."

"No?"

"I was never invited."

"Oh," he downplayed, "you're not missin' much. Most of 'em usually end the night by throwin' up anyway."

Her eyes finally glanced at him. "The closest I've ever come to one of your parties was this morning, when I saw everyone through the bus window."

"See? I told ya you weren't missin' anything."

"You sure seemed to be having a good time."

"Oh," he said. "You mean with Jennifer Cole."

"Yes. The one who has something your friend with the red hair would like to get into, remember?"

"Don't mind Pat. He's just a bit frustrated about having the world's worst strikeout record when it comes to girls."

"The way he talks, I can see why." Ellen's eyes momentarily drifted out of the window, as if this recent conversation about the redheaded boy redirected her thoughts. "I was going to tell you something," she said, trying to remember, "it's on the tip of my tongue, but I can't think of what it could be." She closed her eyes. "Or was it that I wanted to ask you something?"

"Whenever you're ready, fire away."

She gave up, opening her eyes. "It'll come back to me. It always does."

"I guess bein' real smart has its problems. I mean, it must take a long time searchin' through all those data banks."

"No one's really smart," she returned. "Like Will Rogers once said: 'Everyone's ignorant, just in different subjects.'"

"Hey, I like that. I guess when it comes to college parties, I'm the expert."

"And when it comes to literature, I am."

They laughed.

"You have any brothers or sisters," asked Brian.

"No. But I've always wished I had." She gazed out the window at the passing landscape. "As a child, I was always jealous of my friends because they got to go home when it started getting dark and had siblings to spend the rest of the evening with. I never understood why they always wanted their own rooms. I would have given anything to have a little sister or brother. That's probably why I read so many books growing up...for the company." She turned to Brian again. "I was never neglected by my parents or anything, they're great, it's just that there's only so much of the adult world you can take when you're a child."

"Didn't you ever sleep over a friend's house?"

"Yes. And the first time I did, everything seemed so dramatically different than my house that it scared me to death. I ended up having to call my parents to come and get me in the middle of the night," she said in a laugh. "I've had plenty of sleepovers after that, but I guess it's not the same as having sisters and brothers."

"I can vouch for that," replied Brian. "I got an older brother, and he used to kick the livin' sh—" he censored himself, "the livin' *daylights* out of me."

"Just one?"

"Yup. And it's a good thing. If I had more older brothers, I don't think I ever woulda made it through childhoo—"

The bus driver slammed his brakes, causing drinks, magazines, and books to fly everywhere! Passengers nearly toppled out of their seats and into the aisle as the bus fishtailed left, then right, before grinding to a halt—the Greyhound nearly rolling itself over!

"Sorry," the driver's grizzly voice boomed over the speaker. "Traffic jam."

Ellen angrily marched up to the driver. "What are you, a lunatic? Don't you know senior citizens are riding this bus?"

"Sorry Miss, I was blindsided—there's nothin' I coulda done—look," he replied, pointing his callused forefinger at the windshield.

Dead ahead, Ellen's glasses traced the biggest pile-up of cars she had ever witnessed. There were cars smashed into the backs of cars, rammed into the sides of others, crammed underneath trucks, upside down and standing on end! It was as if a ghastly cloud had hovered over the turnpike, raining steel and flesh.

"My God," she whispered, her mouth agape.

"See, Miss? I told ya." The driver snatched the receiver of his radio, requesting a traffic update.

A squelchy voice came over the radio. "Bomb threat in the Lincoln Tunnel," said the dispatcher.

A fleet of paramedics arrived, forming a roadside triage unit.

"Come on, Brian," she called. Ellen opened the bus door and stepped into the freezing cold to survey the scene.

Brian followed her outside, trying not to look at those victims who were suffering the worst.

"You help out over there," she directed, "and I'll—"

"Just a second," he said, turning his back on the gruesome scene, "I don't think I can do this."

"What do you mean," she scolded. "Get over there and help those people!"

"I can't."

"What?"

"I'm...I'm…"

"You're *what*?"

"I'm scared of blood," he admitted.

"I don't care!" she returned.

"Sorry Ellen, but no…I just can't."

"Listen to me, Brian Murray. Those people desperately need our help! Haven't you ever had a first aid class?"

He tried looking at the gruesome scene again, but the sight made him queasy, so he squeamishly stepped back onto the bus.

Brian remained there, in the seat closest to the bathroom. Occasionally, he would glance out the side window where he could see Ellen helping the paramedics by tying tourniquets, or treating for shock, or administering CPR, or, in a far graver case, comforting a young boy whose end was near (for nothing else could be done for him). Ellen's face took on a different appearance to him at that moment; one of an angel—a Godsend, as he watched her hold the hand of a little boy who was just then passing into the next world. Tears streamed down Ellen's cheeks, as if the boy were her own little brother, finding him then losing him all in the same instant.

Chapter 7

New York City

As if the bus ride into the city wasn't disheartening enough. After Brian gave Ellen some much-needed comforting at the Port Authority, and they took a cab to Steinway Hall, she realized it wasn't the same building that Dickens lectured at during his last U.S. performance on April 20, 1868. The inception of Carnegie Hall prompted the owners to relocate, and the original building was demolished in 1916. All that stood now were high-rise apartments called the Zeckendorf Towers. So, even if Dickens *did* hide anything on site, it probably, like he, has long since turned to dust by now.

A scruffy-faced homeless man was sitting on the sidewalk, wrapped in a comforter protecting him from the city's savage winds. Ellen noticed that his socked feet were sticking out of the bottom, in want of shoes. The man poked his hand out of the blanket just enough to reveal his plastic cup; he was so blue from cold that his entire body trembled, rattling what little change was inside his cup.

Ellen reached into her knapsack, but she was unable to produce any change. Instead, she drew out a dollar bill, stuffing it into the man's cup (which stopped him from rattling).

"G'bless ya!" cried the man, looking up at them and attempting to cover his extremities with the blanket. "G'bless ya! You's much kinda den da las' couple dat was lookin' roun' here." His face was so thin it was transparent. "A couple a Scrooges, dat's what dey was!" His hungry eyes peered downward, as if he expected Ellen and Brian to be gone by now and was quite accustomed to talking to himself. He looked back up, surprised they were still there.

Ellen drew another bill, but the man refused her second offering by not producing his cup.

"You saves dat fo' da next one ya see like me. Dat's how we does it in New Yoke."

She gave him a smile instead, and they journeyed on.

"G'bless ya!" he cried. "I sho hope ya fines what ya lookin' fo'! G'bless ya!"

Twilight was setting in, the crepuscular light fading like their hopes of ever finding the second half of the novel. Brian and Ellen meandered through frozen streets; what remained of the city's last snowfall had been plowed against the curb like a dirty Jersey wall of snow, forcing pedestrians to cross only at those intersections containing icy portals.

Brian's leather jacket did little to fend off the frigid winds of the city. "Now what do we do?" he said, shivering.

"I wish I knew the answer," she returned.

He hastened his pace to keep warm. "It's gettin' dark."

"Please," said Ellen, "just let me think."

Brian could only conjure up images of spring break, and Florida, and sunshine, and all the fun his friends were having. "D-d-don't forget," he said, stuttering from the cold, "you told me if this d-d-doesn't work out, th-th-that—"

"I'll fly you to Florida…first-class…I know," she finished.

Having left his gym bag on the Yellow Runt, the boy gave Ellen a sideways glance, envying her fluffy down jacket, and fleecy scarf, and woolen mittens, and knapsack (which even seemed to be keeping her back warm).

"C-c-c-could ya spare a g-g-glove?" he begged.

She plucked off one of her mittens and handed it to him.

"Th-th-thanks."

"I don't know who I feel sorrier for," she said, "that homeless gentleman earlier, or you."

"V-v-very f-f-funny."

"I have to tell you, Brian," she said, "I've exhausted all of my ideas."

His eyes grew angry, but opening his mouth would have allowed some of his hot breath to escape, so he internalized his heated thoughts in an effort to keep from freezing.

"I'm sorry," said Ellen. "I know how badly you wanted to get away for spring break. Instead of eighty-degree weather in Florida, I dragged you here, where the wind chill factor must be ten below. Instead of walking barefoot in the sand, you're trudging through these snowy streets. Instead of being with Jennifer Cole, the most beautiful girl at college, you're—well...you're stuck here with me." Tears started out of her long pretty eyelashes.

Brian stopped her, lifting her glasses, patting her tears dry with the wooly mitten she lent him. "D-d-don't cry," he said, "you'll f-f-freeze to d-d-death." He put his arm around her as they continued traveling into the city's gloaming.

"To make up for this frozen deep I'm putting you through," she said, "pick any hotel you want, and I'll get a room so we can warm up and get a good night's rest. Then tomorrow morning, I'll have you on the first flight to Fort Lauderdale. You'll arrive there before the busses do, I promise."

Brian nodded with a shiver and pointed to the first hotel in sight: the Hotel Delmonico.

When they reached the building, something caused Ellen to pause and stare at the facade. "Delmonico," she said. "Why does that ring a bell?"

Brian pulled her into the lobby and the two were soon nestled high above the city in a magnificent penthouse suite, warm and cozy.

"I'm going to regret this when I get my credit card bill, but we *are* in New York, so we might as well live it up," she said, pushing an express button on the hotel phone. "Room service, please send up a pot of hot coffee and two of the best appetizers, entrees, and desserts that you have. Yes, that will be fine. Thank you."

"You don't have to go overboard," said Brian.

"That's okay. Since I've never been away for spring break, I figure I owe myself a really good one."

"But there's a difference between spring break and springing till you're broke."

"I've been working ever since I was fourteen. It's amazing how much money you save when you never go anywhere."

Brian gazed out of the picture window, looking down at the city. "You said that book I have is worth thousands. How many are we talkin'?"

"Not as much as the letter."

"Yeah?"

"Since the letter is handwritten, it's far more valuable. Unless the second half of the story is found, of course."

"How much?"

"To me, literary-wise, the second half of the book is priceless. It belongs in a museum."

"I'm not talkin' *literally*, I'm talkin' *figuratively*, as in numbers, preferably with lotsa zeroes, ya know?"

"Brian, I wish I could make you understand the true value of what you have. There are far better things in this world to be read than numbers and dollar signs."

"Money is how I bought the book. Money is how we were able to take the bus. Money is how we're able to stay in this suite instead of freezing to death on the street like that homeless guy—and what did *he* want?"

She kept silent.

"Money. That's what he wanted."

Ellen didn't admit it, but knew he made a valid point. Her view of human nature dimmed a bit as she stared out at the city lights that were scintillating in her glasses, dividing the cozy penthouses above from the harsh streets below. When the food and drink finally arrived, she had a hard time enjoying those finer things money can buy, swallowing his statement with every bite.

They dined beside the large picture window of the city, and, when they were through, Brian clasped his hands behind his head and leaned back, as if saying, "Find me a piece of literature anywhere that can satisfy an appetite like *that*." They sipped their coffee, looking out at the lights.

"Tell me, Ellen, why do you think Dickens did it?"

"Sometimes true genius can't be questioned, only accepted."

"But how did he print the book without anybody knowing it?"

"My guess is that Dickens must have printed it himself or had someone close to him at Chapman and Hall do it. I wouldn't be surprised if William Henry Wills was in on it. He was his most trusted and loyal friend."

"I thought you said Forster was his closest friend."

"John Forster was his best friend. But I'm not sure if he was in on it. If he was, don't you think he would have written about it in his biography of Dickens?"

"Yeah. I guess if Forster wanted to make money off Dickens's name, he definitely woulda mentioned the part about hiding the second half of the novel."

"Dickens seemed to have a soft spot for Wills. To him, Wills was like the dedicated, hardworking clerk you always find in his novels. Like Bob Cratchit in A Christmas Carol, or Wemmick in Great Expectations."

"I never read Great Expectations, but I'm an expert on A Christmas Carol. I see it every year on TV."

"You mean to tell me that you'd rather experience the story through the filtered eyes of directors and watered-down interpretations of actors than to get it straight from the fountain? That's like hearsay evidence—entirely impermissible."

"Maybe, but it's a hell of a lot faster."

"How many pages do you think A Christmas Carol is?"

"Hmmm…from what I've seen of his novels, it's gotta be at least a four-hundred pager."

"It's only ninety pages long."

"No way."

"Way. Dickens read it during his final performance at Steinway Hall."

"If I knew the book was shorter than the movie, I definitely woulda read it."

"In fact, at his farewell banquet held for him at—" Ellen's words seemed to hit a brick wall; she froze—in mid-sentence—pondering what she had just said.

"Yeah? I'm followin' ya. His farewell banquet held at…at where?"

"My God," she exclaimed, leaping from the table. Ellen ripped open her knapsack, tearing through her books. "How could I have been so stupid?"

"True stupidity can't be questioned," Brian teased, "only accepted."

"I can't believe it. It was right in front of me all this time!" She dog-eared a page in one of her books, scanned it fervently, then passed it to Brian. "Read this!"

"It says that Horace Greely hosted a farewell banquet for Dickens in New York City at—" *His* words seemed to hit a brick wall. "This is too incredible," he exclaimed. "This is too coincidental. Nunno, no...this is too messed up! This can't be real."

"It is!" she exploded. "I knew the name of this hotel rang a bell. The farewell banquet for Dickens was held at Delmonico's. The Fates may be with us, Brian!"

"You mean *here*? At this hotel?"

"No, not here. At Delmonico's restaurant. And it ties in with the D-E he left in his keynote."

"Deny?"

"Yes! We had the N-Y part of it right, but the D-E part doesn't refer to *of*, it refers to the first two letters of *Delmonico's*. It's not Steinway Hall, the building where he held his farewell *performance*, it's Delmonico's restaurant, the building he had his farewell *banquet*." She pointed to a different paragraph. "See? Dickens showed up an hour late for the banquet. Why? Because he was probably hiding the second half of the novel, that's why!"

"Delmonico's restaurant? Are you sure? How do you even know if this place still exists?"

A smile grew on Ellen's face that stretched from one lens of her glasses to the other. "Because true genius can't be questioned."

Chapter 8

Delmonico's Restaurant

Stepping out of the cab, the classmates were greeted by two huge inviting arms of white marble columns surrounded by brownstone. The sculpted pillars supported a 19th century portico that was so aesthetically pleasing, it seemed a sin no one was using it as a balcony.

A chill ran through Ellen's body that had more to do with the city's atmosphere than temperature. "I know something's here," she said. "I can just feel it."

The chill running through Brian's body, however, had everything to do with temperature. He hurried Ellen (who was still admiring the building's facade) up to the entrance and through the large wooden doors.

A pleasant man with a strong Italian accent met them on their way in. "Welcoma to Delmonico's," he said. "Please tella me you hava reservation?"

In their rush to get there, they had neglected to call in advance.

"Thatsa quite all right," assured the Italian man, smiling. "No problema. I find you nica table, romantica, eh?" He turned to the dining room. "Vincenzo," he called, "a bella tavola for these two younga people."

They followed the waiter to a beautifully arranged table next to the wine cellar, Ellen's eyes scanning the room the entire way. She noticed a newspaper clipping of Mark Twain on the wall, along with several pictures of children and various ships and boats, but not a hint of Dickens.

"Good evening," said the sommelier. "Would you care to see the wine list?"

"No thank—"

"Please," Brian interrupted. "We *are* in New York, so we might as well live it up, right?"

She leered at him.

"We'll take a bottle of...of *this*," he said, pointing at the miniature menu.

"Very well," returned the sommelier, removing the list before departing. He circled the room once, attending to other patrons, then entered the wine cellar beside them.

"You're never supposed to point at the menu," said Ellen, schooling him in etiquette. "If you can't read it, you shouldn't order it."

"I just read the numbers next to it. I figure for sixty bucks, it should be pretty decent. Don't forget that you said all expenses are included on this little scavenger hunt."

The bread soon arrived, and Ellen reminded Brian to employ his napkin on his lap with an "ahem" and a display of her linen.

"Ya see anything yet?" he asked, buttering a piece of warm bread.

"If you're into old ships," she replied, gesturing at the pictures. "On Dickens's last voyage to the U.S., he arrived on a ship named the *Cuba* and left on the *Russia*, but I haven't seen any of those names."

The sommelier returned with the bottle of wine, presenting it to Brian. Ellen couldn't hold back her laughter as she watched Brian tasting the wine, swishing it around the inside of his mouth then gargling.

"Acceptable," Brian said in a pompous tone. "Please, serve the lady then refresh my glass."

"Very well," he replied.

Ellen directed her words at the sommelier, but not with a wine request. "Do you have any Charles Dickens memorabilia on the premises?"

"I'm rather new, but I shall ask the manager."

"Very well," said Brian, imitating him then turning to Ellen. "How about a toast?"

"Sure."

"Since you're the literary expert," said Brian, "I figure you should know some pretty good ones."

"I'm not so sure about that. Some of the best toasts I've heard spouted from the lips of those who partake in the grape."

"In that case, *I* should know some pretty good ones." He lifted his wineglass. "Old college friends never die; they just meet someplace else for a drink."

Ellen chimed her wine vessel against his. "Much more profound than the toast Horace Greely gave at Dickens's farewell banquet," she said.

"How's that?"

"They ended with *God save the Queen*," she replied.

"Would you care to order now?" asked the waiter.

"Give us another minute," Brian said, glancing over the menu. "This Delmonico steak sounds awesome."

"You mean to tell me you still have an appetite after the dinner we had?"

"What can I say—searching for lost treasures makes me hungry." He glanced at the menu. "It says here that Delmonico's invented the Baked Alaska."

"Yes. The one they serve here was Dickens's favorite."

Brian closed his menu. "Ellen, why is it you always have to relate everything to Charles Dickens? I mean... the food, the wine, the way he helped people in that Steeplechase train accident—"

"Staplehurst," she corrected.

"Ya see? That's exactly what I mean. I'm trying to talk to you about somethin' and you catch me on a literary technicality."

"*Historical* technicality."

The waiter returned, and Brian took his frustration out on Ellen's credit card, ordering the Delmonico steak along with some appetizers.

She took a sip of wine. "Brian, remember before when I told you I was an only child, and I had my books to keep me company?"

He nodded.

"Well, I rarely tell anyone this, but the truth is, I was adopted at a very young age." As Ellen spoke, she stared into her glass, swirling her wine. "From what I've been told, my father ran out on my mother, and...well...I suppose she ran out on me, too. She gave me up a few days after my birth."

Brian's eyes turned from frustration to sympathy.

"Please don't get me wrong, I love my adoptive parents more than anything, and I'm thankful they told me. But there's still that burning feeling that gnaws away at you, wanting to know the truth, wanting to know the..." she paused... "*the whole story*."

Brian thought for a moment about what she had said. "Did you ever try to find her?"

She took another sip of wine. "No. It's not that simple. You see, I was born in England, and after the adoption went through, we ended up moving to New Jersey. Lord knows I've always wanted to see England. More than anything in this world I've wanted to see England. But knowing that *she's* there, *somewhere,* well, somehow it's always kept me from going."

Brian was too interested in her story to drink his wine.

"Now, I know you've never read any of Dickens's works—"

"I've read some Cliffs Notes versions," he said, trying to lure her eyes away from her wineglass to coax a smile.

"But whenever I read Dickens, it seems as though he's talking directly to *me*. All of his longing for love and searching for truth seems to be written about *me*. All of his genuine goodness and humility seems to be written for *me*," she construed with great feeling. "His characters were not only the brothers and sisters I've never had, but they were also the parents and grandparents and aunts and uncles I've never known."

Brian leaned in and took her hand, Ellen's eyes moving from her glass to his face.

"You're a remarkable person, Ellen Pipple," he said, staring into her chestnut eyes, the flame of the candle flickering in them, lending her face a soft semblance. He leaned in closer, wanting to kiss her, but a different waiter (one with a French accent) interrupted him, arriving with the appetizers.

"Cheeken Cezair?"

Brian raised his hand.

The waiter was about to place the shrimp cocktail in front of Ellen, but Brian raised his hand again, signaling it was for him as well.

"Bon appétit." The waiter left Brian with both appetizers (along with an awkward glance).

"Funny," Brian said, "suddenly I've lost my appetite."

"I thought searching for lost treasures makes you hungry."

Brian started leaning in again, determined to kiss her this time, but the manager with the Italian accent appeared at the table.

"How isa everything, my younga people? You lika table, eh? Table es beautiful, no?"

"It's lovely," Ellen replied.

He looked at Brian's food. "You lika shrimp cocktail, eh? Shrimp cocktail es good, no?"

"Yeah, it's good," said Brian.

He noticed the boy's Caesar salad hadn't been touched either. "You lika salad, eh? Salad es—?"

"Everything's great," said Brian, "I had a big dinner earlier and it's startin' to settle."

"Whatsa matter?" the manager said to Ellen. "You no lika menu?"

She smiled at him. "Yes, very much."

"You try—you lika." He slid Brian's Caesar over to her. "You mangia, buona."

Ellen took a bite of salad out of courtesy.

"You waiter tella me you lika *Charl Deeken*, eh?"

"Why yes," Ellen returned. "We are very interested in Charles Dickens."

"Charl Deeken lika Delmonico's—very mucha lika Delmonico's."

"Yes, yes...we know," she said.

"I giva you tour after deener. I show you rooma Charl Deeken."

Ellen was ecstatic, looking between the Italian man and Brian. "There's a Dickens room? Thank you! We would like that very much!"

"Buona, buona," he said in parting, "riposa e mangia."

"Isn't that fantastic?" Ellen exclaimed, her eyes widening to the degree that the candle flickering within them turned into a flare.

"Yeah, uh, that's just great," Brian returned, knowing he missed his romantic window of opportunity.

She dug into the Caesar salad. "I'm so excited," she said with her mouth full. "Maybe that's where we'll find it."

"What makes you so sure it's here?"

"I told you," she said, ravenously eating the salad, "I can just feel it. Mmmm, this is delicious, want a bite?"

"No...thanks."

She reached over and snatched a shrimp, dunking it deep into the cocktail sauce before devouring it. "Shrimp's great. You don't know what you're missing."

When the two finished, the pleasant Italian man appeared at their table and proceeded to give them a tour of the restaurant. He showed them a large room that had a placard labeled 'Dickens Alcove.'

"This is the very room in which his farewell banquet was held," said Ellen, taking in the moment. She searched every nook and cranny, but not a shred of evidence even resembling a book was to be found. She even inspected the Mark Twain Alcove (perhaps a barroom where rumors of his drunkenness were *highly* exaggerated).

Trusting her feelings, claiming that it felt as if someone were running a violin bow across her spine, Ellen still insisted something was there.

They returned to the table where she closed her eyes to think. During this pondering process, Brian's eyes wandered through the glass door of the wine cellar, noticing what appeared to be a small, recessed attic door in its ceiling.

"Ellen?"

"Please," she replied, her eyes squinting shut. "I'm trying to concentrate."

Because Brian ceased in pestering her any further (keeping himself *too* quiet), Ellen peeked an eye at him, her candlewicks growing again, her gaze following his gaze up to the ceiling of the wine cellar, up to the tiny recessed door—that violin bow running across her spine again.

"What should we do?" asked Brian.

"It's too high for me to reach. You'll have to go."

"But how?" he replied. "They'll see me through the glass."

"I'll create a diversion." Ellen thought for a moment. "When the waiter comes back, order the Baked Alaska."

"Huh?"

"Then, when everyone's looking at me, make your move—but be quick."

"What are ya gonna do?"

"Don't worry," she replied, "just be sure to look for anything unusual when you're up there; anything that seems like it could contain a book the size of yours."

She hesitantly rose from the table and began strolling past the many pictures on the wall, pretending to view them again, peeping back at their table. When Brian was in the process of ordering the Baked Alaska, she lashed the sash of her frumpy dress around a piece of railing by the staircase. When the waiter left, she started away from the rail swiftly, leaving her dress ensnared, which pulled her entire garment right off her body!

"Aaaaaaaah!" she screamed, all eyes riveting on her.

In a clinging white bra and panties, Ellen stood motionless, half-naked, in the middle of the restaurant.

Brian, who at this point was supposed to make a dash for the wine cellar door, couldn't take his eyes off the girl. She looked directly at him and screamed again, much more animated and contrived this time, but Brian just sat there, helplessly admiring the figure that her dress had been hiding all along. It wasn't until the pleasant manager, in a frantic attempt to cover Ellen, yanked a tablecloth off a newly set table (the resounding crash of chinaware causing a diversion in itself!) that the boy remembered his assignment and made a break for the cellar door.

"Itsa okay," said the manager, covering Ellen with the huge white linen as patrons hysterically guffawed. "Everything es a gooda now, eh?" He raised the back of his hand at the customers in disgust, scolding them: "You shooda be ashamed uva youselves," he chastised. "Ifa es you daughter, you no laugha!" The Italian man's accent and actions were so funny that Ellen couldn't keep from laughing herself, so she put her head on his shoulder and pretended to be crying.

"Thatsa okay, looka, you boyfriend musta be ina restaroom, no be shamed, he no see nothing, no be shamed."

The more he spoke, the more she laughed, burying her face into his shoulder, her tears tumbling down the back of his dress shirt.

"Take easy," said the manager. "You no pay for deener tonight, Delmonico's pay for you deener tonight. You take easy...everythinga okay now."

When her laughter subsided, she tried to look at the man, but his round, olive, pleasant smiling countenance forced her to plunge her face back into his shoulder.

The sheer distress she was seemingly exhibiting prompted the manager to summon not only Ellen's waiter over to her side, but all the waiters, busboys, and wine stewards from every other table were sent into flight as well. If the employees weren't trying to unravel her dress from the railing, they were fetching her water, or coffee, or tiny glasses of liqueurs. When it finally came time for the Baked Alaska to arrive, it was personally served fresh by the chef himself, which seemed to be the only thing capable of calming her down.

When she saw a pair of denim legs dangling from the ceiling of the wine cellar, and Brian drop to the floor (disappointingly shaking his head and shrugging his shoulders), the girl really began to dissolve into tears.

On their way out of the restaurant, the round, pleasant man unintentionally elicited more tears from her by saying, "Coma again and veesit Charl Deeken room soon, eh?"

Chapter 9

A Message

The city loomed so dark and cold, and the two students felt so lost and clueless, it seemed as if they were in a foreign land.

"It's alright, Ellen," Brian consoled, putting his arm around her as they walked down Wall Street. "So, I'm out a few million bucks, no biggie."

"If you're trying to make me feel better," she said with a sniffle, "it's not working."

"I've still got the first half of the story, and the letter," he said, patting his leather jacket. "As long as I come out ahead."

"Are you sure there wasn't anything up there, Brian?"

He pulled her in close as they strolled, her puffy coat helping him keep warm. "I already told ya, the only thing up there was some empty wine bottles and cigarette butts."

"Well, what took you so long?"

"I searched the whole floor, all the way to a window that led to the balcony out front."

"The portico?"

"Yeah—I even jimmied open a window and stepped out on it to look around. Nice view."

"Nothing?"

"Nope." He pulled her closer as they walked, watching the city's lights project off her eyes. "Just graffiti. Someone carved their initials into the rail." He began to bend down in an attempt to kiss the girl again.

"Initials?" she said with a glimmer of hope, not even noticing his advance.

"Yeah. That's all. Initials. Probably the same person who left the wine bottles and cigarette butts."

"What were they?"

"The wine bottles or the cigarettes?"

"No, nunno. The initials," she asked.

"Oh…that." He thought for a second. "P.J.T." Not wanting to miss another romantic window of opportunity, the boy closed his eyes and started to make his advance.

Ellen closed her eyes too, but for a different reason. "Wait!" she shouted, causing Brian to jump.

"What is it?" he alarmingly answered, taking a defensive posture and looking around for whatever prompted her to shout with such fury.

"P.J.T!" she returned. "He left a clue!"

"Who?...P.J.T.?"

"No—Dickens!"

"He did?"

"Yes! P.J.T.! It begins in the eighth chapter of Drood. Those are the same initials above the portal of Mr. Grewgious's chambers at the Staple Inn."

"Yeah?"

"Hand me the book…please!"

Brian partially unzipped his coat, retrieving it for her, his actions inviting an unwelcomed blast of cold into his body.

"See?" she said, leafing through the pages. "P.J.T.! It's one of the recurring keynotes of the novel! It shows up several places," she added, pointing them out. "You really *should* read the first half, Brian."

"So, you're still sayin' he hid the second half of it back there?"

"No. I think I'm beginning to understand now. P.J.T. is just a clue. Maybe it leads to the story; maybe it leads to another clue."

"Yeah, but sooner or later," Brian said, "aren't the clues bound to end up being destroyed?"

"I've thought of that. But we can only trust that Dickens was smart enough to hide the clues in places that would stand the test of time."

"What do *you* think?"

She took a moment before responding. "I think if anybody was smart enough to do it, *he* was. And if anyone is smart enough and adventurous enough to find it, *we* are. Afterall, we've solved two clues up to this point, haven't we?"

"Yeah. I suppose you're right." He zipped his jacket over his chin, and Ellen handed him a mitten. "But where do we go from here?"

"That's simple," she replied. "We must go to—"

"'Scuse me," interrupted a ragged child of the streets, no more than nine. The child approached the two, his clothes grungy and face dirty. A triangular hat made of newspaper covered the top of his head. "I has a message for ya."

"For *us*?" Ellen inquired.

The child scratched the top of his newspaper. "You two *was* the ones over on Fourteenth Street earlier, wasn't ya?"

"Why, yes," Ellen replied, wondering how the child could have known that.

"An' you two *was* the ones lookin' at where the old Steinway Hall used to be, wasn't ya?"

"Why, yes," Ellen repeated.

"An' you two *was* the ones interested in Charles Dickens, wasn't ya?"

Ellen opened her mouth but was too shocked to respond.

"Well," continued the child, "I has a message for ya." He reached into his many layers of frayed rags and produced a plastic cup with a note inside. "I'm s'posta give this to ya right away."

Ellen reached her hand out to him, the hand without the mitten, and the child placed the cup in her palm, slightly brushing her fingers before letting it go.

She remembered the cup. It was the same one she placed a dollar bill in earlier for the homeless man. But instead of loose change rattling inside, there was a ball of crumpled up paper. Ellen glanced at the child's sooty, innocent face. She removed the ball from the cup and unwrinkled it slowly. When her eyes met the paper, a look of terrorizing disbelief filled her countenance that turned her complexion even paler.

Only three words were written: 'YOU IN DANGER.'

Chapter 10

A Guest

"Wfhat the hell kind of a joke is this!" Brian demanded, staring the sooty child down.

"It's no joke, Sir," he said, pushing the newspaper hat onto the back of his head.

"Who the hell gave you this note!" pressed Brian.

"Well, to tell ya the trufe, Sir," said the child, readjusting his paper hat, "the rich people roun' here has their ways of communicatin', ya know, with them teeny phones an' little things that go a-beepin', an' us people of the street, well...we has our own ways of communicatin' too."

"Tell me who wrote this," he pressed, "or I'm callin' the cops!"

"Brian, please!" interposed Ellen. "He's just a child."

"Wif all due respecs, Sir, wouldn't do ya no good anyhow. The police would jus' think I'm tryin' to get a free pass. They'd jus' as soon look at me as put me an' my fam'ly back on the street. They'd says, *'This ain't no Holiday Inn,'* that's what they'd says, cuz they says it before, *'This ain't no Holiday Inn.'"*

Ellen bent down at the child, eye to eye, fixing a smile on him. "What's your name?"

"Wif all due respecs, Miss, I growed up wif so many diff'rent names, I'd has to pick one outta my hat to give one to ya," said the child, emphasizing his remark by removing his newspaper cap and pretending to pull something out of it. "I don't has a name as ya might think. But I'll tell ya what they calls me on the street... they calls me Sonar."

"And why might that be?" Ellen inquired.

"Cuz if anyone ever needs to locate sumpfin', they calls on me, an' I'll fine it for um."

Brian angrily moved in to threaten the child some more, but Ellen held her hand up to the breast of his leather, halting his advance.

"And someone told you to find us," she asked, still bending down at the child, smiling, "is that right, Sonar?"

"Shir is, Miss."

"And they told you to deliver this message too, is that right Sonar?"

"Shir is, Miss."

Ellen examined the plastic cup. "And this person who told you to find us, Sonar, was he a thin gentleman? Scruffy-faced? No shoes? Wrapped in a big blanket?"

"I couldn't 'splain um better, Miss, if he was standin' right here in frunna me now, I couldn't 'splain um better."

She turned her smile to Brian, who still appeared angry. "See? All it takes is a little kindness."

"Kindness?" Brian snapped. "Someone hands you a threatening note and you respond with kindness? Maybe we should wait for someone to pull a gun on us so you can be courteously gracious too!"

"Don't mind him," she told the child. "He's just a little grumpy because he can't go to Florida and play with his friends." She cupped her mitten around his ear, whispering. "He's been placed on academic probation."

Although Sonar hadn't the slightest idea of what she meant, he chuckled until he caught sight of Brian (who was fuming), prompting the child to cut short his laughter, readjust his newspaper hat, and attempt to avoid eye contact with him (like a cute puppy caught rummaging the trash).

"It's from the gentleman we met earlier," she said to Brian. "The one I gave the dollar bill to…remember?"

"The homeless guy?"

"That's the one," she replied.

"Why the hell would he send us a note like this? And even if we were in danger, how the hell would that guy know?"

"Why or how he knows, I haven't a clue. But somehow I know he's telling the truth. As sure as I knew Dickens left something back there at the restaurant, I know he's telling the truth."

Brian let out a visible laugh, his icy breath sending huge clouds in every direction of the city. "Get real, Ellen—they're tryin' to scam us! You're readin' too much fiction!"

She bent down at the child again. "Do you have somewhere to sleep tonight, Sonar?"

"Wif all due respecs, Miss, I always has a place to sleep at nights; so long as there's a park bench, or a doorstep, or a subway vent no one is a-claimin', I has a place to sleep at nights."

She placed her hands on the child's shoulders. "How about you come along with us tonight, and spend the night at our hotel?"

This spontaneous invitation on Ellen's behalf had Brian (who had other plans for the evening) doing a double take and appearing angrier than before.

"Wif all due respecs, Miss, that's very kind of ya, an' ya look nice anuff to take up wif for the night (him, I'm not so sure 'bout), but *you*, why, *you* look nice anuff to take up wif for the night. But, come mornin', I wouldn't want ya takin' me to the place they always takes me to when they fine out I don't has a home. I'd just as soon rather keep my freedoms an' stay on the street, wif all due respecs."

"There ya go," Brian said. "He doesn't want to stay with us."

Ellen squeezed the child's shoulders, as if hugging him at arm's length with her hands. "Sonar, if you stay with us tonight, I promise," she said, removing her glasses and revealing her true face to the child, "I promise that in the morning, you can go wherever you want."

Brian's infuriated face couldn't help but to look at her countenance too, knowing that the child wouldn't refuse her offer. (It would be difficult for anyone to refuse a face exhibiting such niceness.)

"Wif all due respecs, Miss, an' all counts taken into 'sideration, I'd love to take up wif ya for the night. But I don't think your friend here is lookin' too kindly at it."

Ellen looked up at Brian, whose scowl turned into a plastic smile.

"Don't be ridiculous," Brian said to the child, talking through a plastered grin, "I'd love to have ya..." he had to force the last part through his teeth, "*take up with us*."

"There!" said Ellen. "You see? We'd love to have you spend the night."

"Well," replied the child, glancing at Brian who was desperately trying to hold his smile, "if ya really wanna has me as your guest, who am I to argue wif ya?"

Ellen patted the child's newspaper hat. "Brian, can you hail us a taxi?"

"Wif all due respecs," said Sonar, "I'd be mighty happy to catch a cab for ya, since I does it for people all the time. Ya might say it's one of my specialties. I s'pose it'd be kinda nice catchin' one for misself for a change."

Ellen giggled as she watched the child give a loud whistle to a taxi, jumping up and down and waving his hands at it.

"Brian, isn't he the sweetest boy you've ever met?"

"Oh yeah," he said through his teeth. "Real sweet kid, alright."

They arrived back at the hotel and rode the elevator to the top floor. When Ellen inserted her keycard into the lock, she opened the door to a scene of complete disarray.

It was as if a miniature tornado entered from the sliding glass door of the lanai and swept through every corner of the suite! Bureaus and desk drawers were ripped out and upturned! Mattresses, chairs, and bedding were upended and strewn in every direction! Bottles, cans, and snacks from the mini bar littered the room! The only thing seemingly left intact was the spectacular view of the city.

The three carefully stepped into the room, Ellen and Brian aghast.

"Wif all due respecs," said Sonar, "I thought a big fancy hotel like this'd keep the rooms a bit more respec'able."

"Somethin' tells me this wasn't housekeeping," said Brian, checking all the rooms and closets.

Ellen cautiously reeled herself up to the dining room table. "My God!" she said, rooting through her knapsack, "all my written notes—they're gone!"

Brian picked up the standard issue hotel bible from off the floor. Someone had taken the steak knife from their room service order and plunged it into the heart of The Good Book. Brian held it up. "Whoever the hell it is, they mean business."

Ellen slowly meandered through the suite, following her nose to the smell of that frowsty odor again.

"Do you smell that cologne?" she said.

"Smells like a hotel room to me," Brian answered.

She pulled Brian over to the spot she was standing. "You mean to tell me you can't smell that?"

Brian shook his head.

"How about you, Sonar?" She walked him over to the spot. "Do you smell that?"

"Wif all due respecs, Miss Ellen, I has smelled so many nice things since we come into this hotel, they all kinda lumped together in my nose."

"That's what I wanted to tell you on the bus, Brian, remember? When I told you it would come back to me?"

"What would come back?"

"Last night…when you left your book at the library, and I realized it was the original. Some books fell off the shelf behind me—why it scared me half to death! I went around to the other side of the bookshelf and…" she raised her button nose and took a deep whiff, "that's the same cologne. It's such a familiar scent, too. Where have I encountered it before?" she said, closing her eyes in frustration.

"Wait a minute," said Brian. "Are you sayin' the same person who just trashed our room and harpooned this bible was at Hornbake library last night?"

"Yes! They must have overheard me dictating notes! Why—I'll even bet it's the same person who stole my tape recorder!" She lowered herself into the dining room chair. "I feel faint."

Sonar retrieved a bottle of cold water from the refrigerator and uncapped it for her.

"Don't get all worked up," said Brian. "People rob hotel rooms all the time."

"Look around," she said, sipping the water and fanning herself with the room service menu. "Isn't it odd that nothing of value is missing? They're after your book. How else can you explain the missing notes...and tape recorder?"

Brian opened his mouth for rebuttal, but she interrupted.

"And somehow," she said, taking another sip, "the note Sonar delivered ties in. We must try to find that homeless gentleman. He's our only eyewitness to whom-ever it is that did this."

"I'm callin' the police," said Brian, picking up the phone.

"Brian, wait," she said, removing her glasses and splashing her face with some of the water. "Unless you're willing to reveal the motive...meaning *why* someone should threaten us, then call the police." She splashed her face again. "But I warn you, a story like this will be on the front pages of every paper in the free world by the time we checkout tomorrow."

He quickly hung up the phone.

Ellen turned to the child. "Sonar," she said, placing her hand on his shoulder, "the gentleman who gave you the note, is he always on that street corner?"

"'Less the police tell um to move," replied the child. "But even if they has, I know where to fine um. They don't calls me Sonar for nuffin'."

Ellen glanced at her watch. "My goodness, it's almost midnight. We'll have to locate him first thing in the morning. A boy of your age should be fast asleep by now."

"Wif all due respecs, Miss Ellen, it's still early for me yet."

"Nonsense. You're going to have a nice hot bath and get ready for bed."

"Wif all due respecs, Miss—"

"Now!" she insisted.

"Yes, Miss Ellen."

Although she was stern, the child seemed to enjoy being told what to do. And in no time, he was bathed, dried, Q-tipped, manicured, and groomed to such a stately degree, it would be difficult for even one of his fellow friends of the street to recognize him.

Brian, however, did *not* enjoy being told what to do. While Ellen was attending to Sonar, she had Brian clean up everything in the suite so that management wouldn't ask any questions come morning.

Just as it is entirely possible for a person to be jealous of someone who has been dead for a hundred and thirty years, it is equally possible for a person to be jealous of another who is barely nine. Because, as Ellen was tucking the child into the nicest bed in the suite, reading him chapter twelve of *Drood,* Brian was finishing up his cleaning duties, uttering under his breath: "Yes, Miss Ellen. Whatever you say, Miss Ellen. Can you bend over a little more so I can kiss your ass, Miss Ellen?"

The girl gently closed the door of the child's room, putting her finger to her lips. "Try to keep it down," she whispered, "he's asleep now."

Brian cracked open a can of Budweiser from the mini bar. "The kid's used to sleeping on subway vents, Ellen. I don't think he's gonna have any trouble tonight."

"Why—of all the mean-spirited, horrible things I've ever heard—"

"What side of the bed do you want?" said Brian, pulling his white t-shirt over his head.

"If for a moment you think that we're going to sleep in the same—"

"Somehow I peg you as a *left side of the bed* type of person."

"Brian Murray! If for a moment you think that we—"

"But the left and right side of a bed depends on how you sleep, really. If you sleep on your stomach, then it's this side," he gestured with his beer; "if you sleep on your back, it's that side," he again gestured, raising the beer up to his lips on the follow through and taking a gulp. He unfastened his jeans.

Ellen started to resume her objection when her protest was ceased in mid-utterance, her mouth agape. Brian dropped his pants.

"And ya might want to consider keeping your purse close at hand," he said, climbing into bed. "In fact, with that street urchin around, I'll be surprised if any of this stuff will still be here when we wake up tomorrow."

"That's quite enough!" she said. "I've had it with you!" She marched over to the telephone.

"What are you doing?"

"Calling security," she replied. "I'm going to have you removed from this room at once." She rang the front desk.

"You can't do that," he said, propped up in bed, confidently sprawled out in his underwear and sipping his beer.

"No? Whose name is on the registry, hmmm?"

"You wouldn't do that."

"Hello," she said into the phone, "I believe there has been a mix-up in rooms. There's a strange man—no…I take that back," she said, exaggeratingly looking at him from top to bottom, "there's a strange *boy* in my bed and I would like to have him removed at once."

Brian leaped out of bed and into his jeans. "Okay! Okay! You can have the bed!"

"On second thought," she said, looking at him again, "he seems harmless enough...No, that will be quite all right, he's much too small to have to worry about a thing like that. Thank you."

"What do ya mean *too small?*" he exclaimed, zipping up his pants.

Ellen removed a long nightshirt from her knapsack, changing into it in such a fashion that it was impossible for Brian to catch even a glimpse of her.

"Real funny," he said, plopping onto the sofa, clasping his hands behind his head. "I'll just lay here and dream about Florida...and Jennifer Cole," he added, glancing over to see if she was paying any attention.

The girl climbed under the covers, fluffed her pillow, and set her glasses on the nightstand. "That's nice," she replied in a yawn. "Good night."

"Ellen," he said, lifting his head to peek over, "I'm not used to sleeping alone on spring break."

"You have your book. Try reading."

"You know what I mean."

"Fortunately, yes, yes I do. And as I mentioned earlier, I'm not one of your sorority girls back at college."

"I thought since you always let me copy your notes, well…that you kinda liked me."

"And for a while there, I thought that you might have liked me too. It's funny how your mind will lead you to believe what you want to believe. I even wrote a paper on it once for psych class. I called it The Ouija Board Effect." She let go a laugh. "And to think, I actually pictured us spending spring break together working on our papers. What a fool I was. But when you thought I was going to do your paper *for* you; well, that's when I knew you were just using me all along."

Brian lay silent, filled with reproach.

"The only thing that kept you from taking that bus to Florida this morning was the money. I know I had nothing to do with it." She sat up and put her glasses on, addressing him. "But things have flipped around a bit in the past twenty-four hours, Brian Murray, haven't they? Instead of *you* using *me*, *I'm* using *you*. I wouldn't be here without your book." She set her glasses back on the night table, resting her head and lashes on her soft pillow. "What a difference a day makes."

"Yeah? Is that right? How are *you* using *me*? If we ever do find the ending, who says you're gonna get anything out of it, huh?"

"Haven't you figured it out by now, Brian? I'm not in it for the money, or any fame, or glory or greed…and I'm certainly not in it for *you*."

"Oh yeah? Then what the hell *are* you in it for? You have to be in it for *something!*"

Ellen fluffed her pillow a bit more, yawned, rested her head, and then really got the better of him by falling fast asleep.

Chapter 11

The Streets

Sonar appeared from the bedroom that next morning wearing a hotel robe ten sizes too big. Spread before the child was a lavishly garnished table of scrambled eggs, bacon, sausage, ham, French toast, pancakes, a Belgium waffle, bagels with cream cheese, fresh squeezed orange juice, milk, and assorted pastries of every kind. Sonar rubbed his eyes and looked at the table again (to be sure the scene was real) and wasted no time seating himself and stuffing his clean face with one bite of everything, working from the left side of the table to the right, then starting over again like the return cylinder of an old-fashioned typewriter.

"Good morning, Sonar," said Ellen. "Did you sleep well?"

The child became conscious of his poor manners, washing down everything in his mouth with a gulp of milk before responding.

"Wif all due respecs, Miss Ellen, I had the pleasin'est of sleeps las' night that I'm wonderin' if I still ain't a-dreamin'."

Ellen's white teeth beamed at him. "I had some new clothes sent up to the room for you." One of her hands held up a hanger draping a shirt, sweater, and pair of corduroys; the other displaying a box of brand-new sneakers.

The child furrowed his brow. "Wif all due respecs, Miss Ellen, I thought ya told me ya wasn't gonna take me to that place. Ya said that come mornin', I could go wherevers I wanna...'member?"

"Yes Sonar, of course I remember. And I always keep my promise, so you needn't worry. Now, finish your breakfast."

The child smiled at her, then resumed stuffing himself with food.

By this time, Brian had risen from the sofa, stretched, and swigged some warm beer left on the nightstand. He nabbed a copy of *The New York Times* that Ellen had brought in from outside their door.

"Well, I'm glad *someone* slept good last night," said Brian, rubbing his lumbar region and bending backward. "I felt every spring in that sofa."

Ellen laughed. "I'm sure that on your many collegiate escapades you've passed out on far worse things than a couch."

"Yeah, but I always had a girl to break my fall."

She ignored his remark. "There's hot coffee, or are you sticking with warm beer?"

"Brew'll do," he said, finishing his beer and crunching the tin can. "After all, it *is* spring break." He grabbed another can from the mini bar, making his way over to the breakfast table, singing part of *Roadhouse Blues* by The Doors: "*Well I woke up this mornin' and got myself*

81

a beer...the future's uncertain and the end is always near." He opened the paper to the sports section. "Morning, Sonar."

"Mownin', Sir," the child answered with a mouthful of food, washing his response down with some orange juice before continuing. "Wif all due respecs, Sir, I was wondrin' if ya was gonna be needin' the classifies. An' if ya wasn't, if I can has um."

"Sure, here ya go," said Brian, handing over the classified ads section of the newspaper. "But aren't you a little young to be looking for a job?"

"Well, Sir, to tell ya the trufe, I wasn't wantin' um to look for a job." With the finesse of an origami, the child began folding a sheet of the paper, not taking his eyes off Brian. "I was wantin' um to make me a new hat." He placed the neatly constructed product on his head. "The classifies is the bes' thing to make a hat outta, 'cause no one I know will wanna nab um off my head to read um."

Ellen seemed to melt a bit more with each sip of her coffee (and each sentence the child uttered).

Sonar lowered his eyes. "As for me, I couldn't read the paper if I'd wanna. I was never learned."

"You're not missin' much," said Brian, browsing the pages. "Like this, for instance: it's gonna be eighty degrees today in Florida," he said loud enough for Ellen to hear. "The high here in New York should be twenty," he added.

She ignored him again.

"And how about this, Sonar: a record number of college students are hittin' the beaches in Lauderdale."

His eyes skimmed the pages. "And here, in Manhattan, a record number of influenza cases."

Ellen sipped her coffee.

"And this: the water temp in Florida is—"

"That's quite enough!" Ellen asserted, slamming her hand down on the table. "At first, I felt bad about keeping you from going. But not anymore! I'm sick and tired of hearing you whine about it. You're a big boy now, Brian Murray, you know the circumstances, so make a decision and stick to it! Believe me, I'd be more than happy to fly you to Florida now. I'll even pin a nametag on you so you won't get lost."

Brian sat still, like a student being reamed by his teacher.

"So? What's it going to be?" she demanded, steaming, along with her coffee. "Are you staying or going?"

He was almost afraid to answer. "Last night," he said, "last night when I told you about those initials I found at Delmonico's, you were gonna tell me where we go from here. But you never did."

"Fair enough. You want to know where we go from here? Simple. As I told you before, the initials P.J.T. are the same initials inscribed above Mr. Grewgious's portal at the Staple Inn. We must go to the Staple Inn. There, you have it. *Satisfied?"* Ellen emphasized this last word as if daring him to contradict it.

"Y-yeah," he replied in a wishy-washy voice. "I guess."

"Good!" She capped off her coffee with a splash from the pot. "That's the trouble with you, Brian. You never pay attention. That's why you ask questions twice in class. That's why you have to copy other people's notes. And that's why you're on academic probation."

Brian didn't say anything for the rest of the morning. He didn't even ask Ellen for one of her mittens after they checked out of the hotel and made their way onto the icy streets.

Sonar led the way in his new wardrobe, donning, along with his new clothes, a new pair of gloves and a big puffy coat (which resembled a miniature version of Ellen's) to keep out the city's blustery chill. The child looked bright and venerable in his new attire. It was as if all the poverty had been scrubbed off him in the tub the night before and let to drain along with his bath water. In fact, the only trace of indigence that remained on him was the newspaper hat he positioned low on his brow. Though Ellen purchased a fashionable wool hat for him (which he wore, keeping his head cozy), he refused to part with the newspaper lid, citing that it was his trademark.

The three journeyed through areas of New York seldom found on the itineraries of tourists. Soon, they reached the corner of 14th Street, where the shoeless, homeless man who wrote 'YOU IN DANGER' should have been rattling a cup full of change from under his comforter. All that remained, however, was the comforter.

Several homeless people stood around the man's cover in an arc formation, bowing their heads at the blanket, as if in prayer.

"Where is he?" Ellen asked.

"There's only one thing that'd pull ol' Shooey away from his blanket," Sonar replied. He gazed upward. "The Good Lord, Hisself."

Sonar went over to the arc of homeless people to confirm it.

"Where *he* gone to," said one of the homeless men, "not even *you* can find him, Sonar."

"Dis cold weather dun claimed another one!" shouted a broken-looking woman.

"Don't worry, Sonar," added another, "you won't find *his* name on your hat tomorrow."

Sonar rushed over to Ellen, tears starting down his cheeks.

"I'm so sorry," she said, throwing her arms around the child.

Sonar sobbed heavily on her.

"I didn't know he was a good friend of yours," she said.

"None of us out here is friends," the child said between sobs, "we is all more like fam'ly."

Ellen squeezed him tightly, providing a much-needed warmth between them.

"I'm sad for bofe of you too," Sonar said, "you two has been so nice to me, lettin' me take up wif ya las' night, an' feedin' me, an' buyin' me new clothes an' ev'rythin'. Now you'll never knowed who's after ya."

"There, there," she consoled, drawing a few tissues out of her purse and drying the child's eyes, "don't worry about us. We'll be just fine." Ellen beamed at him, and her smile seemed to soak up some of the tears that the tissues left behind.

"Wif all due respecs," said the child, sniffling and glancing at the arc of people who seemed to be awaiting him. "I bes' be on my way."

"Sonar," Brian said, breaking his silence. "Why don't you hang with us till we leave the city?"

This statement surprised Ellen.

"Anyway," Brian continued, "we're gonna need someone to help us find this Staple Inn."

Though Ellen was pleased with the Scrooge-like change in Brian's behavior, she had to disappointingly cut short his bonhomie. "Actually, Brian," she seemed pained to say, "the Staple Inn isn't in Manhattan."

"It's not?"

"No," she said, cringing.

"Where is it then…Brooklyn?"

She crinkled her nose and shook her head sorrowfully.

"Queens?" Brian asked.

She kept crinkling her nose and shaking her head.

"Jersey?" he said, forcing a laugh.

"Try London." She squinted her eyes shut, ready for him to explode.

"*London?* As in *England?*"

She squinted a bit more and nodded her head.

"Well, then…what are we waiting for?"

Ellen's eyes popped open. "You mean you're not mad at me? For not telling you about this before?"

"What difference does it make," Brian replied, "if we gotta go, we gotta go. Let's get to the airport."

"I don't think you understand, Brian. In order to fly to London, we'll need passports."

"So? Let's do it. Where do we get 'em?"

"Oh," she said, "we can apply at any post office really."

"Then we're there!"

"And in a month or so, they should arrive by mail."

"A month?" Brian exploded. "Now I *am* pissed! I can't believe you! Why didn't you level with me about this last night?"

"I don't know," she apologized, "I guess I was too busy thinking about...well, you know, what I told you about at the restaurant. The reason why I could never go to England. Besides, I have this strange feeling that if I ever go there, I'm never coming back."

"Are you tellin' me I'm gonna have to wait a month before flying to London *myself?* So I can look for somethin' that I have no idea of what the hell it is I'm lookin' for?"

"I already thought about that," she said, "and if we were to communicate by email while you're there—even purchase a cell phone in case of an emergency—I could direct you on where to—"

"No chance! You're not gettin' off that easy. If I'm goin', you're goin'!"

"But—"

"No buts! The only *but* there'll be is your butt next to mine on that plane next month!"

A disconcerting haze crept over Ellen's face. "I even thought about that, too," she admitted. "But I'm afraid that a month's delay may be too late. What if the person who stole my notes gets there first?"

"What other choice do we have?"

"Wif all due respecs," the child interposed, "this *passport* you two was talkin' 'bout, is that one of them *book* kinda lookin' things wif your pitcher in it?"

"Why, yes," Ellen replied, "yes it is."

"Well now," said Sonar, "I can get ya one of um."

"A passport?" Ellen said. "I don't think so. It takes weeks."

"Wif all due respecs, Miss Ellen, it might take weeks where *you* come from, but you is in New York. You can get anyfin' you wanna in an hour in New York."

Brian bent down at the child. "Are you tellin' us, Sonar, you know a place where we can get legal passports in an hour?"

"Now wait jus' a second, Sir," he replied. "Wif all due respecs, you is puttin' words in my mouf. I didn't says nuffin' 'bout gettin' *legal* ones."

Brian and Sonar exchanged a mischievous smile.

"So," Brian said, "you know where we can get *illegal* passports in an hour?"

"I didn't says *that* either. I'd never says *that. That*'s even worse than the first words you put in my mouf. I ain't even gonna repeat *that*."

"So," said Brian, letting a few laughs slip out of his smile, "you know where Ellen and I can get *passports* in an hour?"

The child's cheery eyes popped up at him. "They don't calls me Sonar for nuffin'!"

It took less than an hour for the tiny, newspaper-capped tour guide to lead them through a maze of alleyways, where a frayed old man with a dirty, yellowish poodle directed them to an abandoned row house. Within minutes, Brian and Ellen had new passports, driver's licenses, and social security cards to go along with their new names.

"Julio Rodriguez?" Brian said, looking at the name on his passport. "I don't look like a Julio Rodriguez."

"It's pronounced *Hulio*," Ellen replied. "And stop fussing. I don't look very much like a Bwanda Jackson either."

Sonar tried not to chuckle at them but couldn't hold it in (he started laughing so hard that his paper hat fell off his head).

Ellen approached the child, a gush of soberness filling her face as she knelt down at him, looking into his eyes. "Sonar, you know if we could, we'd take you to England with us."

The child looked at Brian.

"She's right," said Brian. "Not just because you're the coolest kid we know, but we could really use someone who knows how to find things."

For a moment, the child appeared to be relishing the thought. He pushed the newspaper hat to the back of his head, looking back and forth between them. "Wif all due respecs, Miss Ellen and Mr. Brian, I would if I could too. But alotta people roun' here kinda count on me to help um out. They need *me* just as much as I need *um*."

Ellen and Brian listened intently.

"Maybe if I was roun' here las' night, ol' Shooey'd still be in his blanket." Tears filled the child's eyes, Ellen dabbing them with her soft wooly mitten. "I really wish I could go wif ya too, but I got responsabillies."

A tear leaked out of Ellen's eye.

"I'm sorry to make ya cry, Miss Ellen. The las' thing in the world I'd ever wanna do is make ya cry."

"That's okay, Sonar," she assured.

"But the streets is my home," he said. "This is where I b'long...wif my fam'ly."

"We understand," said Ellen.

"An' I want ya bofe to know," he said, a bit hoarse in the throat, "that ya bofe will always be in the pleasin'est of my dreams, an' I'll always think back on ya wif the nicest of mem'ries." He gave Ellen one last hug and kiss on the cheek. "You take care now, Miss Ellen. I hope ya fine what it is you been lookin' for." He held his tiny arm out to Brian. "You too, Sir," he said, shaking his hand, "hope ya bofe fine what you is lookin' for."

The lump in Brian's throat kept him from answering, so he gave him a cool nod instead.

Sonar reached into his pocket and pulled out an 1879 Morgan silver dollar. "This is my lucky coin. It's the first valu'ibble thing I ever foun' on the street. It'll bring ya luck while you's there. Maybe it'll help ya bofe fine what you is lookin' for."

"No Sonar," Ellen cried, "we couldn't."

"Please, Miss Ellen, I really want ya to have it." He wouldn't take no for an answer, handing the silver dollar to the girl, who had a difficult time letting go of the child's hand.

Chapter 12

A Flight

British Airways flight 1812 departed John F. Kennedy International Airport at precisely 5:55 p.m. Although a late snowstorm was beginning to make their takeoff look bleak, Ellen and Brian were able to race to the gate and escape New York just in time.

"Well, we got on, *Bwanda*," said Brian, settling into his coach seat. "You know what that means. I get first dibs on the bed when we get to London. Afterall, a bet's a bet."

"I know, *Julio*," Ellen replied, "I know. But who says that we're getting a room in London?"

"What do ya mean?"

"If everything goes accordingly, we should be able to find the—" she paused, glancing around the cabin seats, "*what we're looking for* by nightfall. Then, I was thinking that maybe we could take a train to Paris. I've always wanted to go there in the spring. Have you ever been to France?"

"Does Epcot or Busch Gardens count?"

Ellen let out an angelic laugh, inducing nearby passengers to take notice of her. "No...theme parks don't count."

"Then I've never been to France," said Brian. "Or Germany, England, Japan or any other country for that matter."

A dreamy look came over her face. "Why, Paris is the most..." she hesitated, her eyes shyly drifting up at him, "the most romantic place in the universe."

"Is that why you want to go with me?" he said with a mixture of sarcasm and conceit.

"Don't be silly."

"Then why go to Paris?" he grilled.

"I—I just thought it best that we stay on the move, so that what happened last night won't happen again."

"You mean *not* sleeping with me won't happen again?"

Her shy eyes grew angry. "No. The burglary."

"Ohhh," he skeptically said, "a rolling stone gathers no thieves, is that it?"

She rolled her eyes. "Wake up and smell the day-old keg party, Brian Murray. The whole world *isn't* in love with you."

"The whole world—no," he said, tilting back his seat, clasping his hands behind his head and closing his eyes. "The free world...maybe."

"What an ass," Ellen muttered, shaking her head.

"Thank you," he replied, smoothing the butt-end of his jeans.

"You know why I'd rather not stay in England," she said, her voice turning soft. "I expressed my utmost personal confidences to you—I thought you'd be a bit more compassionate." She quickly turned her head towards the window of the airplane.

Brian popped his chair up. "I'm sorry, Ellen," he said with sincerity, "I forgot about you being adopted."

This caused her to cry.

"I mean—I forgot your real mom lives there."

This made her cry harder.

"I mean—I mean..." He pulled her away from the window and into his arms, squeezing some of her tears onto his shoulder. "I won't mention it again," he said, hugging her.

"Promise?" she cried, sniffling.

"I promise." He gave her a smile. "Or my name isn't Julio Rodriquez."

She let out a saliva-bubbled laugh, like a little girl who was told a joke to stop from crying.

Brian removed a cocktail napkin from his pocket and dried her tears with it.

"I hope whatever's written on that isn't important," she said.

"Not at all," he replied.

The name 'Jennifer Cole' (along with her motel address) dissolved into a smear of blue ink.

"Would you care for a beverage?" asked a pencil-skirted flight attendant, rolling her metal serving cart up to them.

"A cup of Earl Gray tea, please," Ellen replied. She turned to Brian. "When in Rome."

"And for you, sir?" she asked, pouring Ellen's tea.

"I'll take somethin' English too, but with a little more kick to it."

"Tanqueray martini?" the lady suggested.

"Perfect."

"Oliver Twist?"

Brian did a double take. "What?"

"Oliver Twist?" the flight attendant repeated.

"What the hell do you mean by that?" he said, loud enough for nearby passengers to take notice.

"Your martini," replied the flight attendant, observing him oddly. "Olive or twist?"

"Oh," he said with a sigh of relief, "that's cute—real cute. Olive."

"Are you all right, sir?"

"Yeah—yeah. I'm okay." He glanced around at the passengers staring at him. "I get a little nervous flying."

The statuesque woman stirred a martini, serving it up in a plastic cup. The pimento-less green olive had a tiny plastic sword through it. "There's an air-sickness bag here," she informed, opening the pocket of the seat in front of him, "if you should feel the need." She then regarded Ellen. "Let me know if you want to change seats."

Ellen waited for her to stroll the metal cart away before snickering.

"Laugh it up," he said, "I'm glad you find it funny. Someone wants to shish kabob us over an old book, someone who could be on this very plane, and you think it's funny."

"Don't be so paranoid," she said, still laughing, "as long as there are witnesses around, we're safe."

"Don't be so sure," he said, suspiciously smelling his martini before taking a sip, evoking Ellen to laugh louder.

"This is your Captain speaking," said a voice through the intercom. *"Welcome aboard British Airways Flight Eighteen-Twelve. It looks like we're going to enjoy a smooth flight over the Atlantic today. We'll be touching down in approximately seven hours. So sit back, relax, and enjoy the flight. Current temperature at Gatwick Airport... twenty-five degrees."*

"That's just great!" Brian said. "Out of the fridge and into the cooler!"

Ellen desperately tried to conceal her laughter, but the strain on her face and in her stomach overwhelmed her, forcing her to release her gales in tittering intervals.

Chapter 13

Villainry

The bird-faced librarian with steel gray hair, the one who spoke with Ellen and Brian at the lost and found at Hornbake Library, handed the conductor ten pounds.

"Thankee, Ma'am," he replied.

"How long till we arrive in London?" She popped open a large black purse that looked as hard and rigid as her countenance.

"This train should 'ave you there in twenty minutes, Ma'am."

"What time do you have?" she questioned, as if tucking every bit of information into her black shell with her withered, claw-like hand. Tiny scars covered her fingers from the overhandling of library materials whose pages were brazen enough to cross her.

"Precisely 'alf past the hour, Ma'am."

Her pincher plucked a cell phone out of her raven carapace, pulling up the antenna and pressing a button. She brushed her gray streams aside with the device before speaking into it: "I have them in sight... Don't worry, unless they decide to jump off the Gatwick Express, I have them sewn in tight... How long will it take you to get there?... Perfect. You know where to get off for the Staple Inn, right?" She pinched Ellen's stolen tape recorder out of her black shell, turning it around and around in her claw, her stony face glued to it. "No, I'm not questioning your intelligence, just confirming the location... Good. What plans do we have in store for them?... I see... No, I'm not getting cold feet, I just thought you wanted to wait, in case there's another clue... No, I'm not questioning you again... What? You're starting to break up on me... Relax, I'm sitting one car behind them." With her other claw, she wrapped a scarlet-colored scarf around her head, concealing her steel gray hair, peering through the glass of the train door, into the next boxcar, where Ellen and Brian were huddled together.

The librarian closed her phone and began singing in a whisper far more twisted than her claw: "*You take the high road and I'll take the low road, and I'll get the under-grads be-fore ye.*"

Chapter 14

Birds in the Bush

As they exited the Underground at Chancery Lane, and walked along the bustling street, Ellen read aloud from her Penguin Classics version of The Mystery of Edwin Drood: *"'Behind the most ancient part of Holborn, London, where certain gabled houses some centuries of age still stand looking on the public way, as if disconsolately looking for the Old Bourne that has long run dry, is a little nook composed of two irregular quadrangles, called Staple Inn.'"*

"If I had a photo of the place," said Brian, his eyes gazing off in the distance, "I couldn't have described it any better."

Sure enough, these configurations loomed. The little nook comprised a circle with flowers surrounding a fountain that had long run dry. One-half of the circle's flowers were in bloom; the other half dead, as if the fountain erupted every score or so, favoring one particular side or the other.

Two black plaques reading 'Staple Inn' were positioned on either side of a pair of narrow, centuries-old doors, where the initials 'P.J.T.' and date '1747' were inscribed into a piece of aged wood crowning the doorway.

"Listen to this," Ellen said, continuing to read from her paperback version of the novel: *"'In which set of chambers, never having troubled his head about the inscription, unless to bethink himself at odd times on glancing up at it, that haply it might mean Perhaps John Thomas,'* then there's a footnote," she continued, *"'Or Perhaps Joe Tyler, sat Mr. Grewgious writing by his fire.'"*

"What's the footnote say?"

Ellen's thumb fanned the pages to the back of the book. "It reads, *'Not a bad guess. The inscription represents the initials and date of one of the presidents of Staple Inn: Principal John Thompson, 1747.'"*

"Think it means anything?"

"Well, Dickens references it again at the very end of the chapter," she said, fanning more pages and reading, *"'And yet there are such unexplored romantic nooks in the unlikeliest of men, that even old tinderous and touch-woody P.J.T. Possibly Jabbered Thus, at some odd times, in or about seventeen-forty-seven.'"*

The door suddenly swung open, startling them. A painter all in white exited with a bucket of brushes, tipping the bill of his pearly cap at them on his way out, leaving the door wide open.

They peeked in. A work crew was busy spackling, sanding, and painting the finishing touches on the interior of the corner house, converting whatever used to exist there before into an office.

"Well," said Brian, "if there was anything inside—it's gone now."

"Don't be so sure," said Ellen. "Let's give Charles Dickens a little credit. So far, all of his clues have stood the test of time."

"I hear ya. But sooner or later, time does have a funny way of running out."

"Such an optimist you are."

All this time, Ellen's hand was drawn to 'old tinderous and touch-woody P.J.T.,' the milk-tender flesh of her hand rendezvousing with P.J.T.'s dark-tinder, her palm slowly running over it, caressing it, her eyes closing, a look becoming her countenance as if her thoughts were traveling back in time, and that she was linked to that year of '1747', and that she was going to succeed in her literary quest no matter how impossible the clues were that Dickens had left, or what Brian's motives for riches were, or however heinous the plans were by the other party who may also be after it, and after them.

It is not often that a person becomes jealous of an inanimate object. In fact, in the High Court of Law, an inanimate object would most likely be tried, found guilty, and sentenced to death for motives involving *envy* rather than those of *jealousy*. But Brian was viewing Ellen's stroking of 'old tinderous and touch-woody P.J.T.' with a jealous air that filled his complexion with more of a yellowish-hue than a greenish one. It seemed as if Brian could have ripped the inanimate object from the doorway and further weath-ered old P.J.T. by giving the wood a good whacking, he would have done so (if she had allowed it).

"It's in the facade," she whispered, her eyes still closed, as if in a dream.

"What?"

"It's here," she said, her palm still caressing 'old touch-woody.' "Somewhere here in the facade."

"What makes you say that?"

"Trust me, Brian. I've read everything that Charles Dickens has ever written," she said, pausing, "yet, at this moment, I know that I haven't read *everything* Dickens has ever written."

"That makes perfect nonsense."

Ellen broke away from P.J.T., intensely viewing the exterior of the building.

Above the doorway, like the mantel of a fireplace that has long run cold, stretched a shelf running a foot wider than the ingress of the door on either side. Perched atop the shelf, a white glass ball sat upon a pedestal.

She stepped back farther to view the entrance, her face blemished with emotion. "He wouldn't have placed the clue where it could easily be discovered or discarded. He would have placed it here, in the facade, the only part of Staple Inn that he knew would keep."

"I'll just pull the board off and look on the back," said Brian, making a go for the wood.

"No, no," said Ellen, breaking up the would-be scuffle between Brian and P.J.T., but not before P.J.T. drew first blood by piercing his animate adversary with an old but reliable wooden splinter.

"Owww—son of a bitch!" Brian exclaimed, grabbing his wrist.

Ellen took hold of his hand.

"Owww!"

"Don't be such a baby, Brian, let me get it out for you."

"Nuh no," he said, withdrawing his hand. "No way."

"Stop acting like a child." She grabbed hold of his hand again, the two playing tug-o-war with his appendage.

"No way. Wouldn't you love to yank this wood outta me—you'd probably do it nice and slow, too. I'd rather have bamboo jammed under my fingertips."

"Well, all right, if that's how you feel." She threw his hand back at him.

"Ouch!"

Brian went to remove what may have been the Great Grand-splinter (times ten!) of P.J.T. (who may have Purposely Jabbed Through). He sought to find the right angle to grip the inch-long splinter protruding from the underbelly of his ring finger.

"Oh no," he said, giving up on his operation.

"What's wrong now?"

"Blood." A woozy look became his countenance. "I can't take the sight of blood."

Ellen shook her head at him, grabbing his hand again, poising herself to meticulously extract the splinter.

"Rather have bamboo jammed under your fingertips, you say?"

"Please, Ellen, I beg you for mercy, don't—owwww!"

"I haven't done anything yet."

"I'm just practicing."

Ellen's voice took on a ghostly tone as she joked with him: "P.J.T.," she eerily howled. "Exorcise yourself from Brian Murray's body… release him at once!"

"Very funny."

Her specter-like voice (comparable to that of Jacob Marley in *A Christmas Carol*) continued, "Though he has come to steal your treasure, P.J.T., he means no harm."

"Would ya take the wood out already?"

"Hear me," she cried. "Ohhh P.J.T.!"

"Do you want to see me pass out or what? Come on, Ellen!"

"Oh," she said, laughing. "Stop your crying."

"Take it out already."

"Take what out?"

"Stop foolin', Ellen."

"It's out."

"Yeah?"

Brian raised his palm to his face, examining his hand where the only thing remaining on the underside of his ring finger was a tiny red dot. "Hey...I didn't even feel a thing."

Past the dry fountain and dead flowers, above the hedges surrounding the quaint little nook, a steel gray head was positioned in such a way that it seemed to be scouting the goings on of the two students, studying them, as if it were about to pounce upon the unsuspecting undergraduates and strike them down.

The librarian's claw was pinching her cell phone to her ear, speaking into the device with an inferior tone in her voice: "I don't know... I don't know..." as the librarian spoke this, it was evident that these three words she returned to the person on the other end were, by far, the three worst words that she could ever have the misfortune of uttering. Perhaps if any librarian were asked, be it one with a tarnished soul (as her soul was surely tarnished beyond the oldest bookshelf at Hornbake Library), or a librarian whose heart was kind and good-natured (as the hearts of most people who hold this scholarly station are) what the three worst words to say in a library, any library however Public or Private, would be, they would unanimously and undoubtedly retort: "I don't know."

Yet, the chrome-plated crown of the librarian repeatedly offended this Cardinal Rule, persistent on her conveyance of, "I don't know," to the person on the other end, which only seemed to infuriate the caller all the more, who kept prompting her to violate the rule over and over again, smearing her nose in it like a cruel Master does with a dog.

"I don't know... I don't know... Well, I can't very well steal the book in front of the entire city of London."

Regarding this point, the librarian *did* know and was

correct. On one side, where the students were busy studying the facade, there was this quiet little nook of a period long run dry. On the other side, beyond the bookshelf-like hedge the librarian was examining her prey through, existed all of London! If she were to inflict a crime upon them, any sort of crime be it slight, imaginable, or so heinous that it would be *un*imaginable, there would be an entire city taking the stand as eyewitness.

"I don't know... I don't know," she continued. "Well, maybe we should let them find the next clue, then follow... No, I'm not saying that you can't find the next clue, I'm just suggesting that they may still be of some use to us... Yes, I know you want to get there first, and the reasons why... Okay, you stay there, and I'll follow... Wait," she said, listening. "They're coming this way... I just overheard them say that they're going to wait until twilight before returning... I don't know... I don't know... I can't, she's holding it... What do you want me to do, go up to her and tell her the book she has is one-hundred-and-thirty years overdue?... No doubt she'll recognize me. He won't, but the girl's smart—she will... We'll just have to wait until dark... I don't know... I don't know."

She popped open her purse, her claw releasing the phone that descended into her raven carapace, her steel gray semblance paused to the extent that a tourist viewing her over the hedges might have mistaken her for a monument in Trafalgar Square.

Chapter 15

Coffee for Two (or Three)

"Regular for me, too," said Brian. "And I'll pay for the lady's." He handed the cashier a five-dollar bill.

"I'm sorry," said the cashier, "but this establishment only accepts pound notes, sir."

"It's the thought that counts," said Ellen, handing the lady four pounds in coinage (who returned a tenpence).

The coffee shop was situated just off Gray's Inn Road in Holborn, London, not more than a thirty-second walk from where P.J.T. resides at the Staple Inn. However, the two settings were so completely the opposite, it was as if the line between city and country were decided in England at that very cafe, as sure as the time of day is decided by the Royal Greenwich Observatory, perhaps at that very coffee table-for-two, in the very chairs they were settling into.

"The irony," said Ellen, perusing the pages of her Penguin Classics edition of *The Mystery of Edwin Drood*. "It says that the Staple Inn is owned by the Prudential *Assurance* Company."

"That's a good sign," Brian replied, sipping his coffee.

Ellen pursed her lips to her steaming coffee, kissing a sip out of her cup, the heat causing her face to crinkle.

"Tell me again," said Brian, "given we find the ending, how much do you think we figure to make?"

"Don't worry," said Ellen. "If we find the second half of that novel, you'll be rich beyond your wildest dreams."

"Dreams?" he returned. "I'm not in it for wild *dreams*. I'm in it for wild *realities*."

She crinkled her face to her coffee again, sighing out a contented "ahhh" after drinking, as if the caffeine held medicinal properties that were coaxing on her third wind. "And you can't exclude the fame factor either," said Ellen.

"Fame factor?"

"We'd no doubt gain worldwide acclaim as well," she said, pondering, her eyes rising with the steam of her coffee.

"Yeah?"

"Most certainly. People would want interviews and stories about how we came across the book."

"That *I* can do," said Brian.

"And of course, because we were the ones who solved this literary puzzle, we would become the foremost authority on the life and times of Charles Dickens. We could get careers in information and consulting—we could probably even work for the Dickensian."

"That *you* can do."

Her lips kissed her coffee again, and her eyes and thoughts drifted, along with the steam, floating away.

"But I think we'd better postpone Paris for now," she said. "If we find the story, we should head straight back to the States. I have a feeling that once we get back home, everything will be all right."

"Weren't those the famous final words of Amelia Earhart?"

"Very funny," she said, sipping, then gesturing at the window. "It's such a strange feeling knowing that my real mother could walk right by me on that very street, and I wouldn't even know it."

"I thought you didn't want to talk about that."

"I didn't. But being here in England now, somehow I don't feel as bad about it."

"That's good, Ellen, because I had a psych class last semester, and the teacher said it's good to resolve issues from your past; you know, so they don't spill over into your future."

"Sage advice," she said, sipping.

"So, what would you do if you *did* run into your mom?"

"I don't know. There are so many questions I've wanted to ask her, so many things I've wanted to say to her. I've often dreamt about the meeting."

"And what did you dream?"

"Well, at first, when I was a little girl, I always had recurring dreams about seeing my Mom on the back of a subway train, through the glass window, just as it was pulling away. I'd run for it, crying, and she could see me because I could see her crying back. I spent many a night trying to catch that train, but I never could." She kissed her coffee. "In later dreams, though, I do get to meet her, and have a chance to talk to her."

"And what happens?"

"I usually freeze up. That's the worst. When so many emotions well up inside you that you can't say anything. It's like the verbal equivalent of running in quicksand."

"How about recently?"

"Recently, I confront her, and try to talk to her. Words come out of my mouth, but she just can't hear me." Ellen began smooching her coffee rather than kissing it, as her brew drew more tepid. "So...what do you think, Doctor Julio Rodriguez? Am I crazy or not?"

"Sounds like a classic case of resolution conflict, Bwanda."

"You've got that right. Unfortunately, it's a conflict that will forever go unresolved."

"That doesn't mean you can't find closure."

She smiled a sip off her coffee. "My, my, Brian Murray...that psych course *did* teach you a thing or two, didn't it?"

"Oh, it's pretty much common sense. *Parsimony* as they say in the sciences. You just go from the simple to the complex, and don't overlook the obvious."

"Maybe that's why you actually passed that class."

"How'd ya know that?"

"I work in the registrar's office, remember?"

"Yeah, and that reminds me: you might just be the foot in the door of that probationary committee that I need."

"Wait a minute," she returned, "you mean to tell me that if we find the ending and you become rich, you still want to appear in front of the probationary committee? You still want to earn your degree?"

"Hey, maybe you've got somethin' there. They'll probably give me an honorary doctorate; better yet, I'll be a free agent, like in the pros. I'll be able to auction myself off to any college in the country."

"Now, I wouldn't go that far."

"I've always fancied Haaavard," he said with a Boston accent, which quickly turned to a Cockney one: "Or mighbe right 'ere at ol' Oxford."

Ellen laughed.

"No, no...I'm just kiddin'. There's only one way I'm gonna do it," he said. "Maryland's my school, my team, my hometown. They were the only college that accepted me. It'd be treasonous to go anywhere else. It'd be like sellin' out my own state."

"I never pictured you as a loyalist," she said.

"To tell you the truth, I can't wait to graduate so I can stick that big fat diploma right in Mudgrove's face and tell him to kiss it!"

"Wait. Do you happen to know who the chairman of the probationary committee is?"

"Does it matter?"

"It's Professor Mudgrove."

"So, it matters."

"Sorry, Brian."

"Hold on," he suspiciously said. "Why didn't you tell me this before?" He took a gulp of coffee. "You said before that you were gonna help me pass his class, but you never said he headed the committee. You knew I didn't have a chance all along. If not his class, I'd fail the appeal. You knew, one way or another, Mudgrove was never gonna pass me."

Unable to refute, Ellen filled her mouth with coffee.

"Your motive, Miss Pipple," he imitated like Professor Mudgrove. "Pray tell the class what your motive was...we'd all like to hear it."

"I assure you, whatever motive I may have had has changed dramatically."

"Your motive, I do say, Miss Pipple," his imitation continued, "was that you found me completely and utterly irresistible. You were overtaken by my good looks. Overcome by my boyish charm. Overwhelmed by my masculine physique."

"Trust me," she said, "the only thing I'm *over* is *you*."

Brian vainly ran his fingers through his hair. "You wanted to spend spring break studying with me, Miss Pipple, so you could get me alone, fill me up with drink," he said, raising his cup, "and take me home with you."

"Don't include *me* in your wildest realties."

"You make me feel so cheap, Ellen," he joked, breaking character in his own voice.

"Me? Wait till Professor Mudgrove gets a hold of you."

"No problem. So, he heads the committee. I guess he and me will just have to form a mutual friendship for a week or deuce. He'll be nice to me during my appeal, and I'll be nice to him during the interviews; you know, about how his assignment got the ball rolling for us in the first place." Brian took a sip of coffee, cringing not at the beverage but his own statement. "Man! How I dread the thought of kissin' that old man's wrinkly ass!" He swigged his coffee, swooshing it around in his mouth as if ridding the foul taste of his statement. "But I will. I'll do it. *Then* I'll stick that big fat diploma right in his face and tell him to kiss it!"

A few tables away, roosting in a little nook adjacent to them, clad with a scarlet scarf concealing her steel-gray hair, big sunglasses hiding her eyes, her cell phone and claw covering her countenance, the librarian listened intently to the two, taking inventory of them, storing every bit of information she was capable of capturing. It was as if Ellen and Brian's words were traveling over with the steam from their coffees, like a ghostly carriage of ole carrying the day's news.

"Yes," the bird-like woman said into the phone as she sat perched in her station. "Verbatim." Her claw tipped a glass of water to what should have been her lips (though her face was so pointed, it appeared that it would have been just as easy for her to consume the contents by intermittently dipping her beak into her glass). "I don't know," she despondently said into her phone. "All right." She clutched her raven carapace. "Ever the more reason, Norman…ever the more."

Chapter 16

The Port

In Rochester, England, just beyond the Rochester Castle and Cathedral, where the mouth of the Thames joins the strong arm of the River Medway, there arrived by sea a large American vessel delivering goods from the modern day New World.

The hands aboard the vessel were quite apt, quickly tying their lines with fisherman's knots and various other shanks and hitches, as if the vessel were a snug glove fitting onto the hand of that strong arm.

"Welcome to Rochester," hollered a man standing ashore. He had a short pipe clenched between his teeth as he watched the vessel securely moor itself to land.

"We're so loaded that we're bustin' at the rivets," the First Mate shouted from the prow. "You might need an extra forklift if you wanna make it to the pub in time for happy hour."

"You've bloody got it," yelled the man with the pipe, making arrangements as one would at a pub by holding two fingers up to someone in the distance. "What'cha bring me this time, matey?"

"Oh, a little of everything," shouted the First Mate. "Just consider it a sample platter from the good ol' U-S-of-A."

A young boy, his lackluster appearance hinting that he was no doubt the ship's swabby, momentarily disembarked the vessel to hand a crisp white piece of stationery to the man with the stub-pipe, conversing with him for a few moments.

After viewing the contents of the note, the man touched a match to his pipe, puffed out a ring, thanked the lad, and held up one forefinger this time, in a different direction, to a person of a greater distance. The young swabby slogged back towards the vessel where his duties were no doubt just commencing.

A man in a bottle-green coat appeared, blowing a loose fist to rid his hand of the Medway's chill. "Feels like snow."

"Bloody looks like it too," said the man with the pipe.

"What sort of services will you be needing today, my good man?"

"What else—a delivery." He touched another flame to his pipe, giving it a pull.

"What sort of delivery?"

"A land-gram from New York. Bloody important one from what I'm told."

"All my deliveries are important ones, my good fellow."

"Not like this un, mate. Yeh just be sure that this note is delivered. Let me tell yeh the description of the two of 'em," he said, proceeding to impart upon him the portraiture of the recipients, as told by the swab. He handed him the piece of stationery, drew another puff, and tapped his pipe out over his big forearm.

The man in the bottle-green coat took a second to read the note. "If your description is right, it'll be like finding fish in a barrel."

"Let us hope we find 'em soon."

"Of course, my good man, you know it'll cost the usual fee."

"Aye, I'm well aware of your fee."

"One free drink," he said, blowing into his fist again.

"For everyone." He began refilling his pipe with black tobacco. "B'cuz you'll get a drink from *me*, the person yeh hand it to will get a drink from *you*, and the one he gives it to will get a drink from *him*, and so on, and so on, right down the bloody line."

"Let's pray it's not *too* bloody a line, my good man."

"Indeed," he returned, nourishing a flame on his wooden pipe again. "Indeed."

"I trust we're both familiar with the travels of *those* particular lines, my good fellow?"

"The War, indeed. I'm afeared I'm all too well acquainted, mate."

"And pray we never travel them again, my good man."

He consented with a long draw off his short pipe. "Aye. Who yeh gunta go with for the delivery, mate?"

"I'll put the word out, but if they're anywhere near London, Merrywell's our man."

"Merrywell? *John Thomas* Merrywell? The ex-convict?"

"That's him."

"God save us!"

"He's a good man."

"When he's on the bloody wagon. Are yeh sure he's able?"

"He's performing, my good man, so he's able."

"He may be able to perform for the time being, but it doesn't mean he's an able-being who'll perform when the time comes. Isn't there anyone else, mate? 'Ow 'bout Cradwich?"

"He's on holiday. Seems he did a favor for a Japanese gentleman who's buying him one free drink all the way to Iceland, with a few blondes attached to it."

"Well, I just don't bloody want to let our New York connexion down. I owe him several pints now."

"How come you haven't paid him yet?"

"He ayn't bloody old enough to drink."

The man let go a hearty laugh as he tucked the crisp white paper into the inside pocket of his coat. He gave a nod, blew a stiff breath into his fist with a "Good man," then departed, venturing out to shore, as if his bottle-green coat had various other messages of importance to be cast out to sea.

"Bloody Merrywell," said the man to himself, tapping his pipe out. "God save us *and* the Queen."

Chapter 17

A Rook

The gray English sky cast a fluorescent-blue twilight over Staple Inn, giving the facade of the building a surrealistic glow as Brian and Ellen approached old P.J.T.

"You sure this is going to work?" said Ellen.

"Oh, I'm sure," Brian replied, removing a new football from a bag and is packaging.

"For thirty pounds, it'd better."

Brian dropped back, waved his arm in the direction he wanted Ellen to go out for a pass, then lobbed the ball towards her from across the lawn.

Ellen had to hurry under it, stretching her soft hands for the ball and cradling it into her chest.

"Nice catch," said Brian. "I thought you didn't have any brothers."

"I play touch football with my family every Thanksgiving in the Turkey Bowl."

They tossed it to and fro a few more times, Brian holding his arm out for Ellen to lead him in his route.

"Nice spiral," he said, making an over-the-shoulder catch. "You dropped it right in the ole breadbasket. Let's run a play."

Ellen jogged over to him, and they put their hands on their knees, bending over, huddling.

"I want ya to run a post," said Brian, drawing a diagram on his hand with his finger. "Run straight like this, then angle towards P.J.T."

"And let's hope he intercepts it with smashing success," she said.

"Ready..." chanted Brian, "break," he shouted as he clapped his hands together loudly.

Ellen lined up in a flanker position with her hands on her hips, one foot slightly behind.

"On two," said Brian, holding the ball down as if taking an imaginary snap from center. "Ready...set...hut one...hut two!" He faked a handoff up the middle to a pretend fullback then rolled out, running a bootleg left, just stopping shy of the imaginary line of scrimmage, heaving the ball with all his might in Ellen's direction.

The ball whizzed towards her, purposely missing, striking a blow to the marble-colored ball just atop P.J.T.'s head.

But Brian and Ellen's leather ball was no match for P.J.T's glass one. In fact, the jolt of the ball only seemed to splash more of the fluorescent-blue twilight onto the exterior of Staple Inn, causing P.J.T to surrealistically glow all the more.

"If that didn't jolt him, nothin' will." Brian walked over to the white glass ball, glanced around to see if anyone was looking, then attempted to pry it from its pedestal with a long stick. "She's on there pretty tight. But I still think it's behind the wood."

"No," she said. "Look all around. Look at the facade. Look at the way the sunlight seems to fill the ball. It's in there."

Brian gazed at it. "Yeah. Maybe you're right."

Ellen spotted a small boy who was slowly stalking the hedges behind them. He carried a homemade slingshot in his hand, aiming for a rook on the branch of a tree. He drew back his sling and let fire—his rock knocking the rook a good yard in the opposite direction.

"Widdy widdy wix!"

I-ket-ches-Im-out-ar-ter-six.

Widdy widdy wy!

Then-E-don't go-then-I-shy-

Widdy widdy Wake-cock warning!"

As the boy chanted this, he danced a circle around the dead bird, his gaunt figure silhouetted against London's blue gloaming.

"Nice shot," said Brian, nearing the boy.

"Got 'eem dead betwixt the eyes, I did! Widdy wy! Widdy wy!"

"You two should be ashamed of yourselves!" Ellen scolded.

"I didn't do nothin' but plink a rook, lady," the boy defended. "Widdy wy!"

"You took a life, and for no good reason!" Ellen grabbed the boy by his shoulders, pushing him inward at the bird, forcing him to examine his actions more closely. "A few seconds ago that rook was one of God's creatures. It was living, breathing, soaring blissfully to heights we can only dream of. Look," said Ellen, pointing, "she even had a worm in her mouth. Mother was probably on her way back to the nest to feed her babies."

The boy seemed to swallow a dry gulp of crow.

Ellen continued with her guilt trip. "You should feel very proud of yourself, young man, you may have bagged five birds with one shot!"

"Sorry, lady, but I wasn't meanin' to plink more than one of um. Asides, it's the nat-choo-ral order a things." The boy turned his eyes to Brian. "You tole me good shot, Misser, so tell the lady: it's only the nat-choo-ral order a things."

"The kid does have Darwin backin' him," said Brian.

Ellen knelt down, pulling the boy close with a shake, as if to jerk the notion out of him, trapping the lad in the frames of her round glasses.

"The natural order doesn't kill for the sake of killing. They do it to ensure the survival of the species."

"Some particoolar orders 'ave been known to hone their skills on other particoolar orders."

"There are other ways to hone your skills. For starters, I suggest tin cans at ten paces."

Brian interrupted. "Or glass balls, at twenty."

All three slowly looked over at P.J.T., where it appeared as if the fluorescent gleam turned into a blue spotlight now emanating from the ball.

"Widdy widdy wy! You don't think I can plink that, Misser? That ball o'er yonder?"

"No," returned Brian.

"Now wait a minute," Ellen said.

"Stay out of this," returned Brian, "I wanna see how good the kid is."

"You mean *that* glass ball over there on *that* shelf?" said the boy.

"That's the one."

"Brian!" she scolded.

"Ellen, stay outta this."

"Widdy widdy wy! I could plink that ball with one eye tied be'ind me 'ead!"

"I double dog dare ya," Brian goaded. "I'll bet ya that football you can't."

Before Ellen could utter another word, the boy reloaded his weapon, yanked back the sling, and fired his second shot of the day—shattering and scattering the blue light from the ball that exploded in every direction, spilling out the evening twilight, which quickly waned, bringing on the night swiftly.

"Widdy widdy—" before the lad could get the "wy" out, he was off and running, the silhouette of the boy opting for the football over the slingshot, making his way around the hedges, bumping into another silhouette, a much darker one, on the city-side of London.

"Skyooze me, sir," the lad apologized, almost fumbling the football.

The dark figure grabbed the boy's arm.

"It wasn't me, sir! I swar! The one who tole me to do it is over there! He's the one that's darin' people to go a-plinkin', 'e is!"

The larger silhouette loosened his grip, and the smaller broke away, with the faint sound of "Widdy widdy wy!" echoing as he fled.

Ellen and Brian magnetically approached the shattered ornament, sifting through the pieces of broken glass.

Just then, the door of the Staple Inn creaked open, and the two of them froze, wondering if they Perhaps Jolted Thusly old P.J.T. who sought vengeance.

The ghost of a man floated out, white as a sheet from head to toe, rattling what sounded like chains at them.

Their eyes, still bleached from the ball of light that exploded, took a moment to focus, and they realized it was the man they saw earlier donned in a white painter's cap and white painter's clothes. He was carrying a broomstick of empty clanking paint cans over his shoulder.

"What in heavens happened here?" said the painter.

"It was a boy," Brian returned, still a bit startled by the spectre, "with a slingshot." He pointed over at it. "See? He dropped the evidence over there."

"Why would the lad want to do a thing like this?"

"He was going for a bird," Brian defended. "He got that rook over there, see?"

"Pretty nice shot," said the spectre. "Oh well. I'll just have to write it up on the expense sheet." He clanked off towards a work van around the corner.

Ellen and Brian continued sifting through the broken glass.

"Find anything yet?" she asked, fervently examining each shard with her glasses like a jeweler scrutinizing gems.

"No, you?"

She hesitated a moment before answering. "No."

"Maybe there was something inside, and we didn't see where it landed."

"Maybe." Ellen began searching the perimeter of the doorway, and the spectre quietly returned after depositing his noisy chains.

"What the Dickens are you two doing?" said the ghost.

"We're, um, we're just looking," Ellen replied.

"Ohhh," said the friendly spirit, "you've lost something, have you?"

"You might say that," Brian returned.

"Well, what is it? Maybe I can help you find it."

"It's really not ours," said Ellen.

"No?" said the spectre.

"It belongs to a friend of ours," she said.

"I see," answered the spectre.

"We'll manage," Ellen added, "thanks anyway, though."

The ghost headed back to his room at Staple Inn, then turned back. "I'd better jot down the maker for the expense account." He tore a white pad of paper from his pocket as if it were part of his ghostly wraps. "A boy with a slingshot," he said to himself, writing. "Aiming for a bird...hit ornament." The spectre had to wait for his writing to catch up to his words. "The maker," he said, pulling a stepladder out of the building and scaling it. He peeked over the shelf at the pedestal, "Looks like... like...*Trafalgar*."

Ellen and Brian did a double take at the pedestal where the glass ball had rested. When the spectre went back inside the room, Ellen climbed the ladder to see for herself. A tiny bit of blue, crepuscular light remained, shimmering off the pedestal's face like a neon sign, revealing the word 'Trafalgar.'

Ellen let go a scream of elation, rushing inside and hugging the spirit who didn't quite know what to make of it.

In no time, she tore open her knapsack and began sifting through her portable library, studiously researching their next move.

Chapter 18

Trafalgar Square

B rian and Ellen arrived at Trafalgar Square just before seven that night, greeted by the statue of British naval commander Viscount Horatio Nelson mounted high atop his column. Four bronze lions kept guard over him while two beautiful fountains assured that the admiral was never out of his element.

"Who's that?" said Brian.

"Admiral Lord Nelson," Ellen returned, admiring the statue. "A famous sea commander who died at the Battle of Trafalgar in eighteen-oh-five."

"Battle of Trafalgar? What was that?"

"Just one of the greatest naval battles to ever take place."

"Yeah?"

"It was a British fleet that was outnumbered by a larger French and Spanish fleet. The French and Spanish ships formed a huge line like a firing squad, but Admiral Nelson surprised them by dividing his fleet in two and hitting them at right angles."

"Like spearin' a fish."

"Twenty French and Spanish vessels were lost, but not a single British ship."

"Let me guess…Admiral Nelson was knighted by the King and lived happily ever after."

"Not exactly," she replied. "He was fatally shot in that battle…he died a few hours later." She pulled a London travel guide out of her knapsack, flipping to a dog-eared page. "It says here that this site was formerly occupied by run down housing and stabling for the King's horses. It was cleared in 1832 so architect John Nash could develop it."

"I've heard of him," said Brian. "Do you think he was in cahoots with Dickens?"

"Honestly? No. It says here that Nash died in 1835."

"Yeah, but I thought Dickens was born in 1812. That woulda given 'em enough time to know each other."

"But in 1835 Dickens was just starting out as a writer. He hadn't even published the Pickwick Papers yet. Dickens would've known who Nash was, but I don't think Nash would have ever heard of Dickens."

"No?"

"Besides, I don't think Dickens would've had everything in place so early on."

Ellen looked the statue over with a pair of coin operated binoculars stationed in the square. She searched from the top of Lord Nelson's head to the foot of his column, clueless.

"Maybe it's somewhere in the fountains," said Brian.

"The fountains didn't go up until 1939."

"What about the lions?"

Ellen thumbed through a few more pages of her travel guide. "Wait a minute. It says that the four bronze lions were added at the base of the monument in 1867."

"What's that mean?"

"It's three years prior to Dickens's death. That just may be the window we're looking for."

"What window?"

"Remember that five-year gap between his last completed novel, Our Mutual Friend, and the start of Drood?"

"Yeah."

"That's the window. He died in 1870, but the four lions were erected in 1867, don't you see?"

"Yeah, yeah—there *is* a window there."

Ellen gave her glasses a nudge, studying the lions.

"Where do you want me to look?" said Brian.

"You can start on *that* end of the lion," she pointed.

"Great. I get the butt-end as usual."

Brian hopped up on one of the pedestals, and as his hand probed the underside of the lion's hindquarters, two passersby approached, pausing, viewing his actions oddly.

"Sickie," said an elderly lady to her husband.

Not hearing her, Brian glanced at the couple and smiled, causing them to hasten their pace by him.

By nine that evening, Ellen and Brian had gone over every square inch of the square.

"Maybe it's hidden inside one of the lions," she said.

Brian, tired and punchy, started laughing. "Well," he said between guffaws, "I don't think a kid with a slingshot's gonna work this time."

Ellen closed her eyes for a moment, attempting to drown out his laughter. "*Trafalgar,*" she said to herself. "Maybe it spells something if you mix up the letters." She tipped her head back in thought, the moon scintillating in her glasses. "Art-laf-gar...tar-alf-rag—oh, darn it, will you stop that—I can't think!"

"Widdy wy," Brian said hysterically. "Widdy widdy wy," he laughed.

"Well, I don't see any sense in continuing to look tonight. We'll just have to try again tomorrow when it's light out." She meticulously packed up her portable library, frowning at Brian's frivolity. "Aren't you even the least bit concerned that this may be a dead end?"

"Not at all," he said, his laughter subsiding. "Out of anyone I've ever known, Ellen, I think I've got the most confidence in you...in your mind."

"Is that why it was *my* notes you always borrowed in class?"

Brian jammed his hands into his pockets a few times to warm them. "If it's one thing a stupid person knows," he said, walking with her (neither knowing where they were going nor what lay ahead), "it's when they're in the presence of a smart person."

"You're not stupid, Brian."

"Yes I am. Because you were right the other night," he confessed, "I *was* using you for your notes. Just like I met up with you at the library that night so you'd write my paper."

Ellen tucked one side of her dark-brown hair behind the arm of her glasses, exposing the meatiness of her ear that Brian couldn't help noticing as they strolled. (It was as if any visual deficiency in the girl's eyes were made up a hundred-fold in her ears).

"I should've taken the time to see what a great person you are," he said.

Flattered by his remarks, Ellen kept silent, hoping he would continue.

"Even if we did come to a dead end," said Brian, "I wouldn't care. I'm havin' a great time."

"I almost believe that," she said.

"Don't get me wrong, I'll take the money and the fame. But if it doesn't happen, I really don't care."

"You mean to tell me, Brian Murray, that if we reach a dead end, you wouldn't rather wish you had gone to sunny Florida with Jennifer Cole for spring break?"

"Nope."

"I almost believe that, too."

"Besides, Pat Hastings woulda been hangin' around the whole time anyway."

"Pat Hastings?"

"Yeah, the kid with the freckles. You know him. He was in our English Lit class up until he dropped."

"That's right," said Ellen. "Oh my God."

"What is it?"

"He's the one I was thinking of!"

131

"Who?"

"Pat Hastings—that night at the library when the books fell off the shelf. I smelled this peculiar scent, remember? I told you about it the night our room was ransacked. He's the one I've been unconsciously connecting that odor to!"

"Pat? Odor? I wouldn't be surprised."

"No—it was some kind of after-shave or cologne."

"Pat doesn't need to shave. You can count the red hairs on his chin."

"All I know is that I was sitting in the library when I realized your book was authentic, and the books fell, then I smelled it…it reminded me of him."

"You had good reason to. When it comes to odors, it usually *is* Hastings. He cleared out an auditorium once during finals with a silent but deadly—"

"Seriously, Brian, maybe it's him. Maybe he's the one who stole my tape recorder. Maybe he's the one who stole my notes in New York. Maybe he's the one that Sonar's note warned us about."

"Hastings? No way. Aside from the sense of smell, he's harmless."

"It all makes perfect sense. He was in our class. He was at the library that day. He was even on the bus the other morning when I told you about the book, remember? He opened the window and handed you something—probably his or Jennifer Cole's room number. Don't you see? Pat Hastings can be placed at the scene of every crime!"

"Pat? He's not that smart. Plus he knows I'd kick his ass."

"The probability is too high, Brian."

"Never in a million beers, which he's probably consumed by now."

"There's too much evidence to refute it. You have to believe me on this."

Brian laughed. "It's not him, trust me."

"What makes you so sure?"

"He's too much of a loser."

"What if he's here, Brian? What if somehow he followed us? I'm starting to feel frightened again."

"Don't worry," he said, putting his arm around her as they strolled through the square. "Even if it *was* Pat, I assure you, you're safe. I could spot that red hair and freckles a mile away."

More at ease, Ellen rested her face on the boy's shoulder, gazing up at the moon as they made their way out of the square.

"You know what," she said, "I have no idea where we're going."

"I don't have a clue either."

"Good choice of words," she replied. "But don't stop walking, Brian, please." She removed her glasses, closing her eyes. "It feels nice *following* sometimes."

"What do you mean?"

"I'm not sure. But it's like when you're a child, and you fall asleep in the back of your parents' car on the way home from a long trip. That's how I feel right now, and I don't want to get out of the car and go up to bed." She gave a long yawn. "I want to stay right here."

Brian gazed down at her, the moon granting him a picturesque view of her soft semblance, and her tender ear. "I've gotcha," he said, tightening his hold on her, leading the way. "Don't you worry about anything."

She smiled some more moonlight into her face, appearing as if she were falling asleep right there on his shoulder as they strolled. "Where are we going, Brian?" she said, dreamily.

"You leave it to me."

Ellen's white grin beamed more moonlight into her face.

"We might be clueless for the time being," he said, "but it *is* spring break. So we're gonna make a spring break of it."

"We are?"

"Those passports we have say we're twenty-one, so we're goin' clubbin'—or *pubbin'* I should say."

"Ellen laughed. "But you're legal to drink here."

"What?"

"You only have to be eighteen to drink in England."

"Are you bein' Total cereal?"

"What? —Yes, I'm being totally serious."

"Cool. It'll be the first time in my life that I won't have to use a fake I.D."

"That's the good news," she said.

"Uh oh… I'm afraid to ask."

"The bad news is that the pubs close at eleven in England."

"What time is it?"

"I knew this was too good to be true." She opened her eyes, lifted her face from his shoulder, and viewed her watch. "Wow, it's earlier than I thought. We've still got almost two hours."

"Yeeeeee," he shouted, like a college boy returning from a beer run.

The older couple who witnessed Brian fondling the lion earlier were on their way out of the square, his exclamation causing them to hasten their pace by him once again.

"Sickie," said the lady.

Chapter 19

A Shadow Appears

A *wireless* phone they call it? It seems that out of all the phones, the wireless phone is undoubtedly the most fettering in the trade. For the librarian was wending her way across Trafalgar Square as if her phone *had* a wire that was soon reeling her down city blocks, around street corners, through alleyways—like a frantic fish caught on a hook as she helplessly redialed her device, unable to get ahold of anybody.

Rounding a dark street corner of central London, her figure collided with a shadowy silhouette that gaffed her by the arm.

"Aaaaaaah!" she screamed.

The silhouette of a thin man wearing a hat gave her a violent shake.

"Ohhh," she said, catching her breath, "it's only you, Norman...why...you scared the wits out of me."

"Where are they, Ms. Crawley," grilled the dark figure's Oxford English accent.

"Don't worry, they'll be back again tomorrow, when it's light out."

"Where are they, Ms. Crawley?" the dark figure repeated.

"They're going to a pub."

"Which pub, Ms. Crawley?"

"It doesn't matter. They'll be back in the morning."

"I'll ask you one more time, Ms. Crawley," said the dark figure, giving her arm a tremendous shake again. "Where are they?"

"I don't know," was her reply.

The figure released her, stepping into the light of a lamppost.

Professor Mudgrove's pebbly eyes pierced the librarian's countenance (like the tiny sunlight dot of a magnifying glass pierces a leaf aflame). "I told you to stay on them!"

"I'm sorry, Norman. Forgive me."

"*I don't know...I'm sorry,*" he mimicked, "the two phrases I detest the most! You know something, Ms. Crawley? You're starting to sound like my students." The professor trimmed the rim of his Homburg at a pedestrian walking by.

"But they didn't find anything."

"How can you be so sure, Ms. Crawley? What if, after having a few drinks, something dawns on them that they have overlooked? Something, perhaps, that leads them to another clue, another city, another country? What are we to do then, Ms. Crawley?"

"I...I don't know," was her reply.

"Of course, *you don't know*. That's why you are a librarian and I am a Professor. You may constitute the eyes and ears of the university, but I constitute the brain. *Your* job is merely to keep the office stocked and tidy, as would a good custodian or chambermaid, while *my* job is to utilize the information…my job is *to know*. That is why it upsets me greatly when I give you a simple command and you neglect to obey it." He reached his bony hand into the breast pocket of his suit, removing Ellen's notes. "See these, Ms. Crawley?"

"Yes."

"Do you know what they are, Ms. Crawley?"

"Yes...that little brat's notes."

"How about this?" he said, removing Ellen's tiny tape recorder from his side pocket. "Do you know what this is?"

"Yes."

"Do you know how much these items are worth, Ms. Crawley?"

She went to speak, but the professor slapped her face with the notes.

"Not a farthing, Ms. Crawley, these are not worth a single farthing!"

Again, she went to speak, and the schoolmaster slapped her face hard.

"Do you know how much the letter they have is worth, let alone the book?"

For fear of being struck again, she kept silent.

"It is priceless, Ms. Crawley, priceless! Not that such a word exists in the English language, or any other for that matter." The professor tucked the notes and recorder back into his dark coat, trimming his Homburg again. "You see, everything has its price. You, for instance, you are paying yours, now, at my hand," he said, displaying his fist. "*They*, on the other hand, *they* will pay far more deadly a price when I get through with them. Because nothing, I mean *nothing* is going to stand in the way of my finding the story's ending first! And if you play your library cards correctly, Ms. Crawley," he stated, his bony fist turning into a pointy finger that he stabbed into her breast, "I will allow you to gain prominence as my faithful assistant. You will be my *Watson*, my *Friday*, my…my…*Sancho Panza.*"

Still fearful, she kept silent.

"There's far too much at stake to be outwitted by a couple of undergraduate students. Now, I shall pose the question to you for the last time, Ms. Crawley," he said, raising his hand at her. "Where are they?"

Her face, wincing like a dog under the hand of a cruel master, replied: "I will find out."

"Good, Ms. Crawley, good. You go right ahead and look that information up for me."

She situated herself on a park bench, and out of her raven carapace the librarian produced a notebook-sized computer, flipping open the screen and quickly booting it up.

If Ellen Pipple's knapsack can be considered a portable library, Ms. Crawley's raven carapace could be considered the mainframe of Hornbake Library. In no time at all, Ms. Crawley was connected to a super-computer at the University of Maryland. In no time at all, she had a map of Trafalgar Square up on the screen.

In no time at all, the listings of several businesses were being displayed and scrolled.

"What are you doing, Ms. Crawley," questioned the professor.

"I'm listing all the pubs within a one-mile radius of Trafalgar Square," she returned.

"Good thinking, Ms. Crawley. We can then split up and search each one, pub by pub; better yet, we can try to page them."

"We may not have to," she said, her pinchers clicking away. "Most of the bars have cameras, *pub-cams* they're called. We can look for them on the internet."

"Brilliant, Ms. Crawley!" praised the schoolmaster, tucking his cruel hand away in his pocket, perhaps saving it for a later occasion. "I'll never underestimate your researching skills again."

The librarian brought up the University of Maryland's student ID pictures of Brian and Ellen. "I also have a facial recognition system that I pirated," she said. "While we're scanning the pubs manually, the system will be doing it automatically, once it downloads their facial dimensions, features, dominant characteristics, asymmetries and the like."

The shadowy man let go a baneful laugh. "They're no match for us! We have the element of surprise! The resources! Moreover, the intelligence! We shall find it first, Ms. Crawley. I have a grave notion that my students are not going to complete their assignment."

Chapter 20

The Pub

"What'll it be, mate," said a funny-eared bartender.

"Two Guinness and two lemon drops," said Brian, handing him a twenty-dollar bill.

"We only accept pounds, mate."

Ellen handed the man a twenty-pound note.

"Sorry," Brian said to her. "I keep forgettin' about that. One of these days I'm gonna do the money exchange thing."

"Pint or 'alf pints, mate," asked the bartender.

"I don't know," Brian replied. "How much beer is in a pint?"

"Two 'alf pints," quipped the bartender, pausing for a laugh that never transpired. He then held up the different-sized glasses.

"We'll do pints," said Brian.

The bartender slow-poured two beers at the same time, allowing the Guinness to settle halfway through, using his time wisely by sprinkling a packet of sugar onto two lemon wedges. He poured some vodka into a chrome container, shook it, then weaved the liquid into two shot glasses.

"How are you supposed to drink it," asked Ellen, receiving her jigger.

"Sorta like tequila," said Brian. "You suck the sugar off the lemon, do the shot, then bite the lemon."

"I don't know about this."

"It's good—you'll like it. Trust me."

"Okay," she said, "here goes." She clinked his shot with hers then followed through with the procedure, sucking off the sugar, drinking the shot, then biting into the lemon with a sour face (which could be attributed more to the alcohol than the fruit).

"My goodness, that wasn't so bad," she said.

"I major in Abnormal Consumption," Brian joked.

After the bartender finished pouring the Guinness, he placed the pints on the bar in front of them.

They both went to drink their beers, but the bartender stopped them. "What are you tryin' to do, mates, get me fired? This is *Guinness*. You've got to wait for the froth to settle first, let 'er layer up nice an' thick, *then* you can quaff it." The bartender winked at them, then stepped away, traveling down the rail of the bar, leaving in his wake a fist-sized camera that stood above the topmost shelf of the choicest of spirits.

The camera's eye was tilted at a forty-five-degree angle, looking down at the patrons, slowly scanning the room. However, every time the eye impolitely stared in the direction of Brian and Ellen, one of the bartenders or barbacks would traipse by, eclipsing the camera's view of them.

"Here's to spring break," Brian toasted, holding high his pint.

"To spring break," she returned, clanking his glass.

"Spring break's only as good as the person you spend it with," said Brian.

"Here, here," she returned, taking a long creamy pull off her pint.

"Barkeep," said Brian, "two more lemon drops."

"You've got it, mate."

"You'll have to excuse me, Brian, but I'm going to have to skip to the loo before imbibing another dram."

"Huh?"

"I have to use the bathroom before drinking another drop," she interpreted.

"Sure, go ahead. I'll just stay here and keep our beers company."

"Watch my knapsack for me?"

"Sure."

"Don't forget, *everything's* in there."

"Yeah, yeah, I know," said Brian.

The bartender returned with the refills. "Ready?"

"In a minute. She's goin' to the loo."

"I'll keep the shots on ice for you, mate."

A vagrant-looking man donning a weathered top hat and shabby clothes entered the pub, giving a blow at his sooty hands while occupying a barstool next to Brian. He reached into the pocket of his tattered greatcoat and produced a half-smoked cigar, lighting it with a blackened hand. The flame on his wooden match

143

dramatically highlighted his stubbled face. Deep worry lines were carved into his countenance, making the man appear much older than his years.

"Halloa!" he said to Brian. "'Ow 'bout buyin' me a bloody drink, myte?"

Brian looked over at him, the man's disheveled appearance forcing him to place one of his hands on Ellen's knapsack.

"Buy me a drink, an' I'll make it bloody worth yur while, myte."

"No thanks," Brian replied.

"Yeh really ought to buy me a drink," the man urged.

"Can't do it," said Brian, placing his other hand over Ellen's change that was left on the bar.

"Halloa!" said the disheveled man to the funny-eared bartender.

"Well, I'll be!" returned the bartender. "Where 'ave you been keepin' yourself, John?"

"Ohhh, 'ere an' thar, I s'pose."

"Good to see you, mate! The usual?"

"Thot'll be fine," said the man, puffing his cigar. "An' me new myte 'ere is gone to pay fur it." He pointed a black hitchhiker's thumb at Brian.

"I never said I was gonna buy him a drink," Brian asserted.

The bartender filled a birdbath martini glass with ice then snatched a green bottle of Tangeray off the top shelf. "Oh you're payin' for it," the bartender said to Brian. "You just don't know it yet."

"What?"

"Tell me, myte," said the man, his cigar puffing at Brian, "wood yeh 'appen to be in the company of a *lady* this evenin'?"

"Well, yeah...I am. Why?"

"An' tell me, myte," he said, puffing, "wood yeh two 'appen to 'ave been wanderin' roun' Trafalgar Square *arlier* this evenin'?"

"Yeah," said Brian, "how'd ya know that?"

"Joost a lucky guess, myte. Joost a lucky guess."

"Well, you can guess all you want, but I'm still not buying you a drink."

"I can tell thot yeh see through me like I was thot martini glass," said the man, gesturing at the bartender who was holding it, along with the green bottle. The man glanced at the bartender. "Yeh can 'old thot bleedin' drink—it seems me new myte, *Brian*, doesn't wish to pay fur it arter all."

Brian laughed at the man. "Hey, that's pretty good. But you probably heard my friend say my name earlier. Hell, you probably know her name, too."

"Might I inquire as to *'ow* I knew 'bout yur tour through Trafalgar Square then, myte?"

"That's easy," Brian said. "You probably saw us walkin' around there and followed us here to mooch a drink."

The bartender hesitantly slid the green bottle back on the shelf.

"Amazin'!" said the man, removing his cigar from his mouth and looking at the ash, "I've got to bloody 'and it to yeh, myte, yeh coodn't 'ave pegged me better if yeh hit three bullseyes in a game of bloody cricket!"

"I had psych last semester."

"Ohhh, is *thot* 'ow come yur so good at seein' people?" He turned to the bartender. "Thot's 'ow come the lad's so good at seein' people, 'e takes lessons at it, 'e does." He ran his sooty finger across the rim of his tattered top hat. "Well, I'd best be runnin' along. It bloody seems this lad can see through me like I wos a crystal ball!" The man stood from the bar, smoothing his dirty greatcoat. "Pur'aps yur right, myte. Pur'aps I *wos* followin' yeh an' yur lady frien' out and about arlier. Pur'aps I *wos* eavesdroppin' on yur conversation. Pur'aps I *am* joost a bloody bloke off the street who's tryin' to pry a drink out of 'is Amerrycan mytes." He took a long pull off his cigar. "Well, nice to 'ave made yur e-quaintince, Mr. Murray. If you'd be so kind as to furgive me fur attemptin' to pull the bloody wool over yur—"

Brian laughed again. *"Mr. Murray*, that's pretty good too. You must've seen my license when I got carded."

Ellen made her way back to the bar.

"Hello," she said to the man.

"Halloa!"

"Do you two know each other?" she joked.

"Not a'tawl, me dear girl," said the man. "Not a'tawl. But yur frien' 'ere seems to know a lot 'bout me character." He leaned into Ellen. "Personally, Miss Pipple, I think it's them lessons 'e's takin' wot does it."

"How do you know my name?"

146

"He probably saw your license too," said Brian.

"I showed my fake one."

"Well," said the man, "I'd best be rollin' along me merry way."

"Wait a minute," said Brian. "Who are you?"

The man doffed his beaten top hat, bowing over it. "Me name's Merrywell," he introduced, rising back up in a cloud of cigar smoke. "John Thomas Merrywell. A prest'e'digitator by day, a chimneysweep by night." He unbuttoned his greatcoat, revealing a pair of red suspenders that seemed to stretch from his knees all the way up to his ears. "Nice to make yur e-quaintince!"

Ellen couldn't help smiling at him. "And nice to make yours. I'm Ellen, and this is—"

"No need, me dear child, no need. Fur ol' Merrywell already knowed thot. Joost like I already knowed thot yur carryin' *somethink* with yeh. *Somethink* over a score an' a century old."

"How much is that?" Brian asked Ellen.

"A hundred and twenty years," she said.

"How do you know that?" Brian said to the man, threateningly.

"I already tole yeh, myte, if yeh buy me a drink, I'll bloody make it worth yur while."

"Listen," said Brian, moving close to him, "you better tell us how you know as much as you know!"

"Easy now. You can try to put yur 'ands 'pon me, myte, but you'll be the bloody worst fur it."

"Settle down you two," interrupted Ellen, forcing her small frame between them. "If Mr. Merrywell wants a drink," she said, "let's buy him a drink."

The bartender, who all the while was saving the martini by allowing the glass of ice to chill on the gully of the bar top, poured the gin and served the sparkling spirit to Merrywell without hesitation.

"Cheers, mytes." He took a sip and puckered his lips. "Mmmm—joost like me dear ol' mum used to make."

"Are you the one the note warned about?" Ellen asked.

The tattered man appeared dumbstruck. "Now, me dear girl, 'ow do yeh bloody know 'bout the note?"

"So you admit it," she kept on, "you *were* in New York."

"Con't say ol' Merrywell's ever 'ad the pleasure of settin' me foot 'pon land thar; no, Miss Ellen."

"So," she persisted, "then you're working for some-one in New York?"

"You might say thot I 'ave me connexions thar, me dear child; though, like I said to yeh, I've never laid foot 'pon yur soil."

"Who is it?" Brian grilled.

"To tell yeh the truth, mytes, I con't say I've ever met 'im."

"Let's get the police," said Ellen.

"I don't think thar's any need to call the bobbies, me dear. Asides, not mooch a bobby cood bloody do 'bout it."

Brian spun around at her. "And we wouldn't want the cops to find out *why* he's after us, would we?"

A frightened look came over Ellen's face. "There comes a time when it's not worth it anymore."

Trying to change Ellen's view, Brian turned to diplomacy. "Now, Mr. Merrywell, supposin' we were to cooperate with you. How much would you want?"

"'Ow mooch?"

"Don't play dumb with me," the boy continued, "how much money are you lookin' to get?"

"Monies?"

"First," said Brian, "you knew everything. Now you seem to know nothing. Money, Mr. Merrywell. How much money do you want?"

"Why, ol' Merrywell ayn't lookin' fur no bloody pelf."

"What the hell do you want then," Brian grilled. "Fame?"

"Fame? Why, I don't see 'ow I cood get any fame out of it."

"Yeah, right!" said Brian.

By slow degrees, Ellen's face seemed to thaw from her fright. "If you don't want fame or fortune," she said, "what is it that you want?"

"A bloody drink, me dear child. A bloody drink is awl ol' Merrywell wanted from the beginnin'. Arter awl, thot's the way it works. A deliwery fur a drink. Thot's the reasonibble rate of exchange."

"You're losing me," said Ellen.

"Yeh see, the man who gave it to me bought *me* a drink, the man who gave it to 'im bought *'im* a drink, an' so on, an' so on, right down the bloody line. Joost so 'appens thot yur at the end of it, which e-nables me to be the muddle-man, so to speak—collectin' twice, thot is."

"A drink?" she said.

"An' seein' 'ow I've finally got custody of it (though I must say, it's the 'ardest drink I ever 'ad to bloody wring out of any indivijul), I'll render it to yeh." He took a gulp off his martini, emptying a third of the glass, as if wanting to consume it before they changed their minds about buying it. "'Ere yeh go." From the breast of his greatcoat, the vagrant man produced a piece of crisp white stationery, delivering it to the nearer of the two.

"What's this?" said Brian.

"Why," retorted Merrywell, "it's the bloody note." Suspicious that they may renege on the deal, he gulped another third of his martini.

"Note?" said Ellen. "From whom?"

"Yeh might say we got a mutual friend."

Brian unfolded it. "What's this supposed to mean?" he said.

He gulped the last third of his martini. "I don't bloody write 'em, myte, joost deliwer 'em. But, per'aps, yeh might want to take partickler notice of the *way* thot it's writ. An', per'aps, yeh might want to take partickler notice of the stationery on *wot* it's writ."

Ellen snatched the note from Brian.

In a childish scrawl, the note read, 'BaD NoRMiN.'

Ellen flipped the paper over. "Oh my God," she uttered.

"What is it?" said Brian.

"The stationery, it's from the hotel."

"What hotel?"

"Hotel Delmonico."

"In New York?"

"Yes," she replied, turning to Merrywell. "Then you *do* know the person who broke into our room and stole my notes?"

"Ol' Merrywell knowed nothink whatsever 'bout thot, me dear girl."

"How come you know we're carrying something that's over a hundred and twenty years old then?" she said.

"Cos yur carryin' *this*," said Merrywell, giving a swift snap with the sleeve of his greatcoat, stretching his arm out, reaching his black sooty fingers behind Ellen's ear and removing the 1879 Morgan silver dollar from it. He slapped it on the bar top. "Sonar gave yeh this, did 'e not?"

"Yes," she said, "but how did you—?"

"Never yeh mind 'ow ol' Merrywell knows anythink or does anythink, me dear girl, I'm a prest'e'digitator, I tole yeh. Arter all, it's against the rules of the 'andbook."

"What the hell is a prestidigitator?" said Brian.

"A magician," Ellen answered, her frames locked on Merrywell. "So, Sonar's the mutual friend? You know him?"

"Nought personally," explained the tattered magician, viewing his cigar ash again. "The way the grapevine works, no one gets to see mooch of each other. I know of 'im, an' 'e knows of me. Yeh might say *'is* people an' *me* people do each other favors on occasion."

"Do you know what this note means," she asked.

"'Aven't the slightest idear, me child, I'm joost the deliwery man. Yeh might say I'm a prest'e'digitator by day, chimneysweep by night, an' a deliwery man in betwixt." He looked at his cigar. "An' judgin' from the ash on me smoke, it's time to be gettin' along, or I may as well scratch the occupation of *chimneysweep* off me resumé."

"You can really tell the time just by lookin' at your cigar?" said Brian.

"Dependin' on the weather, myte. But yeh see, if me cigar is wet, I can tell thot it must be a-rainin'." He gave his sanguine suspenders a snap, as if it were the exclamation point of his punch line.

"You mustn't go yet," said Ellen. "We'll buy you another drink if you'd like."

"Sorry, me dear child, but I've got an appintmint with a chimney who's got a bad case of the flue." Again, he gave his red suspenders a snap. "Thankee fur the drink, mytes." He proceeded to button up his shabby greatcoat, directing his steps towards the pub door.

"Wait!" Ellen called to him. "If you need to find us again, Mr. Merrywell, for anything, anything at all, we'll be at Trafalgar Square tomorrow morning."

"Thankee, me dear girl, but I must admit thot ol' Merrywell wood mooch rather venture to find yeh at Trafalgar Tavern tomorrow eve'nin'." (If it weren't for his greatcoat, he would have given his suspenders another snap.)

"Trafalgar *Tavern*?" she said to herself, the tiny camera mounted above the shelf fixed on her.

For, when Ellen moved, the camera moved. When she looked into her knapsack, the camera seemed to look into her knapsack. When she got up from the bar and walked down the bar's rail, the camera seemed to rise and follow. And when she exited, the camera surely would have followed too, if not for the tiny metal screws within its steely housing.

Chapter 21

The Tavern

I n *Great Expectations* Charles Dickens wrote: *'Pause you who read this, and think for a moment of the long chain of iron or gold, of thorns or flowers, that would never have bound you, but for the formation of the first link on one memorable day.'*

There exists across the Atlantic, long before any cable was laid to rest on the bottom of that Great Sea, a strong chain of communication forged out of ships, and men, and friendship, and good will that populate every degree of society. For, if not for the shoeless man in New York, Ellen and Brian never would have met Sonar. If not for the swab aboard the freighter that Sonar knew, the crisp white piece of stationery would never have reached the men who unload the cargo at the Port of Rochester. If not for the Captain, and First Mate, and perhaps all Hands on that particular deck, the message never would have made the yawing journey over to England.

After Ellen searched through her wearable library of books with great adoration, like a scholarly marsupial nurturing her infantile information into knowledge, she discovered that Dickens frequented Trafalgar Tavern quite regularly in his earlier days, particularly with his first illustrator, George Cruikshank.

The tavern was located on the southern bank of the River Thames in the Greenwich section of Greater London, where a light snow was just beginning to fall.

Since Merrywell said he was a regular at Trafalgar Tavern, Ellen convinced him to escort them there, paying him the same amount of money he would have procured on his chimney cleaning job (plus drinks).

"I thought the pubs close at eleven," said Brian.

"I bloody tole yeh, myte," said Merrywell, "I'm a regerler 'ere."

"But it's ten minutes after eleven," Ellen added.

"Ayn't yeh never been to an *underground pub*, me dear child?"

"I can't say I ever have," she replied.

"Joost yeh leave it to me, mytes. I'm quite familler with the barmaids."

Every window of the tavern was curtained. And Merrywell gave the door three quick raps with his knuckles, followed by four thumps of his fist.

A frizzy-haired woman opened a small wooden window within the door, eyeing him. "Well! If it ain't John Thomas Merrywell!" she said, closing the wooden window and unlatching the door.

"Hey," Ellen said to Merrywell, "they really *do* know you here."

The woman flung the door open, lifted back her leg, and delivered a kick that struck Merrywell square in his crotch, causing him to double over, his snow-flecked top hat tumbling to the ground and landing upright.

"Yeah," said Brian, "they know him alright."

"Yuh've got some bleedin' nerve showin' up 'ere!" said the woman, Merrywell still bent over and staring into the pit of his hat. "Yuh owe me sixty pounds—so come good with it, or I'll strike yuh another blow what'll make the likes of the first seem friendly—mind!"

"Me e-pologies, Cath'rin," he said in a high voice, "fur whatever I done this time."

"Yuh not only 'ad the bleedin' gall to skip out on yer bar tab, but to do it on *my* shift!"

"I don't 'member, Cath'rin," he said, still trying to compose himself. "Furgive me. I must've been on one of me benders."

"It was a bender alright! Now *un*bend so I can 'ave another blow at yuh!"

Still hunched over, Merrywell drew the said money out of his greatcoat, holding it up to the frizzy-haired woman, who, in one fluid motion, snatched it from his hand, counted it, and crammed it into her brassiere. "I don't normally accept gratuity, but in your case I'll make an exception—come good with it now—mind!"

Merrywell produced a five-pound note from his greatcoat, holding it up. "Thot's awl the bloody pelf I got left, Cath'rin."

"Why, that's not even ten percent!"

Merrywell grabbed his top hat off the ground with both hands by the brim, slowly straightening his back, as if his hat bore a great weight he was attempting to lift. "I swar it, Cath'rin," he said, stepping out of range of the woman's foot, holding his hat low to his groin, "thot's awl I got to me bloody name."

"Yuh give it mouth as if your name's of any worth," she said, snapping the money from his hand and tucking it into her bosom. "What the blimey are yuh doin' 'ere anyway?"

"Me mytes 'ere," said Merrywell, "they want to throw thar eyes over the place a bit, thot's awl."

The woman jammed her hands onto her hips and gave her head a sideways screw; first at Ellen, then Brian, then back at Merrywell, provoking more of her hair to puff out. "An' what the blimey do yuh 'ave to gain fer it? S'posin' I *was* to let yuh in, which I 'aven't made up my mind yet."

"A drink, Cath'rin. Thot's awl...joost a drink."

"Blimey if yuh should ever 'ave the pleasure of wettin' yer lips 'ere again, John Thomas Merrywell!"

The old magician converged on the frizzy-haired woman, placing his hand behind her, on the small of her back, pulling the woman in close. He then proceeded to dip her, pressing his lips against hers as his greatcoat pressed against her chest, making a crinkling sound from the money she kept within it.

"Well," said the woman, softly, her lips letting go, "just one, John."

"Wot I tell yeh, mytes!" he said to Brian and Ellen. "I'm a regerler at this 'ere e-stab-leashmint! Now you kids run along—go 'ave a looksee! Take yur time too, mytes, no need to 'urry it!" He proceeded to make his way over to the bar where a handful of patrons were hobnobbing.

Ellen and Brian exchanged glances.

"We're in," she said.

"Merrywell's got some game," added Brian. "I guess that's what you call a love-hate relationship." He eyed the magician who, by this time, had shed his greatcoat and was in the process of telling jokes and snapping his suspenders at the hobnobbers.

Ellen's eyes circumnavigated the rims of her glasses as she gazed around the tavern. Knickknacks of every size and sort were hanging all about the place. "Let's split up," she said.

"Usually when I split up with friends at the bar," said Brian, "it's to divide and conquer."

"Puh-lease," she replied.

Brian's eyes began scanning the walls as he worked his way around a corner of the pub. He halted at a picture of a skinny boy holding up a bowl of gruel to a bulging-eyed man. "Here's an early sketch of Oliver Twist. And it's signed by...by Cruikshank!"

"Good get," she said, hurrying over to study it.

"Anything here?" he asked.

She lifted the picture off the wall, turning it around, triggering the frizzy-haired woman to shout from behind the bar: "You're to throw yer blimey eyes 'bout the place! Not yer blimey fingers!"

"Sorry," Ellen said, placing the picture back on the wall, "it's for a class assignment." Her glasses spun around at Brian. "Well, it's not like I'm lying to her."

"See anything?"

"I'm afraid not. Come to think of it, I don't know if Dickens would've involved Cruikshank; they grew bitter towards each other in the end."

"Well then," said Brian, "what are we looking for?"

"Hopefully we'll know it when we find it," she responded.

It didn't take Ellen long to stumble upon a large wooden carving set atop a door at the far corner of the pub. "And I think we found it." She stretched her hand up, touching the carving in admiration. "This is it. This is the wooden effigy Dickens speaks of in Drood." She withdrew the paperback version of the book from her knapsack and read aloud to Brian: *"'Over the doorway is a wooden effigy, about half life-size, representing Mr. Sapsea's father, in a curly wig and toga, in the act of selling. The chastity of the idea, and the natural appearance of the little finger, hammer, and pulpit, have been much admired.'"*

"That's him alright," said Brian.

"Get me a lemon drop and a barstool, Brian…please."

"Now you're talkin'!"

Ellen paced the carving from below, examining it from several different angles while Brian schooled the frizzy-haired woman on the definition of a lemon drop. All the while, Merrywell was doing more hobbing than nobbing, partaking in several shots of whiskey with his fellow patrons, toasting "God save the Queen!"

159

"Here ya go," said Brian, hurrying back, setting down the barstool and shot. "You might want to keep an eye on Mr. Merrywell's tab—he's gettin' pretty toasted."

Ellen dragged the barstool in front of the door and climbed onto it, holding her shot of vodka over the little finger, hammer, and pulpit of the carving, as if her jigger were an eighty-proof magnifying glass.

When the ripples of the spirit settled, through the shot glass, in the tiniest of print, emerged the words *'Fechter's gift.'*

"Find anything?" asked Brian.

Ellen answered his question by tossing back her hair, then her shot, in celebration.

Brian joined her, tossing back his jigger as well and shouting, "Yeeeeeee!"

"Yeeeeeee!" Merrywell reflexively returned from across the room, having no notion whatsoever as to why Brian was so jubilantly rejoicing (his faculties so filled with drink that he was nonetheless blissful).

"Pipe down!" said the frizzy-haired woman, slapping the back of Merrywell's head. "Mind! There's no need to advertise yer drunkenness! All we need's the rozzers pokin' their 'eads in 'ere!"

"What'cha find?" asked Brian.

"Fechter's gift," she returned.

"What's that supposed to mean?"

"Charles Fechter was a Swiss actor performing in Paris when Dickens met him. The two became good friends in the eighteen-sixties. Dickens even contributed an essay to the Atlantic Monthly about the brilliance of his acting." As she told this, the two gravitated towards the bar. "As a gift, Fechter sent him a Swiss chalet on Christmas Eve. It was assembled at Gad's Hill Place where he wrote the last words of Drood."

"Where's that?"

"First, it's important to know *what* Gad's Hill Place was, and everything it meant to Dickens. As a boy, young Charles fell in love with the house on the hill, and his father told him that if he worked hard, and became a clever man, he might come to own it someday."

"Did he?"

"Yes. He bought it, fixed it up, and moved there for the last ten years of his life. In a sense, he bought back the happiest days of his childhood."

"That's too cool, Ellen. Not many people can say they did that—I mean—I know people who *say* they're gonna buy back their childhood home someday, but nobody ever does."

"The second half of the novel must be hidden somewhere in the Swiss chalet."

"Does this mean we have to go to Switzerland?"

"No, silly."

"So, where's Gad's Hill Place?"

Pondering over so many different historical connections, Ellen's train of thought seemed to derail like a locomotive, her fragile theory seemingly wrecking with concrete fact. A cloud of gloom began to descend upon her.

"What's wrong?" said Brian.

"The Swiss chalet."

"What about it?"

"It's not at Gad's Hill anymore."

"How do you mean?"

"It's been moved...to a museum."

"Well then…it's gotta be there."

"Yeah," she said, hesitantly.

"*Yeah*? Whatta ya mean *yeah*? You always seem so pumped about these things. What happened to *'Yes!'*?"

"I don't know. You're right—I usually *do* feel more confident. It's just that I don't feel much of anything this time."

"I'll take care of that," said Brian, arriving at the bar. "Two more lemon drops," he said to the frizzy-haired woman.

"An' a bloody shot of rye!" Merrywell added.

The woman began fixing the drinks, shooting Merrywell a sideways glance.

"From everything you said so far, Ellen, it's *gotta* be in the Swiss chalet."

"But it's the first clue we've come across that's not where it should be." She broke open one of her books to verify what she already knew. "Not only has the chalet been moved, but it was disassembled, piece by piece, in which there were over ninety, then moved to Rochester and reassembled again."

"But you said he woulda put it somewhere that'd stand the test of time, remember?"

"Yeah," she sighed.

"There ya go again. Give me a *'Yes!'* Ellen."

Surrounded by her gloomy cloud, she attempted to contemplate it away.

"Come on, you can do it...*Yes!*" He lifted the lemon drops the woman had served up, handing one to Ellen. "Give me a *Y,*" said Brian, clinking her glass with his.

"Y," Ellen returned, half-heartedly.

"Give me an *E,*" said Brian, clinking her glass again.

"E," she returned, wistfully.

"Give me an *S,*" he said, clinking.

"S."

"What's that spell?"

"Yes."

"What's that spell?"

Merrywell took the liberty of helping her, giving it good throat: *"Yes!"*

"Pipe down!" said the woman. "The lot of yuh! Pipe down—mind!"

Merrywell's eyes focused on the woman. "Dearest Cath'rin...may I impose 'pon yur gracious 'ospitality to ask yeh fur a joint of mutton to feast upon?"

"Blimey! I'll give yuh a joint of mutton to feast upon alright!" She held her fist up at him.

Merrywell sat his top hat on the bar, along with his drink, then rubbed his blackened hands together, warming them by friction. He reached into the dregs of his hat and plucked out a perfectly formed red rose. "'Ere yeh go, me darlin'," he said, presenting it. The woman's hair seemed to settle a bit, along with her temperament, in warm reception of it.

"Alright, then," said the barmaid, "I'll see what we got back in the kitchen. I ain't promisin' yuh a joint of anythin', though!"

"Whatever wittles yeh can spar, me darlin'. Whatever wittles yeh can spar."

"I'll be right back," said Ellen

"Where ya going?" Brian asked.

"The loo."

Brian and Merrywell remained at the bar, glancing at each other awkwardly, trying to think of something to discuss that they might have in common.

"I 'eard of ways of gettin' women to say *yes* befur," said Merrwell, breaking the ice, "but 'avin' 'er spell it out? You take the bloody crumpet, myte."

"I heard of ways of gettin' into bars after hours," Brian replied, "but havin' women kick ya in the nuts? You take the cake, man."

Merrywell laughed, sliding one of his two tumblers of whiskey in front of the boy. "At me age, any feelin' I get down thar is welcome."

Brian let go a laugh, the two lifting their glasses and drinking in unison (having found a commonality).

Ellen returned to leave her knapsack with Brian, reminding him that *everything* was in it. She momentarily removed her glasses and cleaned them with a cocktail napkin before heading away again.

"I swar," said Merrywell, catching a glimpse of Ellen without her glasses, "if thot Miss Ellen ayn't the splittin' image!"

"What?" Brian said.

"Thot Miss Ellen," he repeated. "If she ayn't the splittin' image! With 'er spec'tickles off, thot is."

"Splitting image of who?"

"Ohhh...never yeh mind."

"Nevermind what?" said Brian.

"Let's joost say thot me 'eart once went out to a lass; 'er name wos Rosa. An' if thot girl ayn't the splittin' image of 'er!"

"No kiddin'?"

Merrywell gave a fixed stare into his drink, smiling, as if his thoughts were dancing around inside of his vessel (and were far richer than his whiskey). "Bloody asked 'er to marry me. She said *yes* too." He continued staring into his glass, content with the notion.

"So? What happened," asked Brian.

Still appearing mesmerized by his drink, as if he saw pictures steeped in the spirit from better days of ole, the old magician just sat transfixed.

"Mr. Merrywell?" Brian tried tapping him on the suspenders. "Mr. Merrywell?"

"Wot?" he said, snapping out of it. "Wot is it, lad?"

"Did you marry her?"

"Marry?"

"Rosa. Did you marry her?"

"Oh, nunno—no." He took a gulp from his drink. "'Er parents woodn't let 'er 'ave anythink to do with a lad of me upbringin'. Yeh see, I was from the *other* side of bloody town—the *lower* side, thot is. An' she, why, she wos from the *upper* side of town, if yeh knowed wot I

165

mean." Merrywell took another gulp of his drink. "An' d'spite of wot yeh may think, like wot yeh thought me intentions wos arlier, I wos in love with Rosa, not 'er mon-e-tary station in life. B'lieve it or no, myte, bloody pelf doesn't matter awl thot mooch to ol' Merrywell—I make it awl right through the day anyway, with me top 'at, an' me tongue, an' me 'ands, an' wot little else God 'as kindly bestowed 'pon me."

"Whatever happened to Rosa?" said Brian.

"'Er folks sent 'er off to a nunnery. She died thar too, not long arter, of a 'orse an' carriage accident. 'Er parents woodn't even let me 'tend the fyoon'ral. So ol' Merrywell 'ad to watch from afar."

"Ouch," said Brian.

"But I wisit 'er grave ev'ry year, on wot wos to be our anniwersary."

"You must've really been in love."

"Thot I wos, myte, thot I wos." He turned his glass upside down, emptying it. "An' still are."

Brian thought for a moment. "It's probably best not to mention any of this to Ellen. Her imagination can get the better of her at times, and she's pretty sensitive when it comes to these things."

"No worries a'tawl, myte...no worries a'tawl."

The barmaid appeared with spliced sausages neatly placed atop a plate of mashed potatoes and gravy. "So 'elp me, John Thomas Merrywell, yuh better eat these bangers an' mash then be gone! If yuh ask me for one more thing tunnight, I'll bust this plate over yer bleedin' skull, I will!"

Merrywell waited for her to drop the plate on the bar before saying, "Joost one more whiskey, Cath'rin... please?"

She went for his plate to make good on her threat, but he stopped her, grabbing the frizzy savage by the wrist, as if taming her. With his other hand, he reached into the dregs of his hat again and produced from it a piece of chocolate wrapped in shiny silver foil, with a tiny red ribbon. He then presented it to her as if it were the prize of all England. "'Ere yeh go, Cath'rin. Fur you, me darlin'."

"Alright," she said, depositing it into the veritable safe she held in her breast. "Just one more drink. But I ain't promisin' another after that!"

Ellen returned to find Brian and Merrywell eyeing her. "What is it?" she said to them, self-consciously examining herself.

"The splittin' image," said Merrywell.

"What?"

"Nothin'," said Brian.

"Nothink a'tawl," Merrywell confirmed, shoveling sausage into his mouth, filling it as if to keep himself from saying any more.

"The way you're ogling," said Ellen, "you'd think I had a roll of toilet paper stuck to my shoe."

"Two more lemon drops," Brian said to the barmaid, changing the subject. "After all, it *is* spring break."

"Our second pub tonight," she added. "This is a first for me." Ellen went over to one of the windows and drew back the curtain. "Wow! The snow is really coming down out there!"

In the wink of an eye, the barmaid was at the window, snapping the curtains shut. "What the blimey are yuh doin', Missy?"

"It's getting a little claustrophobic in here," said Ellen, pulling open a corner of the curtain. "Besides, look how beautiful it is out there."

"We'll just see 'ow beautiful it is when the bleedin' peelers throw the lot of us in gaol!" said the woman, snapping the curtain back shut.

"Sorry," Ellen apologized, "I keep forgetting about this whole underground pub thing."

"Keep it up, Missy, an' you'll be undergroun' as well…six feet under—mind!"

Ellen made her way back to the bar, and the woman most certainly would not have served the girl another dram of liquor had it not been for Merrywell, who reached into his tattered top hat and produced for the woman a tiny bronze trinket.

Everyone tossed back their drinks, with the exception of Ellen, that gloomy cloud beginning to descend upon her again.

"What's wrong?" said Brian.

"The note," she returned. "I wonder what Sonar meant by 'Bad Normin'.'"

"Who knows."

"I wouldn't think he'd go through the trouble of sending it all this way if it wasn't important. Like with the first note, about us being in danger. And he was more than right about that."

"Stop worrying, Ellen. Drink."

"What if he knows something we don't? What if we're still in some kind of danger?"

"He's a kid, Ellen, drink."

"A wery reliable un," Merrywell interposed, finishing the last of his supper, crumpling up his napkin and throwing it onto his plate. "As fur as men 'bout the street go, me bein' one of um, thot lad's bloody credentials are impeccable! From wot I 'ear, 'e's as good as me when it comes to makin' a bloody deliwery."

"You're not makin' things any better," Brian said to Merrywell. "I'm sure if it has anything to do with danger, we left that in New York. We're in England—thousands of miles away. We're safe, Ellen, so drink."

She tossed back her hair, about to toss back her shot, ceasing. "I'll bet Sonar spoke with someone who was with the shoeless man before he died, the one who saw the person who ransacked our room. I bet he revealed the person's name. My God! He might have even said it on his deathbed."

"I don't think 'e sent the bloody note to say halloa," said Merrywell.

"Think, Brian," she said. "Do you know anyone named Norman?"

"Norman? No. I mean, I've come across a few in my time. Nobody I really know though."

"Norman," Ellen thought. "Are you sure that Pat Hastings's first name isn't really Norman?"

"I'm sure."

"I guess that shoots a hole in my theory. I was certain it was him." She shook her head. "I don't know any Normans either. But why does the name sound so familiar?"

"Drink, Ellen," said Brian, lifting her arm and prompting her to do so.

She threw back her hair again, along with her shot, continuing to contemplate the name.

Merrywell lit up a cigar, and by the time he finished filling the bar with smoke (and himself with drink), he checked the cigar's ash, revealing to all that it was time to go.

Chapter 22

When Shall These Three Meet Again?

The gentle snow graced down upon the three of them like something out of a Dickens' Christmas story.

Merrywell took the liberty of tying a plastic takeout bag given to him by the frizzy-haired woman around the outside of his stovepipe hat, the barmaid perhaps protecting any future procurements the tattered top hat may yield for her.

All three were feeling cheerful, goading each other to hold their heads back and mouths open to catch the pound-sized snowflakes softly drifting down, seeing who could perform this ritual while walking the straightest line as their steps tamped fresh, winding tracks towards Greenwich Station.

Ellen lagged behind, dipping her mittens in the snow, forming a snowball and hurling it at the back of Merrywell—the projectile exploding against the magician's greatcoat like a powdery puff of smoke! When the air cleared, it was apparent to the girl that Merrywell had concocted a frosty projectile of his own, causing her to let go a happy scream as she unsuccessfully dodged his counter offensive. This act of aggression precipitated Brian to bend at the snow and manufacture his own arsenal (barehandedly), launching his own attack against the two aggressive nations.

After this brief flurry of war, being, as he puts it, "a man of the street," Merrywell relayed to them the shortest distance and shortest vehicle and shortest means necessary to get from London to Rochester.

"Please, Mr. Merrywell," said Ellen, "don't feel as if you need to escort us the entire way to the rail station."

"Never yeh mind, me dear girl, never yeh mind. I'm 'appy to 'blige. Joost consider yurselves to be a deliwery of sorts. An' wood yeh look at thot," he said, gesturing at the signpost, "we're awlready at the bloody station." A sad look became his face. "I'm afeared to say it looks like this is where we part, me dear mytes."

"What about you?" asked Ellen. "Where do you go at night?"

"Bein' a man of the street, me dear child, yeh better believe thot I'll be awl up an' 'bout it. Don't worry yurselves 'bout ol' Merrywell. Ol' Merrywell knows 'ow to make the street 'is kitchen, 'is beddin', *an'* 'is stage."

Ellen drew her tiny purse out of her knapsack, reaching inside it, retrieving a fifty-pound note. "Please accept this, Mr. Merrywell, for all that you've done for us."

"Now, me dear girl, I accepted yur pelf afore fur the reason thot I wos missin' me chimney cleanin' obleegations. But as far as deliweries are to be concerned: one free drink, me child, thot's awl...one free drink."

"Please take it, Mr. Merrywell; consider it lodgings for the night."

"Thankee, no. I work fur me pelf by performin'; I like earnin' it the rep-yoo-tibble way. Don't feel the least bit 'umble fur me, dear child; when yur a man of the street yeh got the biggest backyard and nicest view in awl of London!"

Ellen beamed at him, the mammoth snowflakes sticking to her glasses and rosy cheeks.

Merrywell removed her watery spectacles, giving them a few swipes with a neckerchief that he produced from his greatcoat (all the time looking into Ellen's pretty brown eyes) then delicately placed the glasses back on the girl's face. "I s'pose this is where we say g'bye."

"Goodbye, Mr. Merrywell," she said, throwing her arms around him, giving him a squeeze and a kiss. "You helped us in more ways than you know."

"Thankee," he said, doffing his plastic-coated stove-pipe. "I enjoyed 'elpin' yeh. I 'ope yeh find wot ever 'tis yur lookin' fur."

"You're quite a character," said Brian, grasping his blackened hand firmly and shaking it. "Stay cool, Mr. Merrywell."

"If we do find what we're looking for," said Ellen, "is there any way we can get in touch with you?"

"If yeh ever want to find ol' Merrywell, me dear girl," he said with a wink, "yeh needn't look any further than the nearest pub...thot's where you'll find ol' Merrywell."

On that note, the old magician set his stovepipe back upon his crown then snapped both fingers together (as if his suspenders were on the outside of his greatcoat). A puff of magician's smoke accompanied his fingers, momentarily beclouding Brian and Ellen's eyes. By the time the smoke dissipated, Merrywell had long disappeared in the swirling snowflakes, with only the sound of the words "Splittin' image!" filling the black dots of night between them.

Chapter 23

A Ride (and a Lesson, as well)

As Brian and Ellen boarded the train, the cameras at Greenwich Station seemed to be craning their metal necks, allowing their lenses to catch a good view of them.

The ornithic librarian proved her computer skills worthy by hacking into British Rail security, Underground security, and no doubt would have attempted to hack into Her Majesty's Secret Service had the professor and his hard hand wished it.

Professor Mudgrove and Ms. Crawley were travelling in the back of a hackney carriage—the librarian's tiny computer resting upon her lap, the professor's hand resting upon his.

"What was it that you said, Ms. Crawley?" stated the professor's haughty voice, "that they'll be back in Trafalgar Square tomorrow?"

Hard at work, her face buried into her computer, nothing visible but her steel-gray plumage and claws clicking away at her keys, the librarian returned: "Not a problem. We know that the little—" she halted, spying the cab driver looking at her through his rearview mirror.

"We know our eager students," she rephrased, "bought a ticket to Rochester Station."

"And, let me ask you, Ms. Crawley," the professor stated, glancing at the rearview, "when our eager *friends*," he said this latter word in a condescending tone that seemed to correct the librarian's choice of noun, "when our eager *friends* arrive at Rochester Station, will we be able to *take their picture*?"

This question seemed to make the librarian's claws click faster. "Wait…" she replied, with one final click. "Yes! There it is! Rochester Station!"

The cab driver's eyes squinted at them through his mirror. "We're not anywhere near Rochester Station, lady."

"You are mistaken, Ms. Crawley," stated the professor, his eyes likewise squinting, but with a more wrathful slant. "Rochester station is miles away." He held his hard hand inside the other, as if trying to keep it from connecting with her.

On her computer screen, Rochester Station could be seen as a small, narrow, empty platform at this early hour of the morning, being slightly after two o'clock.

"But what about *him*," quizzed the professor. "Our friends' acquaintance at the pubs and honorable tour guide for the evening. The one with the top hat. How are you coming along with *him?*"

This incited the librarian to quickly pull up another window on her screen before furiously tapping away again.

"We should try to acquaint ourselves with *him*, Ms. Crawley. After all, any friend of *theirs* is a friend of *ours*." The professor flashed a crooked smile at the driver in the mirror.

The librarian pulled up a pub-cam close-up of Merrywell's face from the first bar (the cameras being turned off at the underground pub) whereas the words 'Face Rec Sys' titled the page. Numbers rapidly began ascending at the bottom of her screen: the digits on the left comparing faces; the digits on the right being the time elapsing within the search.

"I'm working on it, Norman."

"You were quite adamant about our friends being at Trafalgar Square in the morning, Ms. Crawley. I wonder why they had such a change of heart?"

"I don't know," was her reply.

"Of course you don't know, Ms. Crawley. As I told you once before, that is not your job."

"They didn't find anything at Trafalgar Square, I swear it."

"Oh, I believe you, Ms. Crawley. However, if you examine this matter a bit closer, using logic and reason, you'll notice that it all makes perfect sense."

"Enlighten me, Norman...please."

"Our other friend, Ms. Crawley, the one at Staple Inn, *Mr. P.J.T.*, what were his exact words?"

"Words?"

Not being able to connect with her, Professor Mudgrove nudged the computer halfway off her lap, pinching her flesh and violently twisting it!

"You're not paying attention, Ms. Crawley. You need to put your thinking cap on. Mr. P.J.T. left word for us at Staple Inn. You told me so yourself, remember? You stated that he left a note for us above his door."

The pain induced by this unnatural distortion of her flesh caused her eyes to water, her face wincing as she said, "Yes."

"Very good, Ms. Crawley, very good. You are progressing along nicely. Now, I'll ask you again: what were Mr. P.J.T.'s precise words?"

She took a moment to overcome the pain. "Trafalgar."

"Good answer, Ms. Crawley, good answer. You may pass this examination yet. Now, I'll pose the second question: what do you call a shape that has four equal sides?"

"A quadrilateral."

His wrinkled fingers gave her flesh another painful twist!

"You're overthinking, Ms. Crawley," he corrected. "You must think generally. After all, isn't that your occupation? Providing general information? You must adapt your thinking to this particular assignment. Again, pay attention."

She rubbed her thigh with her claw. "Please, Norman, stop being so—

"Perhaps the driver can answer that one for you, Ms. Crawley." He looked at the cab driver in the rearview. "I beg your pardon, driver. Would you be so kind as to tell me what you call a shape that has four equal sides?"

"A square," he replied into his mirror.

"See, Ms. Crawley, the driver knows the answer." He looked back into the rearview. "May I inquire, *driver*," said the professor, emphasizing this latter word and occupation with disdain, "as to what degree of college you have achieved?"

"If you're askin' me if I've ever been to university—no, sir."

"And may I inquisite, *driver*," he stressed, "as to what degree of high school you have achieved?"

"If you're askin' me if I've ever been to secondary school—no, sir."

"So, may I inquisite, *driver*, as to the age you were when you discontinued school?"

"I was twelve, mate, that's when I called it quits. But look how far I've come," he said, gesturing around his cab and happily laughing at himself.

"See, Ms. Crawley? Age twelve...that's when he *called it quits*."

"Please, Norman, don't—"

"Ah, ah, ah," he said, shaking his bony forefinger in between utterances, "there will be no talking while the professor is talking. Now, let us examine the words *Trafalgar* and *square*. Did our friend, Mr. P.J.T., leave the latter word, *square*, in his note?"

Within this mobile classroom of sorts, the professor was unrelenting in his academic bashing of the woman, going as far as to pit the uneducated driver against her.

"No," she answered, her eyes now watering more from the mental blows rather than the physical.

"You are correct, Ms. Crawley; the word that our friend Mr. P.J.T. left for us merely stated *Trafalgar*." He took a moment to trim his Homburg. "Now, did you happen to notice the name of the pub they ventured to with *him*, our unfamiliar friend, the one with the top hat?" he drilled, pointing his knobby finger at the computer screen where the dimensions of Merrywell's face were still being compared to millions of others.

"Trafalgar Tavern," she said.

"Excellent response, Ms. Crawley, excellent response. You are turning into a prize pupil. Now, I must ask you, do you detect any commonalties between the word Mr. P.J.T. left for us above his door and the establishment *he*," stated the professor, pointing at Merrywell again, "escorted our friends to?"

"Yes."

"Brilliant, Ms. Crawley, brilliant. And since you are in the midst of an academic roll, I shall continue to ask, perchance, if it is possible for *that* Trafalgar to be the one our friend Mr. P.J.T was referring to?"

"Yes."

"Right again, Ms. Crawley. By God, you are red hot!"

The driver interrupted, "Are you two on some kind of scavenger hunt or something?"

"You could say it is a hunt of sorts," the professor replied, his cold tiny pebbles never leaving the librarian's birdlike countenance.

"You've made your point, Norman," she pleaded, preferring for the schoolmaster to peck at her flesh than to bash her brain with any more intellectual measuring sticks.

The professor obliged. Pinching, twisting, *and* pulling at her!

"Please do not interrupt me again," he said, trimming his hat at the driver in the mirror with a crooked show of teeth. "We have arrived at midterms, Ms. Crawley, surely you wouldn't want to jeopardize your academic standing at this point. After all, you are my star student."

"Please, Norman, you've made your p—"

"Tsk, tsk, Ms. Crawley. Now you have gone and done it. I am afraid that I am going to have to punish you." He glanced at the driver before whispering to her, "I will administer it later, when we are alone…after class."

She kept silent, a disturbed look on her face.

"I'll make it simple for you, Ms. Crawley. True or false: with a little bit of logic and reason, we can deduce that our friends will *not* be at Trafalgar Square tomorrow, as you have theorized."

"True."

"True or false, Ms. Crawley: with a bit of logic and reason, we can deduce that the likelihood our friends found something at the tavern is highly probable."

"True."

"Well done. You are almost through with your oral examination. True or false: whatever it is they have found must lead to the town of Rochester."

"True."

He gave her the most vicious pinch, twist, and pull yet! "Not true, Ms. Crawley. Since we don't know what they have found, we don't know if it leads to Rochester." He composed himself with a trim and a smile. "Unless, perhaps, you want to rely on the intellectual interpretations of two undergraduates. Then you may very well footnote them as a reference."

"I see what you mean," she said, afraid to give another incorrect answer. "I understand now."

"That's appropriate, Ms. Crawley. As a professor, it is my duty to bestow knowledge and understanding, however difficult and painful it may be to learn at times." He twisted!

"Here we are," said the driver. "Corner of Park Row and Crane."

"Just a moment," instructed the professor, pulling Ms. Crawley out of the mobile classroom of sorts to speak with her alone.

The professor walked her into the blind spot of the driver's mirrors. "It is imperative that I find the second half of the story first, regardless of what it takes! We shall beat them to the punch—or I will beat *you!* This is what I want you to do...are you taking notes, Ms. Crawley?"

Fearing his earlier threat, she nodded, saying nothing.

"Good. I want you to venture on to Rochester Station without letting them out of your sight, not even if they say they're going to be back at Trafalgar Square in the morning. Are you getting all of this, Ms. Crawley?"

She nodded.

"Good." With the driver's mirrors out of view, his bony hand administered a vicious blow to the side of her face. "I shall take care of business here, Ms. Crawley, then meet up with you there."

Her watery eyes glared at him, the side of her face beginning to redden and swell. As she got back into the Black Cab, she viewed the professor through the window. He was buttoning his collar and trudging through the snow towards Trafalgar Tavern.

Chapter 24

Settlers in Cloisterham

"Somehow or another," said Ellen, staring out of the window of the train as it chugged its way into Rochester Station, "I knew we'd end up here."

The snow had all but stopped since Merrywell performed his disappearing act in London, leaving a blanket of white on the ground in which very few townspeople had trodden this early morning hour.

"How's that?" said Brian.

"Rochester and Chatham have been in Dickens's writings from the beginning till the end—from Pickwick to Drood."

"Well, I don't know about you, Ellen, but I could use a couple of winks. The last time I slept was on the plane."

"I know just the place, too."

"You do?"

"I know everything there is to know about Rochester just by reading Dickens's novels. Maybe we should think of it as the town of Cloisterham while we're here, though."

"Cloisterham?"

"In Drood, Dickens refers to Rochester as Cloister-ham, that way he could move streets and buildings around as he pleased while concentrating on plot. He was such a stickler for accuracy, and there were some realists of the day who would shoot down a story solely for the inaccuracy of its setting." She thought for a moment. "We'll stay at the Blue Boar. That's where Pip lodged in Great Expectations."

"I guess I never read that one, either."

"It's my favorite! And I know it's still here. I'm just not sure whether it's still called the Blue Boar or not. It might be called the Blue Bull now. Dickens stayed there; Queen Victoria too—so we're in good company."

They exited the train, directing their snowy tracks up High Street.

Brian laughed. "High Street, that's pretty good."

"How do you mean?"

"It reminds me of Pat Hastings, the guy you thought was out to get us," he said.

"Why?"

"You saw him hand me somethin' through the bus window. You thought it was Jennifer Cole's number, remember?"

"Yes."

"Well," he said, looking up at the High Street sign again and chuckling. "It wasn't."

"No?"

Brian continued to laugh at his own inside joke.

"Well, then...what *did* he give you?"

"Nevermind."

"No, really…what was it?"

"I'll tell ya someday when you're a little older."

"Oh, I see. You think it will corrupt my innocent mind, do you?"

"You might say that."

"I can handle myself pretty well," she said.

"I know that. Ever since the time you put Hastings in his place at the library."

"Well, if it's something disgusting, I don't want to know about it anyway."

Brian's eyes and body balked as he stood frozen in his tracks. There, on the horizon of the leaden morning, emerged the Norman keep of a five-story castle.

"That's Rochester Castle," she said, equally amazed. She wrapped her arm around his and pulled him along.

Soon enough, the thorny spires of the Rochester Cathedral poked up into view too, as if pointing the way up to the heavens. Ellen drew the paperback version from her knapsack and read aloud the opening lines of Drood: *"'An ancient English Cathedral town? How can the ancient English Cathedral town be here! The well-known massive grey square tower of its old Cathedral? How can that be here! There is no spike of rusty iron in the air, between the eye and it, from any point of the real prospect. What IS the spike that intervenes, and who has set it up?'"* She closed the book.

Brian gazed in awe at the contrasting spectacles: the archaic castle on one side, the ancient cathedral on the other. His mouth was open wide as if it could hold both structures within it, his head ping-ponging back and forth between the two. "That's too cool," he said in a haze.

Ellen's eyes momentarily joined his, then shot off askew, as if the rallying motion of Brian's head had knocked her eyes clear out of bounds. "Pumblechook," she murmured.

This utterance broke Brian's vacillating head into a double take. "Huh?"

"Uncle Pumblechook from Great Expectations. That's where he lived." She pointed over to a funny looking gabled house with timbers and beams.

"You know what?" said Brian, trying to save literary face, "I think I *did* read that one. Uncle Pumblechook was this really cool guy, right?"

"No," she replied. "He was actually the world's biggest ass."

Brian's face gave the appearance of a student being corrected in front of the class.

This time, Ellen's eyes traveled quite slowly in the direction opposite, drifting over to a brick Elizabethan building that was capturing her attention.

Brian's eyes followed. "What's that?"

"Eastgate House," she replied. "It was the Nuns' House in Drood."

"Yeah?"

"More importantly, though, it's the Charles Dickens Centre now."

"You mean," said Brian, "that's where the gift that Fechter gave—"

"Yes."

"You mean, that's the museum where the Swiss chalet—"

"Yes."

"You mean, that's where the book might—"

"Yes."

"I've gotta tell ya, Ellen, out of all the clues he left, this was the easiest to find."

"Don't jinx us now."

In the garden of the Charles Dickens Centre, the Swiss chalet seemed to be growing out of tiny yellow flowers skirting all around it. The diminutive, pretty, pine-stained cottage had white French doors with white shutters and white railing; a Lion Couchant sporting a halberd framed the front. The chalet's wide eaves overhung itself in such a way, it seemed as if it could have been folded up like an umbrella, moved, then reopened again.

A black waist-high gate with the sign 'NO ENTRY' blocked the front, where an artist was meticulously sketching the lion.

"We'll come back and look," she said.

"But why? We're already here."

"I thought you wanted to get some sleep, Brian?"

"I do, but who can sleep now?"

"Let's go," she said, pulling Brian away from the gate. "We'd better go check in at the Blue Boar."

"Come on, Ellen! Let's just give it the once over."

"We'll get some rest first."

"C'mon—I'm used to pullin' all-nighters!"

"Besides, something doesn't feel right."

"What?" said Brian, pointing at the artist in motion. "Him?"

"At the rate he's going, he won't be done for quite some time."

"Want me to hurry him along?" he said.

"True art shouldn't be rushed."

Brian narrowed his eyes at the facade of the chalet. "Maybe it's behind the lion."

She clasped her eyelashes together to better think. "Wait. Something's wrong."

"The story's gotta be there, Ellen. You told me he wrote the last words of it in there."

She opened her eyes, giving up on any further contemplations. "He did write the last words of Drood in there, but it doesn't necessarily mean that it *is* there. Don't forget, this is the first clue we've come across that's been moved from its original location."

"I still say it's here. Either behind the lion or maybe inside the chalet somewhere."

Ellen finally convinced him away from the gate, but not before Brian shouted to the artist, "Is your name Norman?" in which the artist replied, "No, is yours?"

They continued up High Street and checked in at the Blue Boar, now renamed The Royal Victoria & Bull Hotel (ever since Queen Victoria's visit).

The room the door opened into bore two single beds, a bathroom, a desk, and a window overlooking High Street. Their chambers were old but quaint, and the slightly tilted, centuries-old floor felt spongy beneath their feet.

For safe keeping, Ellen hid the original version of the old book under her pillow. Despite the voices of a few passersby in the hallway seeping through the door, they managed to take to their beds and fall fast asleep.

Ellen's face exhibited a wide array of emotions during her state of unconsciousness, ranging anywhere from utter joy at times…to surprise…to sheer terror as her sagacious mind was in the process of defragmenting their travels.

Chapter 25

A Gritty State of Things comes on

Attached to the Royal Victoria & Bull Hotel in Rochester (or Cloisterham, as Ellen prefers) exists a friendly and welcoming pub. Not unlike the other public houses they ventured to on their quest, the Rochester Bar harbors tiny cameras throughout the establishment. Halfway between the front and back bar, little black-and-white monitors were revealing what the cameras projected, giving a wonderful grand tour of the pub and hotel.

Not having to open her computer, the librarian had chosen to situate herself by the monitors, where she was lunching on a plate of roast fowl, testifying that this bird-like creature was not above cannibalizing a member of her own species.

The lunch hour rush was just winding down when a patron entered, an elderly gentleman who occupied a barstool. He received a pint of cider in one hand while opening a newspaper with the other. On the front page of his newspaper the headline read, 'Murder at a London Tavern,' inspiring all those at the bar with newspapers to dolefully shake their heads and comment how sad and bleak the news can sometimes be, the elderly gentleman quipping, "If this world doesn't start straightening up, I'm canceling my subscription to The Times."

When the librarian finished pecking at her plate, not unlike a vulture pecks at the flesh of its prey on the roadside, she wiped her greasy claws on her napkin, never taking her eyes off the tiny TVs, keeping a bird's-eye view on everything.

"Some more," she said, waving her empty glass at a passing busboy, who dutifully refilled it with a pitcher of ice water.

Ms. Crawley sucked each of her talons clean before taking possession of her wireless phone. "Yes," she said, speaking into it. "Don't worry, I've got several eyes on them. Are you still at the chalet?... Have you come across anything yet?... No, no, I'm not questioning you again, it's just that—... I don't know... I don't know... that I *do* know..." she was pleased to say, and with this, she began her brief narrative with the aid of her notebook computer, popping it open. "I was able to access Scotland Yard's records via Oxford University." She read peripherally, never taking her eyes off any of the monitors:

"His name is John Thomas Merrywell, forty-seven years of age, of no fixed address, born and raised on the lower east side of London. He's never been married, with child, but listen to this...he served time in Wakefield prison for the attempted murder of a barrister (wouldn't our friends like to know that). He's a drifter, doing odd jobs ranging anywhere from maintenance work to street performing—Trafalgar Square being his main hub (that's most likely where the little brats met him)... What?... With child?... It doesn't say… What was that? I can't hear you... Oh, over twenty years ago... Say it again?... Reform? Oh, *perform*;" she had to remove her eyes from the TV monitors for a split second to focus on her computer. "He's a magician."

During this entire narrative the waiter had brought the check, and the librarian paid for it without ever making eye contact with her servant.

"Disappear?" she said into her phone. "What do you mean by that?... The newspaper?... No. My eyes have been far too busy for such novelties, why do you ask?... No, I'm not getting smart with you... Okay... I'm sorry... I'm sorry… I don't know."

On one of the hallway monitors, Ellen could be seen exiting the room, quietly shutting the door so she wouldn't disturb the slumber of her classmate.

Slipping off one screen and onto another, the librarian's eyes traced Ellen down the soft winding stairway, past the front desk, out the door of the Royal Victoria & Bull Hotel, which deposited her onto High Street as she relayed the girl's actions over the phone. "Yes, she *did* turn in that direction... I understand, I've got him and you've got her—not that we need *him* for anything, he's of no use to us... No, I'm not saying that we need *her*...I'm sorry… Okay... I'm sorry... Okay... I don't know."

Ellen's tiny shoes tramped through the snow on their way down High Street, back in the direction of the Swiss chalet. By this time, so many other shoes had coursed the same artery that her tracks were no longer distinguishable from the multitude of residents and tourists that preceded her.

The meticulous artist was just putting the finishing touches on his umpteenth sketch of the Lion Couchant before packing up his materials and venturing on.

Ellen's glasses examined every intricacy of the facade for a good half-hour before she decided to ignore the sign and hop the black fence guarding it. The narrow French doors of the chalet were sealed, but surprisingly its old-fashioned key lock was left open. "This is just too easy," she said. Ellen glanced around for a moment, and then quickly entered, closing the doors behind her.

The inside had a musty, cedar smell, the darkness prompting her to produce a penlight attached to her keychain. She adjusted the beam to a wide swath of light and began tracing the walls with it.

Finding nothing in the lower section of the chalet (feeling nothing as well), she carefully followed her beam of light up a narrow flight of stairs to the second floor—taken aback by the reflection of herself in a full-length mirror.

There was an antique escritoire stationed by one of the windows, and she began digging through it, but the drawers were full of modern-day artifacts such as disposable pens, assortments of paper, and an old typewriter (no doubt invented years after Dickens' time on this earth). After flipping through some of the papers, it was evident that the typewriter was most likely used by one of the museum's employees whenever the ambition to write fancied them.

Somehow knowing in her heart that the story wasn't there, Ellen abandoned her search and was about to head back downstairs when suddenly the front door clicked open, startling her. She quickly extinguished her penlight and listened closely. The light footsteps of somebody below could be heard.

"Who's there?" she said.

No one answered.

"I say who's there?" she repeated, shaking with fright.

From the second floor of the tiny chalet, Ellen saw the silhouette of a slender figure with a hat pass by the bottom of the stairwell. She frantically tried switching her penlight back on, but in the process of doing so, it slipped from her hands. The light (still attached to her keys) jingled all the way down to the bottom of the stairs.

"I know I'm not supposed to be in here," she said, trying to elicit a response. "I just wanted to see the inside," she paused... "For a paper I'm writing for class." With each utterance, the girl nervously descended a step or two at a time, stopping, and then listening... "Hello? If this is you, Brian, it's not funny." She paused again, listening. "Are you still there?... Whoever you are, I'll just be leaving now." Halfway down her descent of the staircase, Ellen caught a whiff of that frowsty-scented cologne again, overpowering her altogether.

"Who are you?!" she pleaded. "What do you want?!" After a long pause, she made a break for her penlight, rushing down the remainder of the stairs, scooping it up in one fell swoop and switching on the light.

The beam only revealed an open window at the back of the chalet. A curtain was billowing in and out of it, like a restless ghost desperately trying to escape, that frowsty scent escaping the window as well.

Chapter 26

Philanthropy, Professional and Unprofessional

"It was probably a security guard," said Brian, splashing his face with water to wake himself up.

"It was *no* security guard."

Brian rubbed his face with a towel then threw it over his bare shoulder, examining the circles under his eyes in the bathroom mirror. He ran his hand over the stubble on his chin. "I think I look more worn out now than if I went to Florida."

"I can't believe you don't believe me!"

"I'm still half asleep, Ellen. And I'm in dire need of a shave and a shower." He exited the bathroom and glanced out the window, noticing a small boy below tugging his sled by a rope. To keep out the cold, Brian wrapped the towel around his chest and shoulders like a smock then threw up the sash, poking his head out the window. "Hello!" he called down to the boy.

"Hallo!" the lad returned.

"Do ya know what a disposable razor is?" said Brian.

"I should 'ope so!"

Brian turned to Ellen. "An intelligent boy. A remarkable boy." Then he called back to him. "Do ya know what shaving cream is?"

"I should say so!" returned the lad.

"What a delightful boy," said Brian. "Go and buy it."

"Walk-ER!" exclaimed the boy.

"No, really," said Brian. "Go buy it and bring it here, and I'll give ya five pounds. Come back in five minutes and I'll give ya ten!"

The boy jerked the rope of his sled like an angler pulling in a prized fish, then darted off towards the shops like a shot.

Brian turned to Ellen again. "Do ya think you could lend me ten pounds?" he said, sealing the window. "Just till I—"

"Exchange your money," she finished, unsnapping her purse and handing him the note, "I know, I know."

"Awesomeness."

"But I swear, Brian, I smelled that funny cologne again. That's how I know it's the same person who ransacked our room in New York, and the one who was at the library that night."

"And you still think it's Hastings, right?"

"Who else could it be?"

"A security guard."

"Are they usually in the habit of jumping out of windows? A security guard would have accosted me."

"Then it was probably just a tourist, like you. And he probably thought *you* were a security guard."

"Admit it, Brian. Sonar's note holds water. Even Mr. Merrywell thought so."

"Yeah, but at the time, Mr. Merrywell was holding more drink than the Thames."

"I can't believe you'd put him down like that. After all the trouble Mr. Merrywell went through to find us—and for what? A measly drink!"

"Seventy pounds and several measly drinks," Brian corrected.

"The only money he accepted was the money he would've made working last night. Up until now, his acquaintance has been worth every penny, being he's the one who led us to Trafalgar Tavern. If it weren't for him, you'd still be mulling around Trafalgar Square, probing the ass of a lion."

"I hear ya," he said. "So, did you find anything at the chalet?"

"No."

"We'll just have to go back, then."

"There's nothing to find. I turned the place inside out."

"Well, do what you do best, Ellen...*think*."

"I've been trying. But the only thing I come up with is that strange smell and the picture I have in my head of Pat handing you something out of the bus window. What *was* it that he gave you, anyway?"

A noise that sounded like hailstones striking the window caused them to turn and look. Brian rushed to the window and noticed the boy with the sled reaching for another handful of pebbles, so he lifted the window only wide enough for his mouth, shouting, "Room Two Oh Seven," then quickly closed the sash before more freezing air found its way in. "I can't wait," he said, rubbing his chin. "A shave, a shower, a bite to eat—ahhh."

"Stop avoiding my question, Brian. What did Pat give you? And I don't want any of this *'wait till you're older'* rubbish."

"Alright, alright—if ya really want to know. Maybe it'll set your mind at ease." Brian snatched his wallet off the desk and flipped it open. "This is what he gave me," he said, jamming his finger into it and pulling out a small, wrinkled, crooked piece of rolled up paper.

"What is it?"

Brian smoothed the object with his fingers, giving the ends a twist, molding it into its proper form.

"Wait... Is that what I think it is, Brian?"

"That depends on whether or not you think it's a doobie."

"*That's* what he handed you?"

"That's what he handed me: a joint, a spliff, a bone."

Ellen curiously approached him. "I've never seen one up close before." She removed it from his hand, examining it. "It's much ado about nothing, really," she said, turning it around in her fingers then smelling it. "Rather pungent."

"It's Jamaican."

"Is that good?"

"Yeah, it's good."

"Wait a minute," she said. "I'm surprised at you, Brian. After all we've gone through—New York, the burglary, the passports, the clues—you've jeopardized our entire trip. If customs found this, we would both be in jail right now!"

"Relax, Ellen. It's just a doobie."

A rap came from the door, and Brian went to answer it.

"Wait!" said Ellen, running back and forth with the marijuana cigarette, looking for someplace to hide it.

Brian oddly viewed her. "You're the only person I know who gets paranoid from weed just by smellin' it."

"Where should I put it?"

"Try your pocket," Brian said, twisting the knob and pulling the door open.

Having no dress pockets, Ellen tucked the substance into her bra, sheepishly smiling at the small English child as he entered with his sled.

"I 'ope I'm not in'erruptin' anythin'," said the boy.

"Just a crime in progress," returned Brian with a laugh, plucking the ten-pound note Ellen gave him out of his wallet and handing it to the boy. He glanced at the clock radio. "You owe me change."

"I woulda made it in five minutes if it wuzn't for the woman."

"Woman?" said Ellen.

"The one in the 'allway," said the boy, sliding his wool cap off his head. His ears were blood red. "She saw me comin' to your door with the bag an' wuz wonderin' what wuz inside."

"Did you tell her?" asked Ellen.

"I tole 'er all right. An' I tole 'er to make way cuz I wuz in a wicked 'urry."

"What did she say?" Ellen pressed.

"She asked what the 'urry wuz about, so I tole 'er it wuz a matter of ten pounds. Then she sez she'll give me twenty pounds to look inside the sack. But I tole 'er that it'd be *bad bizness*, that's what me father woulda called it, *bad bizness*."

Ellen bent down at the boy. "What did she say to that?"

"She didn't say nothin', she just boxed my ears and grabbed the bag out of my 'ands. Then she took all but a minute studyin' the shavin' cream and the razors as if they really *wuzn't* shavin' cream and razors."

Ellen covered the lad's ears with her soft palms, offering a soothing touch. "You poor thing."

"It don't really 'urt that much. After all, I got an older brother who thumps me worse than that. What really 'urt wuz that the old witch never made good with 'er promise of twenty pounds. When the ol' crow realized that the labels on the razors and cream wuz what they claimed to be, she just dropped the bag on the floor and went off. That's why I wuz late, I swear it!"

"We believe you," said Ellen. "What's your name?"

"William."

"I'll tell you what, William," she said, digging her hands into her purse, "here's a twenty-pound note." She snatched the other note from Brian, handing it to him as well. "And an extra ten pounds to cover the cost of the items."

The lad's eyes lit. "Thanks, lady! This is the most I ever made on a snow day! And I didn't even 'ave to lift a shovel!"

"Just one more thing, William," said Ellen. "Can you tell us what the woman looked like?"

"Well," said the lad, "she wuz wearin' sunglasses, so I couldn't see all of 'er face. But like I said, she wuz an older, witchy-lookin' sort. She had a neckerchief round 'er 'ead, so I couldn't make out 'er 'air. I guess all I can tell yuh is that she wuz skinny, with a big sharp nose, a little taller than you, Miss...and she don't box ears as hard as my brother."

Ellen laughed at his remark. "Thank you, William. You run along and go sledding now."

The lad jammed the money into his puffy pocket, reeled in his sled, and made his way out the door. "Oh," he said, bending down in the hallway, popping back up with *The Times* in his hands. "'Ere's your paper." Once again, the boy was off like a shot.

"I suppose the woman *he* came across was a security guard, too?" said Ellen, closing the door.

"I must admit," Brian said from the bathroom, making quick use of the shaving cream and razor, "it does sound pretty strange."

Ellen dropped the newspaper on the desk, not noticing the photo of the murdered barmaid highlighting the front page.

"Pretty strange?" said Ellen. "That's all you have to say about it? About everything that's been happening?"

Brian poked his half-shaven face around the corner. "What do ya want me to say, Ellen?"

"I want you to say that—"

"That *what?*" he interrupted. "That we should get hotel security? That we should call the cops? So they can find out that your name's not really Bwanda Jackson and mine's not Julio Rodriguez? So we'll get deported and all chances of gettin' rich—I mean—finding the second half of the novel will be shot?"

"So, you *do* admit it then."

"Admit *what?*"

"Admit that the only reason you're doing this is for the money. What happened to the *'I wouldn't care if we came to a dead end'* bit? Or was that just another one of your famous one-liners you use on the sorority girls?"

"There ya go, bringing up the sorority girls again. I don't know why you're so fixated on them."

"Fixated? You take *one* psych class and all of a sudden you think you're Freud."

"I'm not the one who's got a problem with members of the female sex, Ellen, *you* are."

"You mean that you condone such institutions that kowtow to the way people look and act rather than how they think and feel?"

"I don't know what kowtow means but...yes—yes I do. We need standards in this world. Standards are good."

"And to think," she said, throwing her hands into the air, "I was really starting to like you!"

"Likewise!" he replied, slamming the bathroom door and starting the shower.

"What a jerk!" she said, falling into the desk chair and plopping her purse on the newspaper (inadvertently covering the photo of the frizzy-haired barmaid).

Chapter 27

Tea (and a Confession, too)

Professor Mudgrove parked his rental car off High Street then entered the Rochester Bar. There, Ms. Crawley sat, clinging to the monitors, nesting, like a bird of prey lies in wait.

"What were the contents?" he asked.

"Toiletries," she replied. "Men's toiletries."

The professor didn't seem completely satisfied with her answer, pulling his chair in close. "As I mentioned, you may be accustomed to giving your students at the library general information, Ms. Crawley, general information that they must further research. But all of my courses require specifics. I will ask you once again...for the *last* time," he said, displaying his hand on the table, "what were the contents of the bag?"

"Shaving cream," she blurted, "Barbasol. And razors, Bic—single blade."

"See how easy that was, Ms. Crawley? I ask you a question, and you give me a specific response."

A waiter approached, and the professor ordered a cup of tea.

"Did you find anything at the tavern last night?" she asked.

"You could very well conclude that, Ms. Crawley."

"How did you manage to get in?"

"I offered a barmaid some money. Twenty pounds to be exact."

The librarian pinched open her pocketbook and withdrew twenty pounds, handing it to him.

"But the wench wouldn't accept it," said the professor, taking her money anyway, neatly folding it and tucking it into his small man-purse. "So, I *dismissed* her."

The waiter returned with a pot of tea, pouring a cup for him.

"As they say on the links," said the professor to the waiter, "*it's tee time*."

The waiter forced a smile at the joke before departing.

"Once inside, however," the professor continued, "it didn't take long to find it. You see, if you take the time every now and then to read some of those books you tediously labor on in the form of dusting and cleaning; you, too, might learn something."

The librarian sat quietly, steeping in his remark, feeling equivalent to the teabag within his pot.

"There was a picture of Oliver Twist on the wall," he said, sipping his tea. "Naturally, if you knew anything about Charles Dickens, the clue inevitably ends up here, in this town, at the Swiss chalet."

"What do you mean?"

"It would take too long for me to transfer my knowledge of English literature to you, Ms. Crawley."

"No, I don't mean the clue. I was referring to you saying that you *dismissed* the barmaid."

The professor looked around before answering. "In order for me to expound on your inquiry, Ms. Crawley, it would be wise to notice that the environment we presently share is not conducive to elaborating on specific verbs. However, I can relinquish a noun here and there," by which he leaned over to her and whispered, "Strangulation," then sipped from his cup as if the tea were cleansing his mouth of the remark.

She unconsciously rubbed her throat. "Is that so?"

"Quite. It may not be the most desirable method, but it was certainly the most appropriate for the situation. Swift, quiet, neat—I have often dreamt of performing it on some of my students. However, I suppose a lowly barmaid will have to suffice."

"Who knows," she said, "you may get your wish."

"I don't plan on ever getting that close to them. That's why I have you, Ms. Crawley."

"I know," she responded, still rubbing her gullet.

"Though I don't feel you have neither the strength nor the nerve for it."

"I'm more capable than you know."

"We shall see when the time comes."

"Have you figured out how you want me to—"

"Watch your verbs, Ms. Crawley. You needn't say more. I have considered the..." again, he leaned in and whispered to her, "methodology;" he finished with a rinse of tea.

"You have?"

"Keep in mind, Ms. Crawley, that the best methods are those that can be adapted to a specific situation at a given time."

"How true."

"Given this, and since you feel that you are so much the wiser, what would *be* the ideal situation?"

"Please don't put words in my mouth. I don't feel that I am wiser or more intelligent than—"

"Answer my question, Ms. Crawley."

"The chateau?"

The professor tightened his tea-less hand into a fist, pounding it on the table with a wicked laugh that sent his lipless mouth sucking into his head, leaving a gaping, skeletal hole in his face.

Whenever the professor underwent one of these strange tirades, Ms. Crawley would reflexively wince and cower at him. For the relationship between Professor Mudgrove and Ms. Crawley is an old and disturbing one, dating back a little more than three scores. They are cousins, born exactly six months apart (Ms. Crawley being the younger). Professor Mudgrove's mother got rich hitting a jackpot of sorts, one that takes nine months to pay off. She went to London and returned with the child of a wealthy, married, public official. To keep the scandal from breaking, she was offered a handsome sum, one that kept her family in affluence and arrogance for life. On the other claw, Ms. Crawley's mother remained in the United States and married a man she *thought* was a wealthy gentleman. He turned out to be a grifter, however, leaving Ms. Crawley's mother with nothing but the hospital bill (two bills to be precise, if the beak of baby Crawley were to be counted). The rich sister would often help the ne'er-do-well sister, though not without contingency. Just as the *sisterly* rivalry between Professor Mudgrove's mother and Ms. Crawley's mother was based upon envy, jealousy, gluttony, and all the deadly sins of human nature, so too was the *cousinly* rivalry between Professor Mudgrove and Ms. Crawley, with the professor always maintaining the hard upper hand. Throughout their childhood, young Mudgrove would play the role of the schoolmaster, and he would beat his first cousin if she were ever to insinuate that she was equal to him in any way; be it intellectually, monetarily, or genetically. Oftentimes, his abusive lessons became so horrifyingly twisted and perverse that he violated Ms. Crawley sexually, too. He would first beat her, then molest her, then beat her again with the sick notion that neither urge was satisfied yet. The boy had a violently strange, incestuous compulsion towards his first cousin. As the young Mudgrove swung effeminate punches at her, and performed unspeakable sexual acts on her, he took more the appearance of a bad-seeded girl rather than an ill-natured boy. On one occasion, at the age of ten, Ms. Crawley walked into his room and caught young Mudgrove wearing her training brassiere and panties that he had no doubt stolen on a previous occasion. This provided Ms. Crawley with the only piece of ammunition against him during childhood. To this day, the said ammunition has never been detonated, but there has always been a silent understanding between the two that the incident hasn't been altogether diffused, either. After moving back to the U.S., Mudgrove's mother would occasionally philanthropize her niece, but always made it a point to keep Ms. Crawley a few rungs down in station from her precious son. For instance, when escorting them to the bookstore, she would get her son ten books to her niece's one. When *he* received full tuition to an Ivy League school, *she* had to work at a local library to pay for community college. When *he* became head professor of the English department at the University of Maryland, *she* was third senior librarian at Hornbake Library. To this day, Professor Mudgrove will vehemently deny any blood relation to her or his late auntie, even to the point of referring to them both as 'Ms. Crawley.'

"It is a chalet," he corrected, his laughter subsiding, "not a chateau."

"My apologies, Norman."

"Furthermore, they may not even go back to the chalet."

"Why do we even have to bother with them anymore? We could simply beat them to it, couldn't we?"

"Are you questioning me again, Ms. Crawley?"

"No."

"I believe that you are, and you will have to reap the consequences the next time we are alone."

"Will that be soon?"

"I am afraid not, Ms. Crawley. You need to stay poised here by the monitors from within, and I shall wait in the rental car outside."

"I could get the monitors on my computer if you wish."

"Not a bad idea, Miss Crawley. Not a bad idea at all. Follow me to the car."

"Have I been a bad girl, Professor?"

"Indeed, Ms. Crawley. You have been extremely naughty," he said, cleansing his mouth with the last of his tea.

The librarian sighed in a disturbing tone that was somewhere between a laugh and a cry.

Chapter 28

Illegal Activities

After Ellen took a nice long shower, she felt a little more at ease. Brian tried to convince her there was nothing to worry about; while Ellen, eyes closed, tried doing what she does best.

"I don't feel anything," she said, opening her long lashes.

"I really wish you'd stop sayin' that. I'm not used to hearin' that from girls."

"Real cute."

"You're just in a slump, Ellen. Clear your head."

"I've tried."

"Where'd you put that doobie?" he said, looking around.

"Try the wastepaper basket, which is an appropriate place for it."

"Aw, man." He removed the marijuana cigarette from the wicker bin and straightened it out with a roll through his fingers. "This is Jamaican...you don't throw out Jamaican weed." He scooped a pack of hotel matches out of the ashtray and lit one of the twisted ends, exhaling the smoke in her direction.

"You're crazy."

"C'mon, Ellen. I don't like to smoke alone."

"If you think for a moment that I'm going to put that garbage in my body—"

"It'll get'cha thinkin', Ellen...c'mon."

"No way, Jose."

"It's Julio, remember?"

"I don't care."

"Scared?"

"Right, Brian."

"Dickens wasn't."

"Don't even go there, because there's no credible evidence whatsoever that remotely suggests that Dickens has ever partaken in—"

"Right, Ellen. Like he never hit up any opium. That's probably one of the first things he did with Poe when he visited him in the states."

"You, of all people, have no authority to say—"

"Some things don't need to be said, Ellen. But some things must be done. And I have tasted the apple. Thus, I know when somebody else has tasted the apple. And Dickens did."

"That's so stupid."

"Oh yeah? I read the first chapter of Drood while you were in the shower."

"So."

"There's more people gettin' high in that chapter than a Snoop Dog concert."

"I admit, there are characters partaking in opiates but—"

"I can tell he got high because I get high. Don't ask me how I know. It's like those funny little premonitions you get. But mine have nothing to do with literature. Literature's your department."

"And what's yours?" said Ellen.

"Smokin' da ganja."

"Do yourself a favor, Brian. When the Academic Probationary Committee asks you that question, stick with *hospitality*. It just sounds better."

Brian laughed out some of the smoke that was quickly affecting his faculties.

"There's no credible evidence anywhere that could tarnish Dickens's character," she said, "not even the blacking warehouse."

"Blacking warehouse?"

"A boot polish company he worked at when he was a boy. His father was sent to debtor's prison, and young Charles was forced to work there. Remember how I told you about his happiest days? Well, this was the all-time low point for him; the tragic event that fixated him in childhood for life."

"Then how come that first chapter is so true to life of people smokin' up?"

"Research."

Brian roared.

"He objectively visited opium dens to gain insight."

"*Research*?" said Brian, still laughing. "Yeah, he *researched* alright—like this." He took a long pull off the cigarette, holding the smoke in his head for a few seconds before blowing it in her direction again, comically wiggling his arms in small circles and wobbling during his exhale. "*That's* how he researched." He held it out to her in offering, but she refused, so he attempted a different approach by switching artists: "How about your favorite group?"

"What?"

"Your fab four favorite group."

"The Beatles?"

"Yeah. That *is* your favorite group, *isn't* it?"

"One of them."

"Then you should know that McCartney wrote Got to Get You into My Life as an ode to pot. Look it up if you want."

"That was the sixties, Brian, drugs were viewed as being cool back then."

"They were cool in Dickens' time too, except it was the *eighteen*-sixties."

"If you think I'm going to sit here while you consume illegal substances and attempt to shoot down my idols, you'd better—"

"Okay, Ellen, alright. I don't want to start fighting again. Let's smoke'um peace pipe." He held out the cigarette again in offering. "Here, I've got a bone to pick with you."

"I'm not a sophomore in high school that you can peer-pressure into smoking pot, Brian."

"Good answer. For my side, that is. You're right. You're a mature woman who can take a puff without turning into a heroin addict whose gotta sell herself on the streets of London for a fix."

She allowed him to proceed.

"Have you ever smoked a cigarette?"

"No."

"And you claim to be from New Jersey?"

This time, when Brian offered the cigarette, she accepted it, sniffing a rising helix of smoke. "It does smell rather..."

"Good," he attempted to interject.

"Strange," she corrected.

"Take your time. *Research* it if you wish."

Her eyes were drawn to the hot ash that was slowly burning up the paper.

"I see you admire Pat's work," said Brian. "One thing I can say about Hastings, he rolls a nice doob."

"I feel bad just holding it," she said.

"Sometimes it's good to feel bad. All I'm sayin' is that if you want to try it, there it is."

Her mind began computing.

"And if ever there's a first time to try it—take my advice—the time is now. That's gotta be some of the best bud I've ever tasted!"

"Will it turn me into a zombie or something?"

"No," he said, laughing. "It's fun. You'll like it... really...a lot."

By slow degrees, the cigarette made its way to her lips, and she reluctantly kissed it, drawing smoke into her mouth then releasing a cloud into the room.

"That really wasn't anything," she said, her tender hand passing it back to him.

"That's because you don't know how to inhale. It's why people never get high their first try. You're not s'posed to suck on it like it's a milkshake."

"Oh, that's right, you're the expert...from the hospitality department."

"Here...take another hit. I'll show you."

"Please, Brian, don't say *hit*, it sounds so vulgar."

"Sorry. Take another toke."

"That's even worse."

"How about *puff* then?"

Ellen followed his instructions, kissing it again.

"Now, inhale...breathe it in, like it's your only oxygen supply." He opened his mouth and drew in air as a visual example.

Upon this request, Ellen followed through, the smoke quickly infiltrating her pure mind and clean body that rejected the foreign substance in the form of rapid-fire coughs.

"Congratulations, Ellen, you've officially passed my class."

She held her throat as if it were on fire.

"If ya don't cough, ya don't get off."

"Wa-ter," she said between coughs. "Wa-ter."

Brian quickly filled her a glass.

She waited for her lung contractions to reach three second intervals before attempting to dowse the fire.

Brian took a long draw then spoke while holding in the smoke, "Major expansion of the lungs."

When Ellen's head popped up for air, her pretty brown eyes had a blurry squint to them, her face a silly smile.

"See?" said Brian, grinning, "I told ya you'd like it."

She let go a laugh.

"Are you buzzin', Ellen?" he said in a funny voice.

"Stop."

He teetered over to her, wiggling his fingers, saying, "Buzz buzz buzz buzz..."

She laughed. "Don't do that."

"Buzz buzz buzz buzz..."

"I feel so strange."

"Like you're floating?"

"No, no. More like Alice in the looking glass."

"I never read that one, either."

"Your smile," she laughed. "It looks like the Cheshire Cat."

"Maybe I am," he said, grinning, taking a puff then passing it back to her.

Ellen pursed her lips and drew on it, careful not to inhale too quickly this time. In a cloud of smoke she said, "I suppose I owe your friend Patrick Hastings an apology. Never have I felt more certain that he had nothing to do with anything. All this time I felt as if he meant to do us harm. But, in all actuality, he meant to do us—"

"Good?"

"I wouldn't go as far as to say that. But I should say you owe him an apology too, for calling him a loser."

"I guess so. I didn't think he could cop weed this good."

Ellen's mind began floating away with her smoke. "There was something you said earlier, Brian, that reminded me of something I read in Drood."

"That I didn't think Hastings could get good weed?"

She laughed. "It was when you said that you've tasted the apple; therefore, you know when others have tasted it."

"Pretty prophetic, huh?"

"More like pathetic." Ellen went to her knapsack and unfurled her portable library, removing Brian's original copy of Drood. "I know there's something like that in here somewhere," she said, fumbling through the book, "I think it's in chapter three. Ah, here it is, it *is* chapter three. Dickens wrote: *'Thus, if I hide my watch when I am drunk, I must be drunk again before I can remember where.'*"

"I can't argue with him there."

"It reminds me of a scene in a film I once saw," she said. "The Lost Weekend."

"Lost Weekend? I've had a few. Never heard of the movie, though."

"Have you ever heard of Billy Wilder?"

"Is he related to Dickens?"

She shook her head. "Not at all."

"I'm surprised you know who he is, then." He took another pull off the cigarette.

Ellen thought about the blurb that Dickens had written, knowing that somehow it related to their situation. She thought about many things, her mind never drifting so far as to forget the main objective, however. After all, Brian had *his* main objective, no matter how self-absorbed it may be. And she had *her* main objective, which in many ways, perhaps, is no more selfish than his. And whoever was also after it had *their* main objective. Ellen's thoughts came across Sonar, and Merrywell, and the poor little boy who died while holding her hand on the highway. She thought about "Wicky wicky wye," and the freckled boy, and the night she was alone in the library. She thought about the frowsty scent she's been encountering, almost as if the smoke coming off the cigarette were the foul cologne choking her, and how she encountered it the first time she saw Pat Hastings in Professor Mudgrove's class. She thought about how her real mother could be staying in the very room across the hall, and she'd never even know it. She thought about Princess Puffer who was the opium mixer and addict in *Drood*. And in the deepest part of her heart, she felt a sense that time was running out. The draw of the smoke seemed to draw all of these thoughts and overwhelming feelings into streams of consciousness, where she pondered each one carefully, with a soft semblance.

When she wasn't thinking, they were laughing; when they weren't laughing, they were talking; when they weren't talking, they were smoking; a strange circle of events; nonetheless, a fun one.

"We owe ol' Pat," said Brian between intermittent guffaws, "an apology alright."

Ellen couldn't stop giggling, finding it difficult to pass the cigarette. "All along," she said, "I thought that smell somehow related to him."

"It was *this* smell that related to him," he roared, holding up the cigarette. "We smoked a doob before the first day of class."

She laughed uncontrollably. "All this time...I've been smelling...pot!"

"Pat always smells like pot...more like day-old bong water."

"I remember now...you two arrived late that day."

"And remember what Mudgrove said to me?"

"Yeah," she tittered, "he said you were the perfect example of a student who'd never pass his class."

"I can't wait to find the second half of that novel, Ellen. I've got it all figured out. I'm gonna show up the morning after spring break—no!—I'll show up the *following* morning and take the ten-point deduction! It'll be even sweeter that way! I can picture it now. Mudgrove enters the classroom wearing his hat and clutching that dorky plaid thermos of his. He notices me trying to hide in the back of the classroom, so he calls me out in front of everyone: 'Mr. Murray,'" he imitated, "'I am afraid your assignment is one day late; therefore, I am going to have to deduct one full letter-grade off of your paper.' That's when I walk the length of the room—no—*swagger* the length of the room, slap the complete novel down on his desk, and tell him that I don't have to write the paper because I found the goddamn ending!"

"You shouldn't swear like that, Brian."

"Not make it through? I'll tell him I'm not gonna make it through his class because I've officially decided to retire!"

"Go ahead, keep jinxing us."

Brian laughed. "You're way too superstitious, Ellen. That's gotta be your one fault. All superstition does is make people paranoid, just like religion."

"I'm a karma believer…I think that if you put bad things out there, bad things come back."

"*You*, put something *bad* out?"

Ellen went to the mirror above the desk and viewed herself taking a puff of the cigarette. "Oh my God, look at me! I've turned into Princess Puffer!"

"You look fine."

"I can't even see my eyes!" She took some eyeliner out of her purse and removed her glasses, squinting into the mirror, which made her eyes shrink all the more. "I can't believe I'm doing this," she said, the cigarette poking out of her lips as she traced her eyes with a pencil.

"Guilt trip. Another side effect of superstition and religion."

"You don't feel that if you do something wrong it will come back at you?"

"In the infamous words of Ebenezer Scrooge: *Humbug!*"

Ellen accidentally knocked her purse and glasses to the floor.

"See?" said Brian. He knelt down with her to help gather the contents of her purse.

"Thank you, but I can manage well enough," she said, putting her glasses back on.

"Don't want me to see what'cha got in there, huh?"

"I've nothing to hide."

"I'm curious. Let's see what class valedictorian, literary connoisseur, and Dickens afficionado, Ellen Pipple, keeps in her purse. We have...five sticks of gum."

"Give me that," she said, snatching it out of his hand and dropping it back into her bag.

"We have...two ChapSticks."

"I'll take that, thank you very much."

"We have...one mirror. That's seven years bad luck just waitin' to happen."

"I'll take that please."

"You'd make a great contestant on Let's Make a Deal."

"Very funny."

"What's this?" said Brian. He popped open a tiny ring case. It displayed a rose ring of diamonds and rubies delicately set in gold.

"Give me that."

He held it out of her reach. "This is the coolest ring I've ever seen."

"Careful with it."

Brian took a few more seconds admiring it. "Wow. Let me guess…a keepsake from an old boyfriend?"

She wouldn't say. "Give it back."

"C'mon, Ellen. We've known each other for a half-semester now. I won't judge."

"Long story."

"Then give me the Cliffs Notes version."

"I'm afraid that the end of this story is unknown too. And I've already told you how it begins."

"Well, just continue from the bookmark."

"All right," she said, the two still kneeling. "If you really want to know." She drew a deep breath. "On the day of my thirteenth birthday, my adoptive parents took me aside and explained everything. You see, my father's job, being a Coca-Cola rep, had them hopping from city to city in the states as well as abroad. During a stint in London, they heard of an unwed mother who, along with her parents, didn't want anything to do with the child. As you know, long story short, I was given up."

Brian listened intently.

"My parents, not being able to have children, adopted me through a black market of sorts; you know, through the friend of a friend in England. The ring you're holding belonged to my mother," she paused, gazing at the ring. "It's the only reminder that I've ever had of her. I keep it in a safe deposit box, but I like to take it out from time to time and look at it."

"It's beautiful."

"Thanks," she said. "But I'd trade it for a picture of her any day."

"Your real parents and grandparents are the ones who missed out, Ellen."

"Don't get me wrong, I could never love anyone as much as I love my parents—my adoptive parents, I mean. To me, they'll always be my real parents. It's just that I wish I had a photo of my mother, or could just catch a glimpse of her, if only for a moment. I wonder if she looks the way I picture her in my dreams."

Brian handed the ring back to her. "You don't ever have to worry about bad things comin' back at you, Ellen. You put too much good out there."

The girl smiled at him as she rose to her feet, placing the ring box back into her purse. She went to set her bag down on the desk, noticing *The Times*. Her smile disintegrated as her eyes locked onto the front page of the newspaper.

The photo of the frizzy-haired barmaid was staring back at her.

Chapter 29

The Press

The Times, Thursday, March 30th, 2000: Early this morning, a barmaid at Trafalgar Tavern in Greenwich was found dead just three feet from the entrance of the pub that employed her.

Catherine Penelope Bellswocker, 50, of Blackheath, was the victim of a brutal homicide in which the motive is still unclear. Although the tavern door was left ajar, nothing other than a gun she reportedly kept on her was found missing.

"It appears to be a robbery gone awry," said Chief Inspector Joseph Trundle of the Metropolitan Police. "It looks as if the perpetrator accosted Ms. Bellswocker just outside of the tavern door, a struggle ensued, and the perpetrator strangled her." The inspector stated that during the scuffle the assailant may have appropriated the missing gun.

Witnesses interviewed by the inspector said that a man named John Thomas Merrywell, a convicted felon who reportedly had an abusive relationship with Ms. Bellswocker, was seen drinking at the pub late last night with two American college students. Police are presently trying to locate Mr. Merrywell, who served time in the early 1980s for the attempted murder of a barrister.

"We are calling upon Mr. John Thomas Merrywell, of no fixed address, to step forward," said Chief inspector Trundle. "Until then, he is to be considered armed and dangerous."

Mr. Martin Mintelman, owner of Trafalgar Tavern, is offering a five-thousand-pound reward for any information leading to the capture of the perpetrator.

The CID cordoned off the tavern and surrounding perimeter to preserve the crime scene for Inspector Trundle's investigation. Many local residents have complained that the tavern was often kept open after hours, while patrons of the pub are wondering when it will be reopened. The inspector assured that his inquiry would be brief but thorough. "The Tavern shall be reopened by happy hour this evening," he said.

"This is a most serendipitous scenario—the ideal situation. We could not have hoped for a better one," said Professor Mudgrove, rolling up the newspaper. He reached into the backseat of the rental car, whacking Ms. Crawley with the paper like a dog, awakening her. Several bruises and welts blotted her face and body.

"What is it, Norman?" she said, groggily. "Are you ready to...? Again?"

"No, Ms. Crawley! I merely stated that this is the perfect scenario. It fits together like a Swiss watch."

"What fits, Norman?" She leaned into the front seat, placing her claw on the shoulder of his suit.

"Must I always explain things to you twice, Ms. Crawley? You are worse than an overanxious freshman at orientation. Remain in your seat until you are called upon," he said, throwing his fist back, smashing her square in the nose, sending her into the backseat of the car.

"Sorry, Norman," she said, a streak of blood trickling between her teeth, lending a demented smile to her face.

The professor handed her a handkerchief from his suit pocket. "True or false, Ms. Crawley: Scotland Yard suspects the students' newly found friend, Mr. Merrywell (the ex-convict), to be the perpetrator in the barmaid's murder."

"True."

"You are correct."

She leaned forward, touching his shoulder again with one claw, the handkerchief pinching her nose with the other.

"True or false, Ms. Crawley: Sooner or later, the inspector is bound to apprehend Mr. Merrywell."

"True."

"Correct again."

"Thank you."

"True or false: Mr. Merrywell was already found guilty of the attempted murder of a barrister."

"True."

"Bravo, Ms. Crawley, bravo! I trust you can put two and two together, and give me a fill-in-the-blank answer this time: When the time comes to permanently expel our students from this world, whom do you fathom the inspector will suspect in *their* deaths?"

"Mr. Merrywell."

"Outstanding, Ms. Crawley!" he said, clapping his hands, his lipless mouth sucking back into his head as he smiled. "Mr. Merrywell, the magician, will seem to have made his friends disappear."

"Brilliant, Professor!"

"For having answered so intelligently and expeditiously the questions I have posed to you, Ms. Crawley, I believe some one-on-one time with your professor is at hand."

Ms. Crawley's red-bloodied beak flew from the backseat to the front. And though the sexual act was consensual, the incestual, perverted manner in which it was performed gave more the appearance of a molestation on the part of the professor. He commenced by counting old units of English currency: "Four farthings equal two ha'pennies, two ha'pennies equal one pence, twelve pence equal a shilling..." as he squeezed her leg, he slowly ran his cockled hand up her thigh, fondling her, whereby she soon joined in on the counting, as if she wanted the schoolmaster to both stop and continue his offensive at the same time... "Two shillings and sixpence equal a half crown, five shillings equal a crown, twenty shillings equal a pound, twenty-one shillings equal a guinea..."

Chapter 30

The Old Yarder

Chief Inspector Joseph Trundle of the Criminal Investigative Division of London's Metropolis Police (otherwise known as Scotland Yard) is from what some may say, "The Old Yard." This phrase, however, can be very misleading. Although the inspector has an arsenal of modern-day forensic weaponry at his disposal, and often uses this high-tech equipment and these learned professionals from time to time, his appearance and demeanor seem to be straight out of an Agatha Christie novel.

Neatly trimmed gray hair carpets his head, which his black bowler roosts upon, as if the derby were there to incubate any thoughts that may lead to the hatching of any hunches. Beneath his woolen hatchery, a white mustache, waxed into tiny handlebars (which he has been known to twist from time to time during this incubation process) outlines his long lantern-jaw. An umbrella, which acts as protection on inclement days; a walking stick on fair ones, taps out his strides as he leisurely roves up and down the streets of London. All of these mannerisms, coupled with a plain beige trench coat, seem to unapologetically shout out to all passersby, "I am from the Old Yard!"

Chief Inspector Trundle entered the pub and made his way over to the bar.

The funny-eared bartender who served Ellen and Brian the night before greeted him. "Good Evenin', 'Spector. 'Ow are you?"

"Good but ghastly cold," replied the inspector with a shiver.

"I'm Fiddledew. My boss said to keep me eye out for you. Can I get you a pint?"

"A splash of brandy to take this God-awful chill out of me, my good man, if you will."

The bartender nabbed a bottle of top-shelf brandy from beneath the camera that was overlooking everything. He weaved the brandy into a snifter, placing the bulb-shaped glass in a tin of hot water to warm it up a bit.

"Now," said the inspector, "your employer, Mr. Dimpledorf, said you told him that the two American college students arrived here approximately nine-thirty last night."

"That's right," he replied, drying the snifter of brandy with a clean bar rag before serving it.

"What did they look like?"

"Typical looking Amerrycans. Both white, the girl 'ad glasses, a dress and a satchel. The guy wore a black leather jacket and t-shirt. A James Dean-lookin' sort 'e was."

"Are you sure about these names?" he asked, flipping open a tiny notebook as he administered some brandy into his lantern-jaw, igniting a flush of sanguine in his cheeks like two red light bulbs.

"Carded them meself, 'Spector."

"Just checking, Mr. Fiddledew," he said, hanging his umbrella on the brass rail of the bar, which swung back and forth like a pendulum. "Now, how much time would you say passed between the time the students arrived and the time Mr. Merrywell arrived?"

"'Bout as long as it takes to do a couple shots of lemon drops."

"And what may I ask does *that* consist of?"

"Chilled vodka and a lemon wedge of sugar. Amerrycans seem to fancy it."

The inspector removed his bowler, allowing the rush of heat from the brandy to vent off his neatly groomed hair. "And thereafter is when Mr. Merrywell approached the students?"

"That's right, 'Spector."

The Old Yarder administered some more brandy, which went straight to his cheeks. "You say they bought Mr. Merrywell a drink?"

"That they did. A martini. Tanqueray."

"Odd."

"Not really, 'Spector. Merrywell's quite talented when it comes to gettin' people to buy 'im drinks. In fact, 'e's so good at it, it's a rare evenin' indeed that 'e 'as to pay for 'is own way 'round the rail of the bar."

"You don't say," he replied, twisting the tiny handlebar on the left side of his nose.

"But last night, *that* drink...why, I believe *that* drink was a delivery."

"Delivery?"

"That's right, 'Spector. Merrywell 'ad somethin' for the two of 'em. I 'eard 'im toyin' with 'em, you know, playin' cat an' mouse with the two Amerrycans a bit."

"I am all too familiar with *that* spirit, my good fellow," said the inspector, administering a few more drams of brandy, twisting the handlebar on his right.

"And seldom 'umbled by it, so that's what I read in the papers anyway."

"Now," said the inspector, rolling the brandy around in his snifter, "can you describe to me what it was that Mr. Merrywell gave to them?"

"Looked to me like an ordinary piece of paper. Didn't see what was writ on it, though. But it seemed to shock 'er and offend 'im—I thought 'e was gonna make a go at Merrywell for a moment. And I can't say that that's odd either when it comes to Mr. Merrywell."

"O', a troublemaker is he?"

"I wouldn't say Merrywell *makes* trouble. More like trouble follows 'im round."

"I am all too familiar with *that* spirit, as well," the inspector said into his snifter. "Now," he continued, glancing up at the tiny camera mounted above the shelf, "you have no doubt prepared the videotapes my secretary rang you about, which will allow me to witness this most auspicious encounter first handedly?"

The bartender yanked a white Styrofoam container that looked like a to-go order from beneath the bar, placing it into a plastic bag for him. "I've got your special order right 'ere, 'Spector. Compliments of the owner."

The Old Yarder gave his brandy a few turns in his palm before swishing the remains into his lantern-jaw, lighting up his cheeks again. "On behalf of Scotland Yard, I thank you, my good man, for your time and effort regarding this unfortunate tragedy."

"Right-o, 'Spector. Just one thing before you go, 'owever. It's 'bout Merrywell." The bartender leaned over the rail, so only the inspector could hear him. "'E may be a bit odd, an' it may seem as if trouble follows 'im round, but Merrywell 'as got a heart as rich as the brandy you just quaffed. I'd swear the Good Book on it if I 'ad to. An' if you don't believe me, I can prove it by 'avin' you pay for what you just quaffed, and you'll see 'ow rich *that* is."

Inspector Trundle gave both sides of his mustache a twist before snatching his black umbrella off the brass rail with a *whoosh*, as if sweeping everything that was exchanged between them into his bowler for safe-keeping.

"So 'member that, 'Spector, when you're feastin' your eyes 'pon your special order."

"Well then," stated the inspector, "at no further expense to Her Majesty the Queen, I shall be obliged to take your word on that, my good fellow, and bid you good day." He brushed a speck of lint off his round hatchery before setting it atop his head, careful not to spill any of his eggs. "I wouldn't fret, Mr. Fiddledew. It's not so much your friend's motive that troubles me about this case. It's the college students' motive I can't figure."

"You mean why they would want to murder that woman?"

"No. Why they would hop on a plane to England during their spring holiday when they could have traveled someplace closer, warmer, and less expensive."

"Got me there, 'Spector. Lessen they've got a date with the Queen."

The Old Yarder battened down the buttons of his trench coat and twirled his weighty umbrella around, tipping his hat with it, as if saying to the bartender, "Thank you for the contents within," then forged out into the frosty night; the two red bulbs above his lantern-jaw brightening his way.

Chapter 31

A Date and a Blunder

"Leave your purse, Ellen. I'm buyin' tonight."

"Is that so?"

"Yeah. I exchanged some money at the front desk and I'm takin' you out."

"*Out* as in, *on a date*?"

"That's right. A date. C'mon."

"I still think we should go to the police, Brian."

"No we shouldn't."

"We didn't know Mr. Merrywell was an attempted murderer."

"Ellen, do you really think Merrywell would kill anybody?"

"No, I don't. But in the meantime, we're *his* only alibi and he's *our* only alibi."

"That's even a better reason for us to go out and paint the town tonight."

"This Inspector Trundle," said Ellen, looking at the black and white picture of him in the newspaper, "he's touted as Scotland Yard's finest. We must go to him at once and tell him everything. It's our civic duty."

"And that's the first thing we'll do—right after we find the second half of the book."

"This is no time to be thinking of yourself, Brian."

"We don't know if the book had anything to do with it."

"It's too coincidental. A woman is dead!"

"I know. And we can't change that."

"But we can change the course of how *we* might end up," said Ellen, flipping over the newspaper, exhibiting the picture of the barmaid.

"It's still spring break, Ellen. I say we make the most of it while we can, in all areas. I'm talkin' business *and* pleasure."

"It's like a dream and a nightmare happening all at the same time," she said, looking at her red eyes in the mirror. "Perhaps you're right; maybe we should do something to take our minds off of this for a while." She checked her knapsack to be sure all valuables were safely tucked away. "You're paying you say?"

"That's right. So if anyone ever asks about our date, you can speak good of me."

"Speak well of me," she corrected. "Okay, a date it is, then." She examined her eyes again in the mirror then spun around at him. "Tell me, do I still look high?"

"Whoa! Turn those laser beams off, Ellen! You're makin' me feel like Paul Revere here, walkin' around with those two red lanterns blarin'!" He laughed. "The British are comin'! Two if by sea, if ya ask me."

"Really?"

"No…I'm just messin' with ya. You're supposed to look high. It's one of the requirements of my class."

Brian opened the door of the hotel room, and they passed into the slanted hallway, down the spongy staircase, out of the Royal Victoria & Bull Hotel, spilling out onto High Street. Ellen giggled at the sign.

"See," said Brian, sealing the top of his jacket to shield against the cold breeze whipping up the cobblestones, "that's what I mean about tasting the apple."

"What?"

"You just laughed at the High Street sign because you have tasted the apple."

"Is that so."

"I should write a book on it."

"So, tell me," said Ellen, "does your story include where we'll be dining tonight?"

"I'm in prose-mode. I'll know when we get there."

Along the way they passed a used bookstore, Brian poking his head in at the clerk. "Excuse me, sir, but you wouldn't happen to carry the second half of The Mystery of Edwin Drood, would you?"

The clerk gave a hearty laugh. "That's a good one, my dear boy, a good one indeed! I'll have to remember that one, I will!"

Brian pulled his head out of the store, wiggling his eyebrows at Ellen, and then led the way down High Street.

If it had been ten degrees warmer, he may have considered walking a block or two farther. But being as blustery of a night as it was (the inky sky dumping another load of snow on them), Brian opted for a nearby Italian pizzeria named Giorgio's.

Various hand-blown glass bottles of olive oil appeared to be stretching and twisting their necks at them as they entered.

"I've never seen a pizzeria like this," said Ellen.

"Have a zeat, si'l vous plaît," said the waiter's French accent.

"Cool menu," said Brian. "Look at all those different pies. We'll take a large, with pepperoni," he said to the waiter.

"There eez just one size, Monsieur," he replied.

"Alright, two pepperonis then."

"Better make mine a plain cheese," Ellen corrected.

"Az you wish, Mademoiselle. Anything to drink?"

"I'm in charge of that department," said Brian. "You can pick the food tonight, but I'll take care of the drink."

"By all means," she consented.

"We'll have a glass of your house red," he said, pulling a one-pound coin out of his pocket and extending it at the waiter.

"That eez not necessary, Monsieur." He started away for the wine.

"This has to be the fanciest pizza parlor I ever saw," said Brian.

"So," she said, awkwardly drumming up something to say, the sobriety of the moment reminding her that they were on an actual date for the first time, "how do you like England so far?"

"I pictured it much foggier."

The waiter quickly returned with two house reds.

"The weather's been so strange, really," she said.

"Enough with the small talk, Ellen. Are ya gonna tell me or what?"

"Tell you?"

"Yeah."

"Tell you what?"

"What *you're* in it for." Brian held his glass up to her. "You said you weren't in it for the money and you weren't in it for the fame. Then...what?"

"What do *you* think?" she said, chiming his glass then sipping her wine.

"I'm not really sure. Part of me says you're in it for the same reasons I'm in it, and there's another part that I just can't understand."

"What you can't understand is most likely the reason."

"I know what you think, Ellen. You think I'm in it for shallow, selfish reasons."

"Who am I to judge?"

"You think I'm only in it for the money."

"Who's to say that my reasons are any less selfish than yours?" She sipped more wine. "I was flattered earlier, when you told me that you read the first chapter of Drood."

"Why's that?"

241

"It always gives me a good feeling knowing that I've contributed to someone's appreciation of the arts."

"I guess that's the part I don't understand," said Brian, taking a gulp of wine.

"All my life, Charles Dickens seemed like a close friend to me. I was never alone when I held one of his books, with all of his wonderful characters just an elbow-length away. Remember when I said it seemed as if he was directly talking to *me*—as if I were his only audience? Well, I've got that feeling again, Brian. Nevermore than during this trip—even at this uncertain crossroad. Because he really has been talking to *me*...to *us*."

"And what's he saying now, Ellen?"

"He's saying that the novel is somewhere here in Kent, that's what he's saying."

"Good, Ellen...go with that."

"He's also saying..."

"What?" he urged.

"He's saying that more danger lies ahead. That's why I think we should go to the police."

"But what's he saying to you, Ellen, honestly...what do you feel? Is he sayin' go to the police or is he sayin' go for the story?"

"That's not fair, Brian."

"What's he tellin' you, Ellen? Honestly? C'mon!"

Her hand unconsciously felt an ache in her heart, and, realizing this, she tried to mask the emotion by picking up her wineglass and holding it there (keeping silent).

"I thought so," said Brian.

The waiter served the pizzas with a long-neck bottle of olive oil.

"Hey, you forgot to cut our pizza," said Brian.

"Zee pizza is meant to be eaten with a fork and a knife, Monsieur."

"Not where I come from," Brian replied, cutting it into triangles and proceeding to eat with his fingers.

"Mmmm," said Ellen, opting for the fork and knife, "you should try some of this olive oil, it's simply delicious!"

Brian laughed. "You got the munchies."

"I do?"

"Yeah."

"I suppose that part of your theory really is true then," she said, sinking her teeth into her pizza.

"Consider it but a smaller piece of the greater apple," he said, pouring some oil on his slice, then folding it in half and chomping it.

"You'd make a good Gestalt psychologist, Brian. *The whole is greater than the sum of its parts*."

"Mmmm," he said with a greasy chin, "you're not kiddin'. This stuff *is* awesome." He washed down his bite with a gulp of wine.

"Please," said Ellen, "pass me some more olive oil. Everything tastes so wonderful!"

They feasted and talked for a good while, ordering another pizza to split between them, sampling various flavored oils.

"I've decided," he said between bites, "if I ever get rich out of this, I'm gonna buy my old childhood home back."

"You are?"

"Yeah. The one my folks sold after I left for college—like what you were tellin' me Dickens did at Gatwick Place."

"That's *Gad's Hill Place*."

"I'm not gonna buy some fancy penthouse somewhere. I'm gonna buy a home where I'll be happy."

"I'm glad you feel that way. You flatter me again."

Brian dug into some more pizza.

"Wait a minute," she said. "Come to think of it, *Gad's Hill Place*, that's where the Swiss chalet originally stood."

The waiter brought two more glasses of house red.

"It says in one of my books that..." she withdrew a book from her knapsack and thumbed through the pages, "that Dickens arranged for the chalet to be erected on the opposite side of Rochester High Road, and that he eventually had a tunnel excavated beneath the road, so he could pass from his house to the chalet undisturbed. It was like a childhood fantasy of his youth, *'a secret place among the trees',*" she read. "He even called it The Wilderness."

"That sounds pretty cool. Why do you think he did it?"

"Well, he liked to write there. And we already know about his mistress. He was still married at the time, so he may have used it to conceal his trysts with Nelly. After all, it *was* the Victorian period. They didn't take too kindly to infidelity back then."

"Not like they do today."

"What if..." whispered Ellen, "yes...what if the last clue, *Fechter's gift*—"

"That's the guy who gave Dickens the chalet, right?"

"Yes, Brian...please—wait...I think I'm stumbling onto something."

He kept silent by gulping some more wine.

"What if Dickens isn't referring to the Swiss chalet itself, but rather the precise *location* of the chalet, to the *'secret place among the trees'?*"

"I think you've got somethin' there, Ellen."

She retrieved another book out of her portable library. "It says here that Gad's Hill Place is an all girl's school now. Yes! That's it! We'll head there after dinner and measure out the precise location of where the chalet stood!"

"You've got another one of those feelings again, Ellen, don't cha?"

"I know one of my books has a map," she said, searching her knapsack. "The person who stole my tape recorder and notes would have been better off stealing my books."

From the pub area, a bartender switched on an enormous television (which gave more the appearance of a movie screen), turning the volume up loudly.

"What's going on?" Brian asked the waiter.

"Inzpector Trundle," said the Frenchman, "he is about to announce zee main zuspect in zee barmaid murder… Live… From Zcotland Yard."

Brian and Ellen simultaneously looked at each other and mouthed, *"Merrywell."*

Over by the bar, flashes from the photographer's cameras emanated from the TV, further bleaching the inspector's complexion as he made his way onto the screen. The contrast of his dark bowler and white mustache gave The Old Yarder the appearance of being in black and white rather than color.

"As you know," said Inspector Trundle, "a grave crime has occurred in our fair city this morning, one we here at The Yard are tirelessly working to solve."

Reporters began interrupting with questions: "Can you confirm that the lead suspect is ex-convict John Thomas Merrywell?" shouted one reporter.

"Are the two American students somehow involved?" shouted another.

"I am afraid I cannot answer any questions at this time. However, I come bearing good news and bad news. The bad news is that we were unable to capture clear videotape footage of the two American students. As for the good news, with the gallant efforts and cooperation of the FBI and the CIA, The Yard is in the process of receiving photographs of the two students, which shall be airing momentarily."

"Check please," said Brian.

"Right away, Monsieur," replied the waiter.

"Oh my God!" exclaimed Ellen in a whisper. "They're about to show our faces on TV!"

"That's not a TV," Brian gestured at the gigantic screen. "That's an IMAX!"

"What should we do?" she said.

"I know what *I'm* gonna do." He threw back his wine. "*I'm* gonna get the hell out of here!"

"I'm with you."

"How much do you think I owe?" he said."

"Including the wine, no more than sixty pounds."

"I don't have exact change for tip—how about I just leave sixty-five?"

"This is no time to penny pinch, Brian!"

"Okay, let's bolt," he said, leaving eighty pounds.

As they meandered their way through the bar area to make their exit (being no alternate route of escape), their bodies were framed against the enormous television, as if they were already giving themselves up to the inspector…live…in Scotland Yard.

"Ah, yes," said the inspector. "The photos of the students are coming through now..." Someone handed the inspector a note, which he paraphrased aloud: "I am to interject at this point," his long jaw informed, "that this simulcast from the United States is being aired live via BBC's latest telecommunications satellite, Alpha Centauri."

"Hurry up," she said to Brian… "Move it!"

They couldn't bypass an old, cherub-faced gentleman who was in the process of shuffling his way over to a barstool, trapping them in the pub area.

"What do ya want me to do, Ellen, run him over?"

The inspector continued: "Ah yes, here it comes...a bit more visible now," he stated, his bowler, mustache, and trench coat appearing larger than life on screen as he imposingly stared down from the television at Brian and Ellen. "Okay...jolly good...here they are now..."

"This isn't happening," Ellen whispered to Brian, still waiting for the cherub-faced man to situate himself into a barstool.

The inspector paused, his eyes seemingly fixed on Brian and Ellen as he looked down. "Good heavens!" he proclaimed, his lantern-jaw dropping. "This must be some sort of mistake. *These* are not the same descriptions given to us by the eyewitnesses."

Still dramatically framed on the enormous television, Brian and Ellen gradually turned their faces towards the screen. To the blunder of Scotland Yard, a photo was airing of a Black female, Bwanda Jackson, and a Hispanic male, Julio Rodriguez.

They let go a sigh of relief that deflated them into two barstools.

"I should like to state at this time," the inspector concluded, giving his handlebars a twist, "that there has indeed been a blunder."

The reporters started pitching questions at him again, but the inspector's weighty umbrella just swung back and forth like a pendulum, batting all inquiries away.

"Gentlemen of the press," the inspector stated, "this is not the first time that The Yard has been humbled, and it most certainly won't be the last. So please, take my advice: Do not release any additional information or photos until further review by The Yard. Thank you."

Brian and Ellen's relief turned into cathartic sighs.

"Whew," said Brian, wiping his forehead with the sleeve of his leather. "That was close."

"We narrowly escaped Chief Inspector Trundle," she said, laughing. "We foiled Scotland Yard."

"They're no match for us."

The bartender worked his way up the rail. "What can I get you?"

"Give us two—"

"We really should be going," Ellen interrupted. "Don't forget about that errand we have to run tonight."

"I told you I was taking you out on a date. Besides, if it's been there for a hundred and thirty years, it'll be there tomorrow." Brian directed his eyes at the bartender. "We'll take two lemon drops."

"You got it, mate."

"Merci, Monsieur," said the waiter to Brian, patting his pocket to thank him for the gracious gratuity as he passed the bar en route to a party of eight.

"Ellen, ya think it's too late to get some of my tip back from the waiter?"

"I'd say so. Especially now that you've officially been thanked. But for future reference, you're not required to tip in this country."

"Now you tell me."

The bartender chilled the lemon drops before serving them.

"To our first official date," said Brian, holding his jigger high.

"To our first date," she repeated, clinking his glass, "and a narrow escape."

"Who knows," said Brian, "maybe we'll both get lucky."

"If you're referring to the errand we have to run tomorrow, maybe we will."

They threw back their shots, chasing the vodka with the sugarcoated lemons.

"Ya know what," said Brian, "this looks like a good place to get drunk."

"You're quite the romantic."

He waved to the bartender. "Two more lemon drops."

"There's one thing for sure," she said. "You certainly know how to get your spring break's worth."

"Good. Because I'm thinking of changing my major to hospitality."

Ellen laughed, her smile soon fading away as her thoughts turned serious. "Tell me, Brian...in a way, does it feel like we're doing something wrong?"

"How do you mean?"

"Wrong, you know, like finding something that maybe we shouldn't find. Something that should be left well enough alone; you know, not tampered with. Sometimes the mystery itself is far better than the actual solution."

"Don't go gettin' all Holy Grailish on me now, Ellen. That's just the weed talkin'. We didn't come all this way to leave well enough alone. Anyway, Dickens wanted it to be found, or he wouldn't have set up this little paper chase."

"But there's something almost taboo about the whole thing. I mean, who are *we* to be the ones to find it. What right do *we* have to come over to England and solve the ending of this country's greatest mystery?"

"We're the chosen ones, Ellen."

"Surely you're not going to try to sell me another slice of your apple theory again."

"As a matter of fact, I am."

She laughed. "This should be good. Go ahead, prove your theory, Professor Murray."

"Alright then, I will. We're the chosen ones because you happen to be smart and I happen to be lucky."

"I wouldn't declare that the epiphany of the millennium, but I'll let you proceed, barrister."

"Without *your* smarts, *I* wouldn't be here; and without *my* luck, *you* wouldn't be here."

"A correlation doesn't necessarily show cause."

"If it'll make ya feel any better," said Brian, plucking a cocktail napkin off the bar, "I know a way we can make things right. Lend me a pen."

"A pen? Now I feel like we really *are* back in class," she said, handing him one.

No sooner did the bartender place another shot on the bar than Brian quaffed it. "Now I'm feelin' like I'm back at school, too." He unfolded the cocktail napkin. "Hmmm. How should I start?" he said to himself.

"Start what?"

"My letter...to the Queen."

Ellen laughed.

"I've got it," he said. "What's her name again?"

"Queen Elizabeth...the Second."

He proceeded to read his letter as he wrote:

"Dear Liz Deuce...with all due respect, we have come to rightfully claim the ending of Charles Dickens's last and final novel. How we found the story is a long one. But for now, please allow me to summarize." He thought for a moment, and then scribbled on... *"Remember how the U.S screwed over the throne back in 1776? It's the same thing, really, but this time instead of using a flag, we're doing it with a book."*

"I don't think that's very funny at all," she said.

"Affectionately yours, Brian and Ellen."

He wrapped the cocktail napkin in a white paper placemat, wrote *'For Her Royal Majesty'* on the front, then sealed his makeshift envelope by tying a straw around it and inserting a plastic cocktail sword through each end. "There, our royal seal. That should do. Now you don't have to feel bad about comin' over to this country and stealin' any forbidden treasures. We just informed Her Majesty, the highest authority in England, of our intentions." Brian further sealed it with a kiss then stuffed the envelope into a small, old-fashioned letterbox mounted on the restaurant's wall.

Chapter 32

A Kiss and a Visit

"Well, I'd like to thank you for a wonderful evening, Julio."

"And I'd like to thank you, Bwanda."

The two stood alone in the hallway of the Royal Victoria & Bull Hotel, facing each other in front of the door to their room.

"This might sound weird," he said, "but you have really nice ears."

"Thanks," she returned, "I can't say anyone's ever told me that before."

"Really. They're perfect." He reached his hand out, tucking Ellen's brown hair behind her milky ear, slowly running his fingers down her lobe.

It required very little tugging on that appendage to draw Ellen's face close to his, her lips gravitating towards him. The two closely stared into each other's eyes before succumbing, their lips pressing together, their tongues dancing around the inside of each other's mouth.

"Out of all the spring breaks I've ever been on," said Brian, "this one's my favorite."

"Even with this freezing cold weather?" she said. "I think this nor'easter is following us."

"We'll just have to keep close and stay warm then."

Ellen removed the hotel key from her knapsack.

"So," joked Brian, "are ya gonna invite me in for some coffee?"

"Actually, I was thinking of leaving you standing out here in the hallway." She unlocked the door. "But I suppose one cup won't hurt. Come on in."

"I'll take an advance on the sugar, if you please," he said.

Ellen kissed him again, sending the boy reeling.

"How's that for an advance on your advance?" she said.

"Too much," said Brian, catching his breath. "Let me give you back some change."

He planted a kiss on the girl, sending *her* reeling.

She opened the door with a burst of laughter as Brian hoisted her up, carrying her over the threshold.

"Brian Murray, you're a bad influence on me with all of your drinking, and your smoking, and your lifting. My parents warned me about boys like you. Especially the lifting."

"They've got me all wrong," he said, setting her down. "It's girls like you that give us boys a bad rep, luring us with promises of fortune and fame."

"I've never promised you anything but a ticket to Florida."

"So, then you're not really sure about it, huh Ellen?"

"I'm sure about it. I'm sure it's here, rather. I'm just not sure where."

"One thing *is* for sure, Ellen. We're both here, right now." His hand stretched out again for her ear, pulling her near.

"Is this the final chapter of your apple theory?"

"No, just the beginning."

They passionately kissed.

"What do you call this chapter?" she asked, breaking away, her beautiful eyes still closed.

"The *here and now approach*. It's the kindred spirit that first ignited spring break and kept its flame alive ever since."

"Not bad. It might hold water."

They passionately kissed again.

"*Boy...girl...here...now*," he said, kissing her between each word. "Those are the only ingredients you need."

"You're quite the fundamentalist."

"Fun and mental, yes."

They kissed some more.

"Do I detect a hint of self-deprecatory humor?"

"Maybe. What's that?"

"I think you've finally found humility," she said. "You made fun of yourself. Psychologists say it's a sign of a healthy mind."

They headed for one of the beds when a voice came from the darkest corner of the room: "A 'ealthy mind don't necessarily mean it's a clean un."

Aided by the spongy floor, Ellen and Brian were startled right up to the ceiling!

The flame of a wooden match alit, and out of thin air appeared Merrywell, spread out in a chair, with his red suspenders and tattered top hat. The Old Magician!

"Halloa!"

"Jesus Christ," exclaimed Brian. "You scared the hell out of us!"

"Sorry, myte," he said, touching the flame to his cigar, igniting his tobacco-tainted timepiece. "It wos the only way, though, seein' 'ow I'm on the bloody lam as it is."

Ellen approached him. "I'm so sorry about Catherine, Mr. Merrywell."

"So am I, me dear girl, so am I."

Ellen and Merrywell hugged in a way that communicated neither one of them suspected any foul play on the part of the other. During this embrace, Merrywell's face was aglow, and not from the cigar. It was as if he felt something in her that he hasn't felt in a good while.

"How'd ya find us?" said Brian.

"Yeh *wos* in a pub tonight, wosn't yeh myte?"

"Yeah," said Brian.

"Don't yeh 'member the last think wot I said to yeh wos, myte? Weren't yeh payin' attention to ol' Merrywell?"

Ellen answered for him: "You said that if we ever needed to find you, look no further than the nearest pub."

"Thot's right, me dear child, thot's right. Same think, 'cept only back'ards." He snapped his suspenders and puffed his cigar. "Now, it ayn't any of ol' Merrywell's business wot it wos yeh wos lookin' fur last night, but the lot of us are in pickle-jam."

"I'm so sorry, Mr. Merrywell," said Ellen. "I feel as if I'm to blame for everything!"

"Yeh oughtn't feel thot way, dear child. If it's one think I 'ave a bloody keen eye fur, it's seein' evul in people. Call it a sixth sense from livin' on the streets if yeh want, but I can spot an evuldoer no sooner than 'e steps foot in the pub, no sooner than 'e makes 'is way to the rail of the bar, no sooner than 'e buys 'imself a drink. An' ol' Merrywell knows yeh didn't 'ave any-think to do with it. 'Owever, thot don't mean the 'Specter knows thot yeh didn't 'ave anythink to do with it. An' 'Specter Trundle *always* gets 'is man." He puffed his cigar. "I know, cause thot's who got ol' Merrywell many a year ago."

"You mean," said Ellen, "what I saw in the papers about you being a convicted felon?"

"Aye, thot's right."

"Wait a minute," said Brian, "you were convicted of attempted murder!"

"Aye, thot's right, myte."

"But you weren't really going to kill anyone," said Ellen. "Right, Mr. Merrywell?"

"Wrong, I wos gone to bloody kill 'im." He snapped his suspenders with a puff. "But we 'aven't got time to go into all thot." He looked at his cigar. "Times runnin' out fur us. It's not a question of *will* 'Specter Trundle get

257

'is man, it's a question of *when* 'Specter Trundle gets 'is man. Quite the hawk is 'e. An' if 'e wos good enough to get ol' Merrywell, who makes 'is livin' by makin' thinks disappear, 'e's good enough to get *you*." Merrywell let go a hearty laugh. "I sar 'is blunder on the telly arlier, an' believe me when I tell yeh thot the 'Specter ayn't known fur doin' thot too often. In fact, the last time 'e made a blunder *thot* big wos—well...we don't really 'ave time to get into thot, either. Rest assured, though, I can feel the tickle of 'is mustache sniffin' us out as we speak—The Old Yarder!"

"How many cigars do we have left?" said Brian.

"'Bout five-an'-a-half," Merrywell replied.

Ellen turned to Brian. "We'll have to look for it tonight."

"If yeh don't mind me sayin' so, me dear child, I sar the pictures thot wos s'posed to be yur faces on the telly. I don't know why you'd 'ave fake passports, an' ayn't gone to ask yeh why, fur thot's yur business, not ol' Merrywell's. But every pub-cam in England wos on yeh las' night. Sooner or later *those* pictures are gone to appear. Wherever it is yur 'eadin' to, yeh ayn't gone to get very fur."

"Can you help us, Mr. Merrywell?" she said.

"Well, since *me* face ayn't gone to do yeh no more 'arm at this pint, I s'pose I can oblige yeh."

"Can you get us back to the United States?" she pleaded.

"Well, me dear girl, since 'alf me business 'as to do with deliweries, an' the other 'alf with makin' thinks disappear, I s'pose thar ayn't no one more quallyfied than ol' Merrywell."

"Can you do it by sunrise?" she asked. "Because, what we're looking for—it's very important that we find it."

"I 'ope it's not *thot* important to yeh, because I can get yeh on a wessel thot leaves fur Baltimore in an hour. Thot's yur best bet."

"How about later this morning?" she asked.

He thought for a moment, removing his top hat and scratching his head. "I can get yeh on a freighter to New York. You'll 'ave to work in the kitchen, 'owever, to earn yur keep."

"We don't mind," she said.

"Speak for yourself," scoffed Brian, "I'm still on spring break."

Merrywell turned to Brian. "I'll 'ave 'em put *you* in the bloody scullery," he snapped and puffed.

"What time does that ship leave?" Ellen asked.

"'Bout five-an-a-'alf cigars from now."

Chapter 33

Gad's Hill Place

Ellen flashed her penlight up at the signpost. Emblazoned on the centuries-old wood was the word 'Gravesend.'

"I hope it's not *too* appropriate a sign," she said.

Firmly rooted onto the hilltop, on the road between Rochester and Gravesend, loomed Charles Dickens's old residence: Gad's Hill Place.

"I can see why he fell in love with it," said Ellen.

Two large columns greeted them at the front door like welcoming arms. The bay windows seemed like the lenses of curious spectacles bulging out at them. Smoke poured out of an inviting chimney on the rooftop, filling the air with the smell of burning wood, and Ellen wanted so badly to go inside and warm herself by the hearth.

"Well, I'll be," said Merrywell, lighting up the last quarter-hour of one of his cigars, "Thot's Boz's ol' place. Wot the blimey are yeh lookin' fur out in this country?"

"You'd never believe it if I told you." said Ellen.

"Then ol' Merrywell doesn't want to know wot it is, me dear child."

Ellen popped out one of her books, pinching the penlight between her neck and chest as she breezed through the pages. "Here's the map," she said, walking up to the front door and placing her back against it. She was about to count out paces in the direction of Rochester High Road when the front door suddenly sprung open.

A young girl, no more than seven, stood rubbing her eyes in the doorframe. She was draped in a heavy nightgown and robe. "Hello," said the child.

Ellen bent down at her. "Hello," she returned, smiling. "You're just too cute."

The little girl yawned a "Thank you."

"My name's Ellen, what's yours?"

"Stephanie."

"Well, Stephanie, you know you have a very special school here, don't you?"

"Yes, I know, Miss Ellen." The curls on the child's head bounced around at Brian and Merrywell. "Are you the ones?"

"I beg your pardon?" said Ellen.

The ones we were told about."

Ellen placed her hand atop the little girl's curls. "Told about what?"

"The story," said the child.

"Story?"

"The one they've been telling here for years…that someday people are going to show up at the door and do something wonderful for our school. It's one of our favorite fairytales."

"What do *you* think," said Ellen. "Do you believe it?"

"Oh yes…yes I do!"

"Then we *are* the ones. And we *are* going to do something wonderful for your school."

A large overbearing housekeeper appeared at the door. "Now whut yuh doin' up outta bed at this hour of the night!" she scolded. "Come along, Stephanie, before I have to put yuh in timeout!" She slammed the door on them, but they could still hear her voice. "I warned yuh about talkin' to strange tourists, 'specially at this time of night! Never mind your fairytales, come along now!"

Ellen looked at Brian. "Maybe you're right about us being the chosen ones after all."

"Told ya," he said.

Ellen counted several paces from the door, across the road, into The Wilderness, where the Swiss chalet once stood.

"According to this map, the Swiss chalet was located right in this vicinity," she said. The three of them walked through the thick brush, some of it being a patch of nettles and briars that seemed to reach up and bite the inside of Ellen's hand. "Ouch," she said, shining the penlight down on it.

A large thorn was protruding from her palm, so Merrywell gently pulled the barb out for her, a streak of blood running across her flesh. The magician produced a silver flask from his top hat, splashing a few drams of whiskey on the wound, which wouldn't stop bleeding.

"Amazin' wot brambles can bloody 'ide," said Merrywell. "If yeh don't want somethink found, put it in the middle of a patch o' brambles."

Ellen used a large skinny book like a scythe to hack away some of the vegetation. In doing so, she came across old cricket balls, golf balls, tennis balls, and toys of every size and sort that children abandoned all hopes of finding. There was even the frame of an ancient kite that looked as if it could have dated back to Dickens's day.

"There's poison sumac too," she said, shining her penlight down at the various plants. "Be careful, don't touch anything or you'll be done for."

Merrywell scratched his groin. "Only one bloody think thot ol' Merrywell can't make disappear quickly, an' thot's the bleedin' ivies."

Ellen came across a petrified tree stump, its diameter thrice times the three of them put together. She drew a hardcover version of *The Pickwick Papers* out of her knapsack, using the corner to dig around the edge of the stump.

The book stubbed on a hard, root-like object attached to the petrified cap. Clearing away some debris, Ellen discovered it wasn't a root but rather a piece of iron forged into the same Lion Couchant with halberd that frames the Swiss chalet back at the Dickens Centre.

"I have a feeling we're at the homestretch," said Ellen. She cleared some more debris away, digging the dirt around the outline of the lion. She examined it for a minute then carefully twisted it with both hands, reuniting the internal keys and turnstiles that were over a century-and-a-quarter old, giving rise to a massive hinge on the far end of the stump that slowly creaked open, the earth beneath them opening up before their very eyes.

Brian stepped back. "Jesus!"

"A different part of the secret tunnel," Ellen said.

"Ol' Merrywell's not seein' anythink nor wants to know anythink. Thar's somethinks out in the Old Country thot oughtn't be disturbed."

"Come on," said Ellen, leading the way with her penlight.

Brian anxiously followed, climbing into the stump.

"Ol' Merrywell's just gone to remain out 'ere an' 'ave a few puffs in the night air if yeh don't mind."

"You're coming with us," Ellen ordered.

He puffed his cigar. "Don't want to know anythink thot's not ol' Merrywell's business."

"Now!" said Ellen.

He quickly obeyed, climbing in.

The tunnel led back across the street beneath the main residence of Gad's Hill Place, where it ended just below a massive cobblestone ceiling with an iron door cut into the center of it.

Ellen ran her hand over the ceiling, causing some blood from her palm to get onto the cobblestones. "It feels warm," she said. "We must be right below the hearthstone." She shined her light on the trapdoor. "There's the hinge, so you could lock and unlock it from down here or inside the fireplace."

"Look!" said Brian, pointing at the ceiling.

The three of them gazed upwards.

Ellen's blood had outlined part of a letter etched into one of the cobblestones. She studied it intensely. "Mr. Merrywell, may I borrow your cigar?"

"So's long as yeh don't tell ol' Merrywell anythink thot ayn't 'is own business, yeh can gladly burrow me cigar. 'Ere," he said, handing her the stump of his stogie. "Toilin' with it is gone to waste fifteen minutes off our clock, 'owever."

Ellen vigorously rubbed the ash-end of the cigar into the crevice of the cobblestone, as if trying to erase whatever she was attempting to read. The more she rubbed, the more the inscription began to appear through the black ashes of Merrywell's timepiece. In Old English lettering emerged the words:

Where... Durdles... Takes... Jasper.

The **p**-letter of the text had a stopper plugged into its hole, so Ellen sacrificed one of her nails, breaking it on the cork with a grimace.

A glistening, gold-plated key fell out of the letter, clinking onto the stones below.

Ellen picked up the key, transfixed on it, her lashes closing for a moment. "Of course...it's in the crypt."

"The crypt?" said Brian.

"In the story itself, that's where Jasper drugs Durdles with laudanum, and steals his key to the crypt."

"What's laudanum?" said Brian.

"Yeh don't want to be messin' with *thot* brew," replied Merrywell, "take me word fur it."

"It's liquefied opium," Ellen answered. "They used it for medicinal purposes back in those days."

"Where *is* this crypt?" said Brian.

"Underneath the Rochester Cathedral." Ellen held up the golden key. "It fits together with the story. A puzzle within a puzzle. And I have a feeling that this is the final keynote...literally." She tucked it into the breast pocket of her coat for safekeeping.

"Ol' Merrywell don't want to know anythink, don't want to see anythink, an' don't want to 'ear anythink."

Ellen directed the beam of her penlight onto Merrywell's cigar. "Time to go," she said, pointing the way out of the tunnel.

Chapter 34

A Distinguished Visitor

I t was two in the morning when, off in the distance, the headlights of a lone car on the road overpowered Ellen's penlight during its long approach.

Snow had begun to fall again, blurring the space and visibility between them.

A Rolls Royce Phantom IV stealthily approached the trio, forcing them to hold their hands up at their eyes to thwart the Phantom's brightness. The stately car passed them, then traveled a good quarter mile up the road before making a k-turn and heading back.

Ellen sandwiched herself between Brian and Merrywell. "You don't think this is the person who's after the same thing we are, do you?" she said.

Brian and Merrywell walked Ellen off the road, the boy grabbing a stick and some stones for protection.

"Jus' stay close to Ol' Merrywell," he said, his blackened hands removing his top hat as he clutched it upside down by the brim (as if magic were his only defense).

"I've never seen a limousine so magnificent," said Ellen, watching the Phantom slowly slice through the snow as it passed again. It traveled another quarter mile up the road and turned, beginning another approach.

The three of them ducked down in some brush by the roadside.

"Maybe they're lost," said Ellen, trying to catch another glimpse of the magnificent auto. "Maybe they need directions."

"*You* can go ask if ya wanna," exclaimed Brian.

"Ol' Merrywell don't see anythink nor wants to know anythink," he said, bracing his hat.

The car slowly swooshed to a stop. And the driver exited, pulling a flashlight out of his chesterfield coat, shining it down in the brush at them. "You! There! Show yourselves!"

"What do you want from us," Brian shouted, cocking back one of his stones.

"Get up here," shouted the driver, "the lot of you! Present yourselves at once!"

"Make us!" said Brian.

The driver brandished a revolver from his chesterfield coat, pointing it at Brian.

"Allow me to present myself, I'm Brian Murray."

"Drop that, what you've got!" said the driver.

Brian complied, releasing his primitive weaponry.

"You too," the driver shouted at Merrywell.

The old magician complied by setting his stovepipe atop his head, still whispering to himself, "Don't see, 'ear, nor knowed anythink."

"Present yourselves!" repeated the driver.

The trio climbed back onto the roadside, and to their relief, the driver tucked his gun back into his chesterfield. "Didn't mean to frighten you. But you were threatening first."

"What do you want?" asked Ellen.

"It's not a question of what *I* want," said the driver, "it's a question of what my *passenger* wants." The sleeve of his chesterfield extended towards the rear of the Phantom, his gloved forefinger pointing to the door.

"Wot I bloody tell yeh?" said Merrywell. "It's the 'Specter! 'E done sniffed us out awlready!" He gave a hearty laugh, igniting a new cigar as if he had the God given right to smoke its entirety before ending his game of cat and mouse with the inspector. "The Old Yard Bird!" Merrywell roared, "'E's a sly 'un, 'e is!" he said, puffing. "An' I know The Old Yarder is 'earin' everythink I'm bloody sayin' at the moment, cause 'is bloody ears are *almost* as good as 'is bloody nose!" He laughed some more, choking a bit on his smoke. "*Almost* I say. An' if yeh want to know 'ow I bloody knowed thot, I'll tell yeh 'ow I bloody knowed thot!"

"You are mistaken," said the driver, wrapping his white-gloved fingers around the ornamental handle of the rear passenger door. "It is not an *inspector* who wishes to see you. It is a *lady* who wishes to see you."

"What?" said Ellen.

The driver pushed the button on the handle, pulling the door open.

There, properly poised in the backseat of the automobile, sat Queen Elizabeth the Second herself! Unmistakable! The Queen of England herself!

Merrywell was taken aback to the degree that his cigar fell out of his mouth, his hat off his head, spilling all of his cards, and trinkets, and coins, and chocolates, and trickery (even a tiny rabbit made its way onto the roadside).

"Ol' Merrywell don't see anythink nor knowed anythink," he incoherently muttered.

"Please," the Queen proclaimed, "*do* come in out of the cold."

The driver patted his chesterfield. "I hope you understand now the reason for the precautions I had to take."

Awestruck, their frozen faces just gaped and nodded.

"Let's move along now," said the chauffeur. "Better do as Her Majesty says."

They climbed aboard the Phantom, with the exception of Merrywell, who remained outside, gathering his cigars and trickery.

"Come on," Ellen said to him.

"If it's awlright, me dear child, ol' Merrywell's gone to just wait out 'ere an' catch a breath of—"

"Now!" ordered Ellen.

He quickly obeyed.

After situating herself in the grand auto, Ellen realized the impoliteness of the moment and attempted a curtsy that sent her plopping into the velvety-covered couch.

"Good morning," the Queen greeted, "I'm Elizabeth."

"Yes," said Ellen, her face overcome with paralysis, "I—I know."

"And you might be...?" said the Queen.

"My apologies, Your Royal Highness, please allow me to present myself: I'm Ellen Pipple, of College Park Maryland, um...the county of Prince George's."

"You needn't be so formal, dear girl," said the Queen, the diamonds in her tiara then glinting at Brian. "And you, my dear boy?"

"B-B-Brian," he said.

Her diamonds shined on Merrywell.

"Me name's Merrywell, an' I don't see, nor 'ear, nor knowed anythink," he blurted, "anythink a'tawl."

"I don't believe you do," retorted the Queen, as if understanding Merrywell's mumbling to be truth.

"I have a feeling that you know why we've come," said Ellen, her eyes fixed on the Queen.

"Yes, dear...yes I do."

"But...however did you know?" Ellen asked.

"You addressed me earlier in a letter, did you not?"

"Why," Ellen returned in disbelief, "yes, but..."

"You signed your names to it, dear girl, did you not?"

"Why," she returned, "yes, Your Highness, but..."

"You placed the letter in a letterbox, did you not?"

"Why, yes, yes, but—"

"Then why in Heaven's name would you be surprised that I should pay you a visit?"

"My goodness," said Ellen. "The letter! I'm so sorry about the impoliteness of the letter's tone and the utter crudeness of its—"

"No need to apologize," the Queen interposed, fixing a stern glance at Brian. "It doesn't take analysis from a handwriting expert at Scotland Yard to determine which one of you wrote it."

Guilt of the letter was written all over Brian's face.

"In days of yore, one would have been beheaded for such correspondence," the Queen eloquently stated, her eyes outshining the diamonds of her tiara as she glared at the boy.

Brian took a hard dry gulp of air. "I didn't put a stamp on it," he said, feebly attempting to defend his actions.

"You needn't a postage stamp when corresponding with the Queen in this Country," Her Majesty informed, shooting down his defense.

"That's right," said Ellen. "Wow! That was fast."

"Let's just say that I have my own *London Eye*, and they had it expedited," said the Queen. "For good reason, as you know, and can see."

This utterance started Merrywell up again, swearing to himself (and unintentionally the Queen) that he neither saw, heard, nor knew 'anythink.'

"Are we in trouble?" Brian asked.

"That's not for me to decide," returned the Queen. "That's for the inspector to decide."

"You mean," said Ellen, "you also know that we're wanted by Scotland Yard?"

"Since I have yet to see your pictures on the telly, for I shall wait till this morning's paper to read *that* news, who am I to say that you are wanted?"

"Then you *do* know about the book," said Ellen.

"Oh, I know about the book all right, dear girl. As did my Mother, my Grandmother, and my Great, Great Grandmother."

"You mean," said Ellen, completely overwhelmed and astonished, "Queen Victoria?"

"Precisely." She opened a small compartment in the corner of the Phantom, displaying a warm inviting tea set for four. "How do you prefer your tea, Miss Ellen?"

She felt as if she were in a dream again. "Two sugars, please."

"And you," said the Queen to Mr. Merrywell, most hospitably.

"Joost the same, please," he replied (as if he wasn't going to taste *anythink* either).

Her tiara pointed to Brian again. "And how many *lumps* would you like?" she said, in a harsh tone.

Intimidated, the boy sheepishly replied: "No lumps for me, thank you."

"I thought not," retorted the Queen, courteously preparing their tea and serving her guests first.

"I've read somewhere," said Ellen, "that Dickens would have been more than happy to tell your Great, Great Grandmother, Queen Victoria, about the story's ending; that is, if she had wished to know. But nothing

I've ever read suggested that he had ever shared confidences about it."

(This utterance started Merrywell mumbling again.)

"And so, she wished it," said the Queen, "and so, Mr. Dickens had told it." Her Majesty raised her teacup in cheers, toasting them.

Merrywell broke from his mumbling, raised his cup, and reflexively cheered: "God save the Qu—" before halting, realizing she was actually in his presence.

"Yes?" said Her Majesty.

Merrywell's stubbled face turned into a knot as he desperately sought an alternative ending. "God save the..."

Her Royal Highness patiently paused.

"God save the... the... the Country!" Merrywell finished.

"God save the Country," the Queen repeated. "*All Countries*," she added.

The foursome tipped and sipped their tea in unison.

"You see, dear girl," the Queen continued, "my Great, Great Grandmother, Queen Victoria, became very good friends with Mr. Dickens. They corresponded quite frequently through the post."

Ellen listened in amazement.

Her Majesty sipped some tea. "They got along rather famously as pen pals. There is much that remains to be found, my dear girl, between the pages of their story. Perhaps of *everyone's* story."

"'Ere, 'ere," said Merrywell, tipping his tea and drinking.

"So then," said Ellen, with tremendous fervor, "you know how the story ends?"

"Just because my Great, Great Grandmother wished to know the ending doesn't necessarily mean that I do...not yet, anyway. It would have to be a grave day, indeed, when I should take to peeking at the ending before it is discovered." She politely sipped. "You are correct, Miss Ellen. Mr. Dickens stipulated very clearly to her that he would be happy to reveal the ending, but in turn, she would have to grant him a trifle of a favor. Of course, she consented."

"Please!" Ellen pleaded. "I beg of you! If you know the ending, tell me then!"

"Per Mr. Dickens' request, dear girl, and on my solemn promise to my Great, Great Grandmother's solemn promise to him, the true ending is not to be revealed, the true ending is to be found."

"You mean," said Ellen, "you're going to allow us to continue on?"

"There are certain events that not even Queens should interfere with, dear girl. Especially in those regarding the writings of Charles Dickens, and the confidences he shared with my family."

"How did you find us?" Ellen asked.

"Come now, Miss Ellen, you know there was only one of two places it could have been."

"You mean, Gad's Hill or the cathedral?" said Ellen.

In an effort to reveal no more than her Great, Great Grandmother (or The Squire of Gad's Hill) would have wished her to reveal, the Queen silenced herself by sipping her tea, suggesting that she may not know *what* the ending to the mystery is, but she certainly does know *where*.

"It's in the crypt, isn't it?" said Ellen.

"As I have told you," the Queen proclaimed, "there are some things that should not be interfered with. Some things that are best left to run their own course, to find their own endings." She finished her tea, inviting them to do the same, their time together growing near.

"You and your family have been true to your promises all along," said Ellen, still overcome by her personage. "Why, you're the most honest, loyal, utmost traditional person I've ever met!"

"You humble me, dear Ellen. If there are three things that I wish my dynasty to be remembered by, they are Honesty, Loyalty, and Tradition."

"So, you're going to let us go find it?" she said, "just like that…Scot-free?"

"Free is how we prefer our Scots, dear, and all people, especially visitors whose hearts are as good and noble as yours. Likewise, that is how Mr. Dickens preferred it. He said that the best would come, and the best would find it."

"I confess," said Ellen, "a woman's death may have come about this."

"That's very unfortunate, my dear girl."

"Is that all? Don't you want the Royal Guards to capture us or question us or something?"

"Who am I to judge?" said the Queen. "Just because people go meddling around in my affairs doesn't mean that I should go meddling around in theirs. Besides, that's what we have a Scotland Yard for. In fact, I am quite confident that the inspector is more than capable of performing his duties."

"Wot I tell yeh!" Merrywell said to Ellen. "Wot I tell yeh! I can feel the tickle of The Old Yarder's mustache as we speak!"

The Queen gently took the girl's hand, squeezing it in a grandmotherly way. "It has been a pleasure making your acquaintance, Miss Ellen Pipple, of Prince George's County, Maryland," she said. "You too, Mr. Merrywell." Her tiara then pointed at Brian. "As for *you*, young man, regarding *your* correspondence," she stated quite firmly. "If you ever address me in that manner again, if you ever address *anyone* in that manner again, so help me, Mr. Brian Murray, I will have your head!"

Brian unconsciously loosened his collar, taking another dry gulp of air, chasing it with the last of his tea.

The Queen gave Ellen a wink. "Nevertheless, I am glad that you informed me of your intentions, regardless of the vagrant manner in which you had gone about it."

"Your Majesty," said Brian (most sincerely), "I'm so sorry for the way that I—"

"It's too late for apologies," she retorted, giving Ellen another wink, the girl's soft brown eyes taking in the Queen's semblance.

"Why," said Ellen, still admiring her, "lately I feel as if I'm in a dream."

"No," the Queen corrected. "You feel as if you're in a *story*."

Ellen gave her a smile. "You're right, and nevermore than at this very moment. For, in a short while, I'm going to read the ending of the greatest literary mystery of all time!"

"My dear girl," proclaimed Her Majesty, "it already *is* the greatest literary mystery of all time."

On that note, the Queen pressed a button, and the driver's chesterfield swiftly appeared, his gloved hand readying the door for her guests to depart.

"I would offer to drive you to your destination," the Queen stated, "but I wouldn't want to interfere with—"

"With the natural course," Ellen interposed, "with us finding our *own* endings."

Her Majesty smiled. "Perhaps Mr. Dickens was right. Perhaps the best *has* come."

"Thank you for the tea, Elizabeth," said Ellen, "and the delightful conversation. Please allow me to bid you farewell."

"No," returned the Queen. "We shall meet again. There are certain formalities that must take place in these situations—but I have said enough, and should say no more, and will simply welcome your farewell, and bid you mine as well." The Queen's eyes welled up, revealing the countenance of a little girl beneath her tiara (her childlike eyes sparkling far more brilliantly than her diamonds). "Travel safely, my dear friends, wherever your stories may lead you." Her delicate hand dabbed a handkerchief to her eyes, and, as she sat there, she gracefully gave the appearance of a China Shepherdess. "Godspeed to you," said the Queen, "especially in those sentimental areas of family and friends that Mr. Dickens wrote about."

After the three exited, the driver sealed the door, and the Phantom elegantly faded into the snowy stillness of the English countryside.

Chapter 35

A Good Walk

"I think she's cute," said Ellen, huddled between Brian and Merrywell as the three trekked their way back towards the Rochester Cathedral. The snow seemed to be turning into a moist fog that was wrapping around them. "There's no other word to describe Her Majesty's face but *cute*."

"Real cute," said Brian. "She threatened to cut my head off."

"Thar's worse thinks thot she cood've threatened to cut off, myte," said Merrywell with a chortle. "Yeh bloody know wot? 'Er 'Ighness *is* rather cute!"

"See, Brian? Mr. Merrywell thinks so, too."

"What would ya call a person threatening to shoot me then, a goddess?"

"More like a god*send*," said Merrywell, puffing his timepiece as he and Ellen laughed.

"You know what," said Ellen, "you're just jealous because out of the three of us, she liked you the least."

"That's only because of the letter. And it's a good thing I wrote it, or we never woulda met her."

"She didn't fancy yeh at awl, myte...yur joost tryin' to fool yurself."

"She liked me," said Brian.

"Not a'tawl."

"Okay, I'll say *respected*, then," he rephrased.

"Try *despised*, myte," said Merrywell, puffing.

"Or perhaps *loathed*," added Ellen.

"What's this, open season on Brian Murray? I feel like one of those foxes those hounds chase, and you two are on horseback hunting me down in the English country-side."

"We ayn't 'untin' yeh, myte. Asides, it ayn't *jackass* season," he said with a puff.

"How are we doing on time?" Ellen asked.

Merrywell checked his cigars. "Four hours to go, me dear child."

"Then we have plenty of time," said Ellen. "I can't believe the Queen has been hospitably waiting all these years."

"What do ya mean," asked Brian.

"Hospitably waiting," she said, "like when she politely served us tea, she served us first."

"If yeh don't mind me sayin' so, fur ol' Merrywell can't swar no more thot 'e ayn't seen, 'eard, nor knowed anythink, but from wot the Queen said of Brian, I woodn't ask 'is 'pinion when it comes to matters of politeness *or* 'ospitality."

"Thanks for the endorsement," said Brian.

"No 'arm intended, myte. It joost so 'appens thot when it comes to matters of politeness an' 'ospitality, thar ayn't no better 'thority than 'Er Majesty the Queen, thot's awl I'm sayin', myte. I'm not tryin' to be cheeky." He looked at Ellen and laughed. "Awl right, maybe I *am* tryin' to be a *little* cheeky."

"Tallyho!" said Brian.

"Yeh know 'ow you an' Miss Ellen go fur schoolin'? Same with 'Er Majesty. An' when it comes to them two royal subjects, politeness and 'ospitality, yeh might say she's majored in 'em both."

"She likes me," said Brian.

"Yur kiddin' yurself, myte."

Ellen switched on her penlight. "It looks like we're getting that fog you mentioned, Brian." Her light only worsened their visibility, causing Merrywell to fire up another hour's worth of their time—the cigar's red ash doing a better job than the penlight. "This curtain of fog is coming from the Higham marshes," she said. "The River Medway is to our left...I think."

Since they could no longer navigate horizontally, for they couldn't see more than a few feet in front of them, Ellen was forced to glance up and find Polaris, navigating vertically via constellations, slightly adjusting their course as they drifted along, huddled together in the ghostly sea of fog.

"Did yeh bloody 'ear thot?" said Merrywell, doffing his hat for security.

"Hear what?" said Brian.

"If I didn't knowed no better, I'd bloody say thot those are footsteps I 'eard."

Their lump of bodies abruptly stopped, listening...

"I don't hear anything," said Brian.

"Me neither," added Ellen.

They hesitantly continued on.

"Thar it goes again!"

They stopped…listening….

"Blasted! I can only bloody 'ear the damn think when I'm walkin'!"

They ventured about five more steps when Ellen stopped Merrywell. She untangled a frayed paper bag from around his foot.

"Oops," said Merrywell. "'Ow'd *thot* get thar?"

Brian seized the moment to get in a shot. "Mr. Merrywell doesn't need Inspector Trundle to arrest him. A wet paper bag will bring him in."

The old magician laughed.

"Mr. Merrywell," said Ellen, "what were you talking about earlier?"

"'Ow do yeh mean?"

"You know," she said, "implying that the inspector's sense of smell was far superior to his sense of hearing."

"Oh...thot." He chortled as if it were an inside joke between him and the inspector. "Like I said afore, thot's Merrywell's business."

"We shared our business with you," said Brian.

"Ol' Merrywell made it quite clear to yeh thot 'e never wanted nothink to do with yur business. Yeh might say yeh 'eld me down an' forced yur business down me weasand."

"Come on, Mr. Merywell," Ellen said, "tell us about the inspector...pleeease?"

They drifted a while longer before Merrywell gave in.

"Well, awlright. Yeh see," he said, following his glowing ash, "many a year ago, the 'Specter wos called 'pon by The Yard to track ol' Merrywell down arter I wos on the lam fur the attempted murder of that man. This wosn't just no ordinary man, neither. This wos a barrister from the bloody 'Igh Court!"

"Why'd ya want to kill a barrister from the High Court?" asked Brian.

They drifted some more before he responded.

"'E tried keepin' ol' Merrywell from the only woman 'e's ever loved—an' bloody succeeded in the long run, too. 'Cept it took the 'Igh Court, Scotlan' Yard, an' Wakefield prison to stop me from seein' 'er!"

"Rosa," said Brian.

"Thot's right."

"Who's Rosa?" Ellen inquired.

"The only girl he's ever loved," Brian replied. "He told me at the tavern the other night. Her parents were rich and didn't want her to marry him, so they sent her to boarding school."

"No, no, myte! Yee've got it awl wrong! It wos a nunnery! If yur gone to tell someone's bloody business, man, at least tell it right."

"Sorry," said Brian.

They drifted along.

"It's the 'Specter who yeh inquired 'bout, me dear child, so it's the 'Specter thot I'm gone to tell yeh 'bout."

"Fair enough," said Ellen.

"Anyhow, the 'Specter wos sent out to get ol' Merrywell, bein' the attempted murder of a barrister as it wos. An', fur the first time in The Old Yarder's career, it seemed as if 'e coodn't get 'is bloody man. The papers writ thot ol' Merrywell disappeared into thin air! Thot's wot they writ—the lot of 'em! Thot ol' Merrywell disappeared into thin air! An' thot's joost exactly wot I done! Ha!" he puffed.

"Where'd ya hide?" said Brian.

"I 'opped from pub to pub at first, but The Old Yarder wos gettin' wise to me, an' me disappearin' acts wos becomin' more an' more frequint. In fact, 'e showed up at one of me performinces once befur *I* did. Thot's when I 'ad to find the best 'idin' place of awl."

"Where?" asked Ellen.

"Well, arter searchin' ev'ry 'ouse in London, the Old Yard Bird finally got clever…an' searched 'is own."

The three of them laughed hysterically.

"An' 'e never wood've caught me neither," he said, guffawing between words, "if it wosn't fur me bloody cigar 'abit—the Old Bird smelled me smoke one night while 'e wos sleepin'…" his laughter forced him to pause… "I wos bloody 'idin' right under 'is own bed!"

The three roared as they trekked on, Ellen celestially guiding them through the marsh's ghostly brine.

Chapter 36

A Lost Book Found

The spires of the Rochester Cathedral emerged from the fog long before the building ever did, providing a splendid beacon for the weary travelers. In fact, one could argue that the cathedral never really came into view at all, the ghostly fog from the marshes enveloping it from the bottom up, as if the spirits of all those at rest had suddenly left their crypts and were slowly rising.

Ellen reached out to touch the door of the apparition to see if it was real. "Okay," she said. "I'm not dreaming." Her penlight scanned a travel guide. "We're here, at Gundulf's Tower. We need to get down the Pilgrim Steps, past the Presbytery, a right at the South Choir Transept, and down the stairs to the Crypt."

"Ow 'bout we joost follow yeh?"

She smiled. "That works, too."

"How do we get in?" said Brian.

"Maybe if I try the key." She removed the golden key from the breast of her coat, about to try it on the door when Merrywell interposed.

"This is a 'ouse of God, me dear girl. God's door is awlways open." He reached out and demonstrated this by turning the knob and pushing the door ajar. "See?" Removing his top hat, he stepped inside.

The door of Gundulf's Tower allowed some spirits of the night to sneak in, a long thin stream of fog eerily appearing to lead the way for them, down Pilgrim Steps, past the Presbytery, and to the South Transept, where there existed a brass memorial to Dickens.

"This is ironic," said Ellen. "Dickens always wanted to be buried here in Rochester."

"Is he?" asked Brian.

"No... His grave is actually in the Poets' Corner of Westminster Abbey."

She took a deep breath then followed the stream of fog, down into the bowels of the ancient crypt, Brian and Merrywell following close behind.

White, lozenge-shaped tombstones were scattered about the large musty chamber, highlighted by the flickering of candles with winding-sheets, which protruded out of thin, waist-high candleholders.

"I wonder which one it is," said Brian.

"In the story," said Ellen, "Durdles tells Jasper that he uses a hammer to tap out the hollow tomb."

"Where the hell are we gonna get a hammer?" said Brian.

"There's got to be something around here," she replied. "Go have a look."

Brian frighteningly glanced around. "*I'm* not goin' *anywhere*!"

"Allow ol' Merrywell to be of some assistance." He reached into his top hat, slowly extracting a long cane.

"Wow," said Brian, "that's pretty good!"

"I've 'eard of dead audiences befur, myte, but this beats awl," he said, gesturing at the tombs.

Using the sash of her frumpy dress, Ellen fastened a loose piece of marble to the cane and began tapping on each of the stone graves with it. "I feel something."

"Which one?" said Brian.

"No, not with the cane." She followed a wisp of fog branching over to another part of the crypt. "It feels like I'm getting warmer."

"Go with it, Ellen."

The girl trailed the wisp to an unmarked tomb along the wall. "I think I'm red-hot." She knelt down at the blank tomb and ran her hand over it. "I know I'm red-hot."

"Go, Ellen!" Brian encouraged.

She tapped along the crypt: *Thud, thud, thud, thud, thud, thud, **ping!***

"That's gotta be it!" Brian rejoiced.

The banging of the makeshift hammer caused Ellen's palm to start bleeding again, some blood getting on the tomb, trickling down into a tiny notch at the head. She examined the crevice closely, noticing that her blood formed a pattern similar to the bit on the end of the gold key.

"I think I found the lock," she said.

"Yes!" exclaimed Brian.

"Well...here goes." She placed the key into the notch and gave it a twist.

A series of levers and pulleys from beneath the crypt started turning, meshing gears, causing iron chains to become taut, giving steady rise to the tomb below!

Brian turned to Ellen. "Are you sure he's not buried here?"

A pine-stained wooden shelf with the letters 𝕮.𝕯. painted in gold lettering unfolded, the shelf popping open, galvanizing the three of them.

Atop the shelf, a small, red-carpeted portmanteau with two twinkling silver buckles like eyes presented itself most astutely, as if saying, "Here I am! Good get! You found me!"

Ellen took a few moments to gain her composure before nearing the tiny portmanteau.

"Thot Boz wos a sly 'un, wosn't 'e?" said Merrywell.

"Quite the Dickens," said Brian.

She touched her fingertips to her lips, then her heart, before running them over the sanguine exterior of the suitcase.

"I guess whatever you're in it for comes down to this," said Brian.

Ellen's mild hand carefully unfastened one of the silver buckles, giving the illusion that the portmanteau was winking, then she unfastened the other. "I'm so scared," she said. "What if the Queen was right? What if it already *is* the greatest mystery of all? Could what

289

we're about to reveal ever meet the critics' expectations? The public's expectations? *My* expectations?"

Brian and Merrywell listened to her as she marveled aloud.

"There's also the Droodians, each with their own denominations; some believing it's Jasper who killed Edwin; some thinking it may be Reverend Crisparkle or any of the other characters; and some who don't even think Edwin's dead at all. My God, what are we doing?"

"Bringing closure," said Brian.

"On top of that," she said, "you've got the Thuggee theories that trace back to a cult in Asia."

"Open it," said Brian.

"What if the religious people in the story turn out to be the evildoers? What if the opium smokers are the righteous ones?"

Brian placed his hands on her shoulders from behind. "What do *you* think, Ellen?"

By slow degrees, she gently peeled back the top of the portmanteau where a letter rested atop a package wrapped with old, yellowed newspapers of the day.

Ellen picked up the letter and read aloud:

"'Congratulations, Intelligent Reader, for you have proven the worthiest of all detectives, indeed, by solving The Mystery of Edwin Drood! Well done! As a token of my appreciation for your hard work and dedication, this letter is to certify that its bearer is entitled to all riches pertaining to these lost writings, including all royalties hereinafter. In good testament, I have endorsed this note with my signature, as well as those of my three

*distinguished witnesses: Mr. John Forster, my dear
friend and advisor; Mr. William H. Wills, my trusted and
faithful companion; and Her Majesty, Queen Victoria,
my royal friend. (I trust these witnesses satisfy any
reputability requirements?) God Bless you, Gentle
Reader, for remember that the true ending of your own
story lies within you, however you wish it to be.'"*

Ellen's hands began unwrapping *The Daily News*,
which was dated June 7, 1870, the yellow hue of the
newspaper changing to blue as she dug through.

"My God," she said.

"What?" asked Brian.

"This wrapping paper," she replied, "it's stationery...
it's *Dickens's* stationery!" Her glasses began scanning
the papers. "There are scores and scores of his personal
notes here—he didn't burn them after all! I knew it!" As
Ellen read, she had to pause from time to time, wiping
her eyes, her tears getting in the way of his writings.
"Here are his notes from Great Expectations," she cried,
"and David Copperfield...and here are some from A
Christmas Carol!" She dug a little deeper, crying a little
harder. "And letters he sent to Queen Victoria, and
letters she sent to him!" When the girl finally came upon
the second half of the leather-covered book, which
perfectly fit like a puzzle piece onto the first half, her
legs were incapable of holding herself up anymore,
giving way, Brian catching her as she fell back. He
folded his arms around the girl's waist, holding her up
until she composed herself. Ellen then rejoined the two

halves of the book back together by snapping the leather straps from the second half onto the tarnished snaps of the first, reuniting the two half-stories once and for all.

"From what you've been saying," said Brian, "I bet we can auction these notes and letters off for millions of dollars."

"Millions of *pounds*," she corrected, foggily, still overcome by the gravity of the moment.

"Wot are yeh bloody waitin' fur?" said Merrywell, flashing the remainder of his cigars at them from under his greatcoat. "Look 'ow mooch time we've got! 'Ave a looksee then pass it on awlready! I'm bloody dyin' to knowed the endin' of the story meself!"

"You've read the first half?" Ellen asked him.

"Of course I bloody read the first 'alf, me dear child. Dickens is standard coursework for schoolin' in this country. So get on with it awlready...please 'urry up an' throw yur eye over the bleedin' think!"

"*I* haven't even read the first half yet," said Brian.

"Then yur gone to 'ave to wait till I read the endin' arter Miss Ellen. Thot's only fair. Yeh shood be required to read the first 'alf befur bein' allowed to read the second—ayn't thot right, Miss Ellen? Shoodn't 'e 'ave to read the first 'alf first?"

"Now wait a minute," Brian protested, "I'm the one who found the—"

"Mr. Merrywell's right," said Ellen. "That's only fair. Consider the first half of the novel to be a prerequisite." She handed Brian her paperback version of the book.

"Look on the bright side, you've already made it through the first chapter."

For the first time in his life, Brian *wanted* to read a book, so he situated his back against a tombstone, paperback in hand, and pulled up a candlestick.

"In the meantime," said Merrywell, "I better run off an' make the final necessary arrangemints. I've still got one final deliwery to make. Fur, in joost a few hours, ol' Merrywell's gone to perform 'is greatest trick yet...'e's gone to make the lot of yeh disappear!"

Merrywell leaned down and kissed the girl on her forehead. "Joost in case somethink shood go awry fur ol' Merrywell along the way (fur, I can feel the tickle of The Old Yarder's mustache as I speak!). Yeh knowed where Rochester Castle is, don't yeh?"

"Yes," said Ellen.

"Yeh knowed where the River Medway behind the castle is, don't yeh?"

"Yes."

"Yeh know wot a wessel is, don't yeh?"

"Yes."

"Well, thot's precisely where you'll be catchin' yur ship, me dear girl."

Ellen's glasses looked fondly at the old magician. "You're always welcome to visit us in the States."

"I awlways did fancy seein' New York. But me place is 'ere fur now. Anyway, yeh might say I've got some unfinished business with the 'Specter."

Something about the notion of parting with him made Ellen sad. "Thank you, Mr. Merrywell," she said, hugging him with a long squeeze. "We couldn't have done it without you. Be careful and hurry back... please!"

"Thar thar, me dear child...ol' Merrywell will be back fur the endin'. Don't yeh worry 'bout thot." He removed Ellen's glasses, his smiling eyes taking in her face. "The splittin' image," he said.

Upon these words, the old magician disappeared, vanishing into a cloud of smoke, which quickly joined the rising fog outside, floating into the darkness of the ancient English Cathedral town.

Ellen comfortably situated herself, pushing her back up against Brian's tombstone, repositioning the winding sheets of the candlestick so that the two of them could share the candlelight together. And they read.

Chapter 37

A Six-Storied Keep

"That was the second greatest experience of my life," said Ellen, reflecting on the novel's ending as they walked across the lawn of Boley Hill, en route to Rochester Castle.

"Yeah?" said Brian, "what's the first?"

She shyly looked up at him. "Our kiss."

The fog was still rising, halfway up the castle by this time, promising a beautiful morning within the next half-hour (or half-cigar, perhaps, according to Merrywell's timepiece).

"Do ya know what I'm going to do, Ellen, after we get back home and turn in our papers?"

"Yes. You're going to put Professor Mudgrove in his place."

"Well, yeah, I mean after that."

"No," she said, giggling. "What are you going to do?"

"I'm gonna take *you* to Paris."

"On another date?"

"Exactly. Consider it a continuation of spring break—hell—we can have an endless spring break if we want! The spirits have allowed us to do it all in a few nights," he joked. "But this time it's gonna be legal, with real passports and everything. This time, I'll officially be escorting Ellen Pipple, not Bwanda Jackson. And there's not gonna be any Merrywells or Sonars or inspectors gettin' in our way either." Brian shifted the sanguine-carpeted portmanteau to his other hand, putting his free arm around Ellen and rubbing her in an attempt to rid them both of the pre-dawn chill.

"Sounds romantic. Of course, we'll have to pass through Scotland Yard first, to tie up any loose ends with the inspector about Catherine's death."

"Why? We didn't have anything to do with that. For all we know it was just a coincidence."

"Hopefully it was. But I wouldn't feel right if we didn't, Brian."

"They might have a fuzzy picture of us on TV or in the papers somewhere, but they don't know our names. We're in the clear! It's all downhill to the river—straight across the Atlantic—and back to the good ol' U-S-of-A!" he said, starting to sing: *"Over the river and through the woods to grandmother's house we go..."*

"Don't go jinxing us again, Brian."

"There's nothing to jinx. We did it, Ellen! We solved The Mystery of Edwin Drood!"

"Let's wait till the whistle blows...the Captain's whistle, that is. Then we'll know we're in the clear... then we'll know we're safe."

"Hey, check that out!" said Brian.

The fog was encircling the castle's five-storied keep like a medieval wreath, a teaspoon of eager sunlight casting a brilliant red shimmer about it.

"Amazing," said Ellen, stopping to take in the view.

Out of nowhere, a giant, bird-like creature swooped down on Boley Hill, knocking both students to the ground, but not before snatching the portmanteau out of Brian's hand and flying off in the direction of the castle!

"Are you all right," he asked, helping her up.

"Yes, yes, I'm fine."

He started after the thief.

"No Brian—wait!"

The bird seemed to fly into a crack in the wall of the south-east turret, Brian searching for the opening before darting through a narrow wooden door that was left open.

"Let it go, Brian!" she screamed, trailing behind.

He stormed Rochester Castle, chasing the bird up the steep winding stairway; the bird having a good story's worth of a head start up the Norman keep.

The castle's thick walls of coursed rubble projected a reddening glow from the sun-laced fog circling above, the wreath gradually rising higher and higher to the top.

"Your life's not worth it!" Ellen shouted as she stepped inside, her voice echoing throughout the castle. "Brian! Come back!" Ellen began to cry as she headed up the stairs. "I want *you* for the ending!" She switched on her penlight. "I just want *you* for the ending," she cried. With each step up the castle's keep, the girl somehow felt in her heart that she was getting farther and farther away from ever coming back down again, causing her to sob heavier. Her life flashed before her eyes in the foggy red gleam, weakening her legs, stalling her ascent.

Brian finally arrived at the top, the crimson haze making it difficult to see.

Through the fog, the gray-haired librarian appeared, slowly unwinding her scarlet scarf.

"Wait a minute," said Brian, catching his breath. "I know you!"

As Ellen struggled to climb the stone-carved staircase, she caught wind of that frowsty-scented cologne, along with Brian's cigarette, which triggered her mind into a stairwell of thoughts. "Thus," she said, as if talking to the fog, "if I hide my watch when I am drunk, I must be drunk again to remember where." She let the scent and fog waft over her for a moment as she stood there. Her mind immediately drifted to the face of Pat Hastings. Then her thoughts drifted to what Brian had said about being high on the first day of class. "But it can't be Pat," she said, "he dropped Professor Mudgrove's class the first week of—" Her sentence fell away, as if the fog had lifted her words to the top of the keep and cast them over the side. "My God, how could I overlook the obvious like that?" Her glasses lit up with a red glare as she raised her eyes upward.

This utterance seemed to revive a new vitality in Ellen, compelling each step she took to become stronger than the one before, her legs soon taking chunks at a time out of the steep staircase as her puffy coat and frumpy dress ascended the castle.

"You're the librarian!" said Brian.

Ms. Crawley cackled at him, her claws clutching the portmanteau.

"Give it back!" Brian insisted. "That's ours! We found it!"

A familiar voice came from the fog: "Once again, Mr. Murray, you are letting your ignorance precede your actions."

"Professor Mudgrove," Brian exclaimed.

The miserable old man stepped out of the fog, trimming his Homburg with one hand, brandishing the gun he had stolen from the barmaid with the other. His face was grotesquely disfigured with red bumps, welts, and lesions of every size and degree. "Pardon my appearance, but I happen to be highly allergic to poison sumac."

Brian stood frozen.

"As your Professor," he said, pointing the gun at him, "may I have the distinct pleasure of informing you that you will not be passing my class this semester, Mr. Murray." He cocked back the trigger. "And, as Head Chairman of the Academic Probationary Committee, may I have the distinct pleasure of informing you that I am expelling you from the University of Maryland." His lipless face caved into his festering lesions as he smiled. "And, as your executioner, may I have the distinct pleasure of informing you that I will be expelling you from this world, Mr. Murray, permanently," he said, scratching the lesions on his face. "So, step back, over there, and have a seat." He pointed the gun at his head.

"What's wrong, Mr. Murray? Are you upset because you won't have the opportunity to (how did you so eloquently phrase it?) stick that big fat diploma in my face and tell me to kiss it?"

The librarian seemed to be aroused by these words, running her claw over the professor's shoulders as he held the gun on Brian.

"You killed a woman over this," said Brian.

"Poor choice of verbiage, Mr. Murray. I wouldn't say *killed*. I consider it more along the lines of *decreasing the surplus population*. Bumping off a bumpkin if you will."

"I won't!" Brian retorted.

"Just like the accident that held you up on your bus trip to New York. Though, I must admit, serendipity played a major role in that. I only intended the bomb threat to slow you down; I never imagined it would wreak havoc to the degree that it would actually kill and maim so many people. Oh well," he shrugged, "discoveries such as these often occur at the loss of innocent lives."

"What are you gonna do?" said Brian, seated on the castle floor.

"I'll give it to you in fifty-fifty format, Mr. Murray. I can shoot you here, or you can jump off the keep over there. At least you'll have a few extra seconds to live that way. Which do you prefer?"

"Don't jump!" said Ellen, finally reaching the top. "He just wants to make it look like an accident!"

"On time as usual, Miss Pipple, I was expecting you to show up for finals." The professor kept his gun on Brian as Ms. Crawley grabbed the back of Ellen's hair. "I see you still do Mr. Murray's homework for him."

"Your reasons for wanting the story are by far the most selfish, evil, and twisted of all!" she decried.

"Miss Pipple, as I have mentioned to your friend before, he has solely been using you for your mind all along." The professor reached into his coat, removing Ellen's tape recorder. "I think this belongs to you?"

"Yes!" she replied. "My notes too! You couldn't solve the mystery yourself! You had to have us solve the mystery for you, and then steal it!"

"A mere conjecture on your part, Miss Pipple."

"Then why didn't you kill me when we were alone in the Swiss chalet?"

"I had my reasons, Miss Pipple."

"Your reasons being that you couldn't buy a clue, let alone find one!" Ellen looked back and caught a glimpse of the librarian, who was still clutching her hair from behind. "Isn't that right, Ms. Crawley? Tell the truth, didn't Professor Mudgrove need me to research all the information for him?"

Fearing the professor's hard hand, the librarian kept silent.

"Answer her, Ms. Crawley," said the professor. "Tell her how I knew all along where Dickens hid the ending."

Ellen continued her condemnation. "I let Brian copy my notes, but I never once did his homework for him!

You, however, *you're* the one whose homework I did! You're nothing but a no-good plagiarizer! An academic fraud! A cheat!"

The professor scratched the itchy bumps and lesions on his face harshly.

"And now you want to accept all the accolades, though you're not even deserving of a footnote in any of this!"

Professor Mudgrove became frustrated at his student, taking it out on Ms. Crawley by punching her face for not immediately flying to his defense, causing her to let go of the girl.

"It's a classic tale," said Ellen, "a tale that dates back long before Dickens's time: The student outwits the schoolmaster!"

The professor became enraged, scouring his face, breaking open some of the lesions—pus and blood oozing down his flesh. "Tell her, Ms. Crawley!" he demanded, raising his hand at her again. "Tell her I knew where the ending was all along!"

The ornithic librarian spoke through her bloodied beak, "Norman—I mean—Professor Mudgrove knew the entire time where to locate the story," she feebly affirmed.

"Why didn't you kill us back at Gad's Hill then?" said Ellen. "Or near the marshes?"

The professor trimmed his hat. "If it weren't for the Rolls-Royce, Miss Pipple, I would have."

"You had plenty of time before and after," said Ellen.

"Tell her, Ms. Crawley," he said, shredding his face, "tell her I knew it was in the crypt!"

Not feeling Ms. Crawley's arguments were convincing enough, the professor turned his weapon on her this time, bashing some of the woman's teeth out of her head with a pistol whip.

"Thstop it, Norman!" she screamed with a lisp, her front teeth missing. "Thstop it! Or thso help me I'll…"

"You'll *what*, Ms. Crawley?" he said, raising the gun at her.

"Thso help me I'll…I'll…I'll…*tell!*" she squawked.

The professor proceeded to smash any remaining teeth from her head with the gun, bashing her over towards the edge of the keep.

"I caught the profesther wearing my underpanths," she said between blows, "he thstole my bra and underpanths and was wearing them!"

This disclosure infuriated the professor to the degree that he beat the woman right off the ledge of the keep, sending the flightless bird plunging more than a hundred feet down to her death!

The professor's Homburg spun back around at Brian and Ellen. "There is one thing Ms. Crawley was correct about," he said, directing the gun back at them, "this castle *does* have a view to die for."

Brian was about to stand from the floor and make a go at him: "You son of a—"

"Easy, Mr. Murray," said the professor, positioning the weapon closer to Ellen's face, "the triggers on these old dueling guns are quite sensitive. I don't want to be the undertaker of any undergraduates just yet."

"You lured us in here," said Ellen, "it's the only way you could get rid of us *and* keep the story!"

"You always were my brightest student," said the professor, trimming his hat and scratching.

"I could never be your student," she retorted. "I don't believe in what you teach!"

Professor Mudgrove held the gun up to Ellen's temple, tossing back a tress of her hair with the end of the barrel. "There are things I can teach you, Miss Pipple; how to count old English currency, for instance."

"Leave her alone!" said Brian.

"You stay in your seat, Mr. Murray, and no harm will come to either one of you...not yet anyway." The professor began running the back of his bony, pus-filled middle finger down Ellen's cheek, caressing it. "Repeat after me," he said to the girl, "Four farthings equal two ha'pennies, two ha'pennies equal one pence, twelve pence equal a shilling..."

Having no choice, Ellen began repeating after him: "Two shillings and sixpence equal a half crown, five shillings equal a crown, twenty shillings equal a pound, twenty-one shillings equal a guinea..." then she flashed her penlight in a wisp of haze streaming between them, which acted like high beams in the fog—the yellowish light bleeding the red haze into an orange blur, momentarily blinding the wicked man.

Brian leaped at the professor—two shots rang out!

When the fog began to lift, Professor Mudgrove could be seen dropping his pistol and clutching his midsection. A gaping bullet wound the size of the lipless hole in his face was revealing his bloody insides, the force of the shot causing him to steadily backpedal. He greedily grabbed the portmanteau, but the weight of it made him stumble backwards all the more. To keep from falling, he released the treasure, which catapulted him towards the ledge. The hideously disfigured professor tripped over a low portion of the stone rubble wall, over the side, and plummeted headfirst to his death below... landing next to his twisted, broken cousin.

Chapter 38

The Dawn

66 **A** re you alright?" Brian asked.

"I think so," Ellen returned. "What happened?"

"Halloa!" called a voice. The old magician appeared before their very eyes; the stub of a cigar clenched between his teeth.

"Mr. Merrywell!" Brian thankfully said. "You saved us!"

"Yeh might say I 'elped. But I'm not the one thot saved yeh."

"What do ya mean?" said Brian.

Inspector Trundle's mustache materialized through the red fog, along with his black derby, beige trench coat, and umbrella, which was smoking from one end.

"I always carry this umbrella in case of inclement weather," said the inspector, lifting the end up to his mustache, his lantern-jaw blowing smoke out of the umbrella's barrel.

Ellen and Brian looked at Merrywell.

"Wot can I say? The Old Yarder bloody sniffed me out on me way back from the wessel." Merrywell went over to the side of the castle, peeking down at the two mangled bodies that the sun was bringing into view. "Ewww," he said, cringing at the ghastly sight. "Kind of gives new meanin' to *the break of dawn*."

"It was your cigar that once again gave you away, Mr. Merrywell," the inspector stated. He looked at Brian and Ellen. "As for you two, it was your motive. Funny how it always comes down to motive. I couldn't figure out why two college students would want to brave the elements on this side of the pond as opposed to going someplace nice and warm for holiday." He gave the handlebar on his left a twist. "I determined that you must have been looking for something, some sort of *MacGuffin*. When viewing the videotapes of your meeting with Mr. Merrywell, I noticed the pub's camera was working manually, along with several others out and about London. Her Majesty's Secret Service verified they weren't spying anyone that particular night. That's how I knew there was a third party involved, a technologically advanced party at that, who was seeking this MacGuffin as well." He gave his right handlebar a twist.

"But how did you trace us to Rochester in the first place?" asked Ellen, her hand tight against her heart, perhaps from all the drama that had unfolded.

"Simple," returned the inspector, twirling his umbrella. "Just as it was Mr. Merrywell's cigars that gave him away, it was your drinks. I merely had Scotland Yard ring every pub in England last night to see if they had served any *lemon drops*. It took me no time at all to trace you both to Giorgio's."

"I bloody told yeh I felt the tickle of 'is mustache!" said Merrywell, his laugh falling off the top of the castle as he glanced over at Ellen, the rising sun lifting any remnants of fog off the keep, allowing him to view her hand. "Yur 'and is bleedin' again, me dear child."

The girl removed her hand from her heart, looking at the blood. Then she opened her coat.

A fatal wound caused by Professor Mudgrove's gun was shot into her.

"It's not my hand that's bleeding."

Brian and Merrywell rushed over to her, examining the massive hole in her chest.

"I thought you said you were alright!" Brian said, gently lying Ellen down on the castle's stone bailey. The boy began to cry as he held her, his tears mixing in with her blood.

"Please, Brian," she said. "Don't cry."

Brian looked at the magician for help, who sadly shook his top hat and cigar (as if both were empty).

"I thought you can't take the sight of blood?" she tried joking.

"I can't." Brian's eyes sought Inspector Trundle for encouragement, and though he was already phoning for an ambulance using the handle-end of his umbrella, the inspector sorrowfully shook his derby and jaw.

Brian turned his eyes back on Ellen, realizing that whatever words he was about to say had better count, for their studentship, companionship, and friendship were quickly coming to an end.

"You were right at first," Brian admitted. "I was in it for the money. I was a selfish ass who couldn't think about anybody but himself."

"What you *were* in it for doesn't matter," said Ellen. "It's what you *are* in it for that counts." She started to cough foggy breaths, as if her spirits were visibly escaping her body.

Brian tore his leather jacket off and covered her. "Is there anything I can do to make you more comfortable?"

"Kiss me."

He did.

"I don't think I'm going to make it to Paris," she said.

They held each other.

"Do me a favor, Brian, please?"

"Anything."

"On the first nice day," she said, beginning to lose her sweet breath, "I mean, on the first most beautiful day...when the birds are singing and...and the smell of spring fills the air...think of me, will you?"

"I will," he said, fighting back his tears. "I promise."

She gasped a cloudy breath. "Take the ring out of my purse...you know the one."

In doing so, he came across Sonar's silver dollar, which she wanted him to keep. Brian then removed the gold ring of diamonds and rubies from the box.

"Place it on my hand...please."

He did so, delicately screwing it on Ellen's ring finger. Brian then whispered something in her ear, punctuating whatever he said with a kiss on her soft pink lips.

"Mr. Merrywell?" she called.

"I'm right 'ere, me dear girl," he said, his eyes fixed on the ring.

"You don't think that…" she had to catch her breath… "that you could make one last delivery for me…do you?"

"Wot's thot, me dear child?"

"Can you make sure that…" she paused again… "that I'm sent directly to heaven?"

Merrywell leaned down at her, touching her tender hand, and the ring, kissing her forehead. "Thot's one deliwery you won't need me fur." His tears seemed to smooth the creases and stubble on his face, making him look younger.

She mustered all of her senses to focus on Brian, who was still struggling to hold back his tears for her.

"I think that…that you understand what I was in it for now," she said, smiling at him.

Tears once again streamed the boy's face.

"Don't be sad…" she consoled, "our story's not over." The lights of her bright eyes began fading. "Whenever you want to visit me…all you have to do is…is open one of the classics…because you'll know I've visited there before." Her voice turned to a whisper. "We'll meet between the pages…in the most wonderful places."

These were to be Ellen's final words as she let go of her last precious breath of life with contentment, looking up into the dissipating mists high above, which spread the morning sky out before her.

Chapter 39

A Ring and a Trick

A few seconds later, off in the distance, a ship's horn blew from the Medway, as if awaiting two more passengers.

"Thot's the engagement ring I gave Rosa," said Merrywell, wiping the tears out of his eyes with the sleeve of his greatcoat.

"You're a liar!" Brian cried, still protectively holding Ellen atop the castle. "That ring was Ellen's! It belonged to her mother!"

Merrywell's eyes riveted on the inspector.

"He is right, Mr. Merrywell," proclaimed his lantern-jaw. "That *is* Ellen's mother's ring."

"Don't tell me, 'Specter, thot I can't 'member the ring I gave the only woman I ever loved! Arter awl, it took a good many shows an' a good many chimneys to pay fur the likes of it!"

"Likewise," said the inspector, setting his jaw on Brian, "that *is* the ring Mr. Merrywell gave to Rosa."

Brian and Merrywell looked at each other.

"I am afraid, Mr. Merrywell, that you have been on the wrong end of an improperly balanced scale, for a long while now."

Merrywell gave a look suggesting he was beginning to put the puzzle pieces together, the pieces of his own story that the inspector was confessing.

"Yes, Mr. Merrywell," his long jaw pronounced, "your feelings are correct…Ellen was your daughter."

Merrywell broke down, collapsing on the castle's stone bailey, weeping.

"I am sorry, Mr. Merrywell, but when Rosa went away to the convent, she was *with child…your child.* She did not die of a horse and carriage accident as the coroner led us to believe. She died of a broken heart… while delivering your daughter."

Merrywell sobbed harder.

"I know this because Ellen's grandfather, the barrister, told me this."

"Alas!" cried the magician. "I shood 'ave murdered 'im!"

"I understand your feelings," said the inspector, "he did his best to hide it, especially from me. Working at the High Court of Justice, he had several political ties. One being with the coroner. I never saw Rosa's body."

Merrywell's watery eyes glared at him.

The inspector continued. "By the time I figured it out, your daughter had already been comfortably living in the States for two years. You, on the other hand, were residing in Wakefield prison, a broken, penniless man."

"Maybe it wood've bloody snapped me out of it," Merrywell cried, "did yeh ever think of thot? Maybe the dear child just might've pulled me spirits up out of the dregs. Did thot ever bloody occur to yeh?" He let go an

312

agonizing groan. "I shood've killed the bastard! I spared 'im though, you of awl people knowed thot, 'Specter, I bloody spared 'im!"

"I know, and I did my best to spare *you*. That's why I had you discharged the moment I found out. If you will recall, you received an early release."

"I shood've bloody killed 'im!"

"But you are not a murderer, Mr. Merrywell."

"But *'e* wos! 'E denied me *two* lives!" he bawled. "Thot of me wife *an'* me daughter! 'E'll bloody rot in hell fur it, too!"

"I know there is nothing I can do that will change anything. But I should say that I spoke with him recently, and if you will permit me to say so, his life has been far worse than any life I've ever known. And I do not mean his disbarment or in any monetary sense. I am speaking of the Highest Court who is punishing him," he said, his eye and jaw glancing upward. "For he has lost every person ever dear to him, and he continues to suffer each and every day that he outlives them."

"'E don't knowed wot suffrin is!"

"He suffers because he could have known his daughter and granddaughter but chose not to. You, however, Mr. Merrywell, you have had the chance to know Rosa and Ellen, however brief the time and coincidental the circumstances."

Merrywell broke down again, knowing the inspector's words to be true.

The ship's horn blew again, accompanied by the faint sound of a captain's whistle.

"The scales of justice, however," pronounced the inspector, "when so heavily leaning in one direction, often have a way of tipping themselves out." He realized his words didn't quite sink in. "Let me restate to you, Mr. Merrywell, that when one side of the pendulum so heavily favors one particular side of the clock, it is only a matter of time before it balances out."

Merrywell looked at him, perhaps knowing what he meant. "Well then," he said, wiping his tears with his sleeve, "if thot shood be the case, allow ol' Merrywell to perform one las' trick fur yeh."

"Very well," said the inspector.

"Of course, for this trick, I'll need a volunteer," he said in a most sober tone, "'Ow 'bout you," he said to Brian, trying to elicit a smile, "the one with the leaky eyes." He went over to the boy, whispering something in his ear, but Brian shook his head, not wanting to let go of Ellen. He whispered something else, and after a few more whispers, Brian took one last look at Ellen, giving her pretty face one last kiss before complying.

The inspector allowed him to proceed.

"Now," said Merrywell, "I'll give the lad an ordinary box, like the one we've got right 'ere," he said, grabbing the red-carpeted portmanteau and tapping both sides of it with a magic wand he produced from his hat. He handed the suitcase with its silver-eyed buckles to Brian, and then proceeded to remove his greatcoat, draping it over the boy, covering his entire body, along with the portmanteau, giving the grand illusion that his coat was suspended in midair. After a few moments, he continued. "Now, I'll say the magic words, abracadabra, 'ocus pocus, make the lad an' the box begone in me smokeness." After pausing a few more moments, his greatcoat (which somehow really *was* suspended in midair!) fell to the ground with a puff of smoke...Brian and the treasure being well on the way out of the castle.

With all remnants of smoke and fog dissipated, the inspector went over to the side of the keep, watching a man with a short pipe, and another with a bottle-green coat, directing Brian up the gangway. Shipmates were reeling the boy in before the barge steadied up the Medway in good trim. The Old Yarder gave both sides of his mustache a twist.

"Let the lad go," said Merrywell, falling back with his daughter's lifeless body. "'E didn't 'ave nothink to do with anythink. It's ol' Merrywell thot yeh want." His watery eyes bent over his child.

"Very well," said the inspector.

"Joost let me sit 'ere by 'er side, joost a little while longer," said Merrywell, hugging his little girl.

"Very well."

Merrywell removed Ellen's glasses, holding his face close to hers as he cried: "'Ave I no tricks left in me hat? 'Ave I no time left on me cigar?"

After a few moments of silence, with the sound of approaching sirens growing louder in the distance, the inspector spoke:

"Perhaps I should inform you, Mr. Merrywell, that I had a rather interesting conversation with the Queen."

Merrywell kept silent.

"Scotland Yard and Buckingham Palace have had an amiable relationship for many a year. In fact, you might say that she considers me to be her *London Eye.* And during my interview with Her Royal Majesty, I discovered that Charles Dickens and Queen Victoria had a similar amiable relationship, particularly when it came to correspondence."

"I woodn't know."

"Oh, but you *do* know, Mr. Merrywell, because Her Majesty knows you personally; I questioned her about it myself. And there is one thing to be said about the Queen: she hides nothing from The Yard. I ask her questions, and she tells me truths."

"She's a good lady."

"Likewise, Mr. Merrywell, she says you are a good man."

"Don't believe everythink yeh 'ear."

"Well, believe me when I say that Charles Dickens and Queen Victoria stipulated that if ever a certain *mystery* was solved, his coffin would one day be exhumed from its resting place and returned here to Rochester, where he had always wished to be buried."

Merrywell just sat there, embracing her.

"And it has also been stipulated that the party who finds a certain, shall we say, *MacGuffin*, will one day receive burial in *his* place at Westminster Abbey."

With tears streaming down his cheeks, Merrywell smiled at his daughter. "Did yeh 'ear thot, me dear child?" he wept. "Yur gone to be buried in the Poets' Corner of Westminster Abbey."

Chapter 40

The Ending

Stretched out on a chair aboard the ship, his soiled apron proving his dishwashing duties in the scullery were completed, Brian finally finished reading the ending of *The Mystery of Edwin Drood*. As the barge made its way back west, he went to the stern of the ship. One by one, Brian tore out pages from the old book, casting each one to the frigid Atlantic where they sailed like kites for a good while, the pages climbing high into the air before diving header-first into the ocean below. The boy then ensured the two half-covers of the book were fastened together tightly, securing the snaps and winding it with fishing line (so they would never let go). He then relinquished the ancient-looking cover to the icy brine, forfeiting the treasure forever.

"Now only you and I will ever know the ending!" Brian shouted out to the sea.

Ellen's adoptive parents were informed of the tragic news by Inspector Trundle, and, with an invitation by the Queen, they were flown to England for a private ceremony and interment in the Poets' Corner of Westminster Abbey. Out of respect for the family's wishes, no further mention of a MacGuffin was ever made public.

As for Professor Mudgrove, it was stated in the papers that he was linked to The Barmaid Murder. *The Times* wrote that he was shot and killed by Inspector Trundle who witnessed the professor push his cousin, Ms. Crawley, to her death, then threaten the life of an innocent bystander: one John Thomas Merrywell.

Although the ending of the story was never found, there were priceless letters that had been discovered. For, at the all-girls school at Gad's Hill Place, a parcel was addressed to a young girl named Stephanie who received the gift among the excitement of her schoolmates; the children's ogling eyes hurrying her to open it. Within the old newspapers of the portmanteau were numerous letters that Charles Dickens and Queen Victoria had written to each other over the years. A secret benefactor listed the orphanage as the trustee, so the multi-millions in correspondence would keep the school and its fairytales flourishing forever! It was evident in the eyes of the curly-haired little girl that she was reflecting on her meeting with Ellen that night on the porch, knowing quite well that Ellen made good on her words: that something wonderful would happen.

All of the lost notes pertaining to Dickens's novels were also discovered (with the exception of *Drood*). The secret benefactor used the procurement to purchase and maintain a nice home for Sonar and his family.

Never again would they have to brave another harsh winter on the streets of New York.

Spring weather had finally arrived, Brian witnessing its glorious splendor out of his classroom window at the University of Maryland, an empty desk behind him.

The new teacher for English Literature 401, a stout, turtle-looking man with a bald head and big Adam's apple, was passing back term papers at the close of class, dropping them facedown on the students' desks.

When Brian flipped his over, **B-** was printed on the cover in big red lettering, along with a special note from the teacher that read: *'Very creative, but it couldn't possibly have ended that way!'*

Brian could only laugh as he gathered his books, including such authors as Dickens, Hemingway, and Poe, as he made his way out of the classroom.

"Yo Bry!" called the redheaded boy from down the corridor. "Where the hell have ya been?"

"Studying," he replied, walking down the hallway in a fog.

His sunburnt freckles followed Brian. "You missed an entire *lifetime* on that trip, man!"

He thought for a moment. "I know."

"Whatcha doin' with all those books?" They traveled down the long corridor, a warm beam of sunshine brightening the door's windowpane at the far end.

"I've got some reading to catch up on."

"How'd ya make out on that paper?"

"Passed."

"Congrats—you survive another year! Good thing you didn't go with us to Florida after all. By the way, did ya ever try that smoke I gave ya?"

"Yeah."

"That stuff was killer, wasn't it?"

Brian remained silent; his eyes fixed on the sunbeam that was growing brighter in the door's window.

"Hey, whatta ya say we go out for a beer or three? We can kinda-sorta make up for lost time on spring break. How 'bout it, Bry?"

"I can't," he said, straightening up his books as he began to exit. "I'm meeting an old friend."

The young man held tight to his literature as he banged through the heavy metal door, out of the corridor, and into the sunshine of a beautiful day.

THE END